ON
THE
THIRD
DAY

ON THE THIRD DAY

Piers Paul Read

Random House
New York

C.2

Grateful acknowledgment is made to Penguin Books Ltd. for their kind
permission to reprint excerpts from *The Jewish War* by Josephus,
translated by G. A. Williamson. Copyright © G. A. Williamson, 1959, 1969.
Reprinted by permission of Penguin Books Ltd.

Library of Congress Cataloging-in-Publication Data

Read, Piers Paul
On the third day / by Piers Paul Read.
p.   cm.
ISBN 0-679-40089-3
I. Title.
PR6068.E2505   1991   823'.914—dc20   90-53476

Manufactured in the United States of America
9 8 7 6 5 4 3 2

Book design by JoAnne Metsch

The third day, he rose again from the dead.
—The Apostles' Creed

ON
THE
THIRD
DAY

The discovery of a crucified skeleton,
possibly Christ's, sets off a theological
and political controversy.

Prologue

The Israeli archaeologist Michal Dagan, once a professor at the Hebrew University on Mount Scopus, later director of the Staedtler Institute of Archaeology in West Jerusalem, lived with his wife in that leafy quarter of the city called Rehavya. Their flat had three bedrooms, one for the parents and one for each of their two children. That of their daughter, Anna, was rarely used; she had been to school in the United States, and was now studying in London.

The son, Ya'acov, sometimes called Jake, was in the army, and only lived at home from time to time. In 1988 he was stationed in Jerusalem, attached to a unit of military counterintelligence headed by Colonel Yehuda Lomish. He worked in plain clothes, driving every day from his parents' flat in Rehavya to a military compound on the Ramallah Road. The professor never asked what his son did from day to day, content that it was undoubtedly of some importance to the defence of the Jewish nation, not just from its external enemies but also from those within, who at that time were organizing the *intifada*, the protests and demonstrations by Palestinians and Arabs against the Israeli occupation of Gaza and the West Bank.

One evening in late May, Ya'acov abandoned his usual discretion and, over the supper table, began to tell his parents about his work. Because of the *intifada*, it was now necessary to eavesdrop on the Arabs in their sanctuary on the Temple Mount. Existing devices on the hills surrounding the Old City were proving inadequate, and a decision had been reached to go in from below.

Michael Dagan was familiar with the excavations that had already taken place beneath the retaining walls of Herod's Temple. Since the conquest of the Old City in 1967, a tunnel had been dug under the Muslim quarter adjacent to the Western Wall, linking the area around Wilson's Arch with the cisterns under the Via Dolorosa. Israeli archaeologists had itched to know what lay on the other side of the wall, but they had always been prevented from excavating under the Temple Mount itself by the religious sensitivities both of the Muslims above and of the Orthodox Jews in the Ministry of Religious Affairs. But now the needs of security seemed to have overridden all other considerations, and a decision had been made to go through the Western Wall at a point at the northwest corner where it bisected an old cistern and blocked the Hasmonean watercourse from the Damascus Gate.

The point Ya'acov made to his father was that if the work was left to the sappers and engineers, they might overlook and inadvertently destroy objects of great archaeological importance. He himself had some archaeological training, but had neither the knowledge nor the experience to judge the importance of what his unit might find. Therefore he had asked his superior, Colonel Lomish, to let his father be a part of the operation and allow him to enter first through the Western Wall.

Michal Dagan could not refuse. His wife, Rachel, directed a doubting look across the table, and asked Ya'acov who, beyond Lomish, had authorized the operation. Her son's answer was vague, but it satisfied his father. Whether legal or illegal, dangerous or safe, it was an unique opportunity to gain access to the whole labyrinth of caves, conduits and cisterns known to be beneath the mosques on the Temple Mount, and to have remained untouched since the destruction of the Temple by Titus.

The operation proceeded in great secrecy, with five young sappers in plain clothes working under Ya'acov and two fellow officers, Mordecai and Asher. It took more than three weeks to cut around the stone, and another week to dislodge it, inch by inch. At the beginning, Dagan visited the site almost every day, but there was little he could do to help. Since progress was slow and he had other work to do, he tended to leave it to Ya'acov to tell him when he was needed. It was almost a month after the work had started that Ya'acov came home and told his father they hoped to remove the stone the next day. Early in the morning they both went to the plaza in front of the Temple Mount, and were met there by Asher, Mordecai and the young sappers. They walked along the tunnel to where the massive block of stone protruded from the wall, held up by a tangle of scaffolding, chains and pulleys. It took another two hours to edge it out of the wall, and so tight were the blocks around it that when it finally swung free there was no movement whatsoever, simply a black rectangular hole leading to the other half of the bisected cistern.

Dagan peered through, inhaling the musty air, then shone a flashlight into the darkness to look for the level of the floor. They had assumed that it would be lower and that they would need a ladder to reach it, but instead found that there was a shelf of rock only a few feet down. Michal pulled himself through, followed by Ya'acov, Asher and then Mordecai, who carried with him a powerful lamp attached by a cable to the circuits in the tunnel. The light revealed a large cavern, similar to other cisterns of the Roman era with which Dagan was familiar. The ledge on which they were standing was at the base of a pillar that must have stood at the center of the cistern and was carved out of solid rock. The floor was about fifteen feet beneath them, and to reach it Mordecai called for a ladder, which was passed through to them from the other side of the wall.

Ya'acov went down first, to make sure it was steady for his father. Dagan went next, followed by Mordecai with the lamp, trailing the cable behind him. Their first instinct was to look up to see if there was an entrance to the cistern from above, then to look around the wall to find the outlet from which water would have flowed to other cisterns beneath the Temple itself. It was only when he was standing on the shingle that had collected at the lowest point that Dagan noticed a large earthenware jar, cracked and lying on its side.

The jar was not unusual. Like the cistern, it was of a kind common to the period, used for storing olives or grain, with a wide neck and a tapered stem. It was too large to have been used to draw water from the cistern, and perhaps for this reason had been left submerged under the surface. It seemed of no immediate interest, and while Ya'acov and Mordecai searched the roof of the cavern for a place where they might plant their bugs, Dagan searched for the opening that would lead through a conduit to the cisterns beneath the site of the Holy of Holies.

It was only after he found the opening, now walled up from the other side with masonry from the Herodian period, that Dagan returned to the jar. He knelt and peered in. The beam of his flashlight fell on what remained of a wooden lid, jammed about halfway down the jar. If he moved the lid, the wood would undoubtedly crumble. He asked Mordecai to fetch tape and a plastic sheet, intending to bind the jar to prevent it from splitting open where it was cracked, and then to remove it from the cistern to the laboratories at the Staedtler Institute.

It was Ya'acov who pointed out that it would be difficult to carry the jar up the ladder and through the hole in the wall without disturbing the contents. Dagan agreed, and when Mordecai returned they unrolled the plastic onto the shingle and gently lifted the jar onto it. Mordecai held the lamp, while Ya'acov and Asher separated the two halves of the broken jar, lifting one off the other like the lid from a box.

Dagan crouched to examine the skeleton. "How curious," he said. He took a magnifying glass from his pocket and looked more closely. Ya'acov, Mordecai and Asher watched in silence. Then the professor glanced up, his face pale. "We must touch nothing," he said. "Leave everything exactly as it is. We must have a witness to this, another archaeologist—someone, above all, who is not a Jew."

PART
I

PART

1

Among the world's most celebrated archaeologists was Father John Lambert, an English Simonite monk. His order, founded by St. Simon Doria in the Middle Ages to copy the Bible onto parchment, had evolved over the centuries into a community of celibate scholars who ran schools and universities all over the world.

Exiled from England after the Reformation, they did not return until the late nineteenth century, when they were invited by Cardinal Manning to found a Catholic university in London. A site was bought in the borough of Paddington, and the money raised to build a large church in the Gothic style, which would be attached to a monastery for fifty monks. When the idea of the university came to nothing, the Simonites founded a school instead. Some of its pupils later joined the order, together with other English Catholics who had received their education elsewhere. By the early 1960s, the small group of Irishmen, Frenchmen and Germans who had reintroduced the Simonites to England, had grown into a community of forty or fifty Englishmen, renowned for their learning and papist zeal.

By far the most distinguished of these was Father Lambert. He had entered the monastery as a young man but had spent little time in London. In the 1950s, he had studied under the French Dominican Roland de Vaux, at the Ecole Biblique et Archéologique in Jerusalem, had later taught at Tübingen, and for a time

9

at the Simonites' own Pater Noster University in Seattle. In 1969 he came back to Europe, to the Pontifical Biblical Institute in Rome, but only returned to England in 1975, as professor of archaeology at Huntingdon College, part of the University of London.

Father Lambert was at that time around forty, a tall, vigorous man with close-cropped hair, pale blue eyes, and skin that had grown tough and dark from digging under the burning sun. He was considered an ascetic by the other monks because he mortified his flesh in a way that was quite out of fashion. His expression was stern and his manner remote, even forbidding. Few people called him "John" or even "Father John"; it was always "Father Lambert." Yet despite this austerity he had a gentle manner; he was always kind; he was often funny. People traveled across London to hear him preach, and his lectures at Huntingdon were so popular that they drew students from many different faculties, some of whom sat around the lectern like groupies at a rock concert.

His reputation went beyond academic circles, and though several of the English Simonites were eminent in their fields, Father Lambert was the only one who could be called a celebrity. He was often asked for his opinion on various matters by the national press, and was invited to appear on television, but neither his fame nor his dedication to uncovering the past had ever distracted him from his obedience to his calling as a Catholic priest. He said Mass every day, at an altar in a church or at a table in a tent, and when in London he would sit in the confessional for an hour every Saturday morning, waiting for penitents who rarely came.

Every summer Father Lambert spent two months in Palestine, working on different excavations with Michal Dagan, a man he had known for twenty years and one of his closest friends. It was an unlikely friendship. Dagan was a committed Zionist and Father Lambert a Catholic of an uncompromising kind. Each had always respected the other's learning and skill, but they would never have chosen to work together had cooperation not been forced upon them by political considerations. The Israelis unquestionably ruled Palestine, but some of the most important archaeological sites had been controlled by Catholics since the time of the Crusades. It had therefore been thought appropriate for Professor Dagan to work with a Catholic and for Father Lambert to work with a Jew.

Though they shared an enthusiasm for uncovering the Palestinian past, each man was inspired by a different vision. To Dagan,

God had made a Covenant with the Jews that gave them Palestine. To Father Lambert, God had made a new Covenant with all who believed in Christ that gave them the kingdom of Heaven. Dagan wanted to inspire the disparate groups of modern Israelis by re-discovering what the Romans destroyed, so as to make a nation fit for the coming of the Messiah. For Father Lambert the Messiah had already come; he hoped to unearth the stage upon which He had played out the drama of His life. Their convictions were incompatible—if one was right, the other was wrong—but when men sweat together, eat together and sleep under the same stars, a bond is forged between them, and they were now such close friends that Michal Dagan had sent his daughter, Anna, to study under Father Lambert in London.

In early June, 1988, soon after Corpus Christi, Michal Dagan telephoned Father Lambert and asked him to come to Jerusalem immediately. To Lambert, it was an odd request. The term at Huntingdon College, where he lectured twice a week, was not over. In addition, he had to prepare a paper for the Congress of Biblical Archaeologists being held in Oxford in July, and to attend meetings of the organizing committee. Dagan was coming to the Congress, and Father Lambert had planned to return with him to Jerusalem for his usual season of excavation. This was all known to the Israeli, yet he still insisted that Father Lambert drop every-thing and take the next flight to Tel Aviv.

Father Lambert agreed to go because he trusted Michal Dagan. He received permission from his prior, Father Godfrey—a for-mality—and told his secretary at Huntingdon College to cancel his appointments and reserve a plane seat. To neither did he give the reason for his precipitate departure; this he confided only to Brother Andrew Nash, who was both a Simonite monk and one of his graduate students.

At the age of twenty-eight, Andrew had almost completed his seven years' probation as a member of the order. In six months he was due to take his vows and be ordained as a deacon. He was considered by the other monks to be a valuable addition to their number. There were few vocations to the priesthood, and intel-ligent young men usually went into better-known orders such as the Jesuits, Dominicans or Benedictines. What had drawn Andrew to the Simonites was the personality of Father Lambert himself. He had first seen him on the podium of a lecture hall at Huntingdon College at a time when Andrew was not even a Catholic, let alone a would-be priest. His father had been an agnostic, his mother an atheist, and the Anglicanism he had been taught at school had been so bland that he had gone up to London University with no beliefs at all.

Father Lambert had overwhelmed Andrew. It was not just his lectures which had impressed him, but the way in which his ambitions soared above the mediocre values of the times. While every other member of the older generation, particularly his parents, seemed to pursue banal objectives—more money, a faster car, a better job, a new wife—Father Lambert had devoted his whole life to a striving for sanctity and a search for truth.

Other students who were impressed in this way did not go on to become Catholics, let alone monks in the Simonite order, and some of those who knew Andrew's background felt that he had joined the Simonites only because he had found in John Lambert a better father than the one nature had provided. It was also thought that the spectacle of his parents' unhappy marriage had led Andrew to consider a celibate life, something some of the young women at Huntingdon had reason to regret, because he was both good-natured and good-looking, with shaggy black hair and perpetually rumpled clothes that, as a concession to his calling, were dark in color—gray flannel trousers, with a black corduroy jacket or sweater, and a blue-denim, open-necked shirt.

Some doubts had been expressed by the novice master in the early years of Andrew's novitiate as to whether his vocation was a genuine call from God, or the immature emulation of a man he inordinately admired. After graduating from Huntingdon, he had been sent to study theology at the Simonite house in Rome. He had returned as determined as ever to become a Simonite monk, and had been considered sufficiently mature by the prior both to proceed toward ordination and to return to Huntingdon College as one of Father Lambert's graduate students. It had also suited the community, because no other monk was available, to assign him as an assistant to the man who was now the most distinguished member of the order. This was why Father Lambert had told Andrew about the mystery surrounding his summons to Jerusalem, and why his student was impatient for his return.

Father Lambert was due back on Saturday morning, exactly a week after he had left, but when Andrew came in on Friday evening from the college he was told by Gerry, the old Irish porter at the monastery, that Father Lambert had already returned.

"When did he get in?" asked Andrew.

"This morning," said the Irishman, "and I can tell you, Brother, he looked terrible. I think I would say he was ill."

"He always gets jet lag," said Andrew, "and he may not have slept much on the plane."

"Then you'd think he'd rest," said the porter, "but he was out again almost as soon as he came in, and then in and out, with hardly a cheerful word, which is very unlike the Father."

"Is he here now?"

"I think so, but I can't be sure because I haven't been at the door for most of the afternoon. They asked me to help them with moving the chairs down at Our Lady of Victories for the jumble sale, which is tomorrow, so I went off with Father Godfrey's blessing . . ."

Andrew left the porter still talking, as he had learned to do over the past few years, and walked through the tiled monastery hall to the broad stairs of polished wood. Floor polish was the prevalent aroma around the place, sometimes mixed with the scent of incense wafting in from the church after High Mass on Sunday. He climbed the stairs to the first floor and went to his room.

It was not yet dark outside, but his window was overshadowed on one side by the Gothic church and on the other by a wing of the monastery itself. He took out the books and papers from the Air France airline bag which he used as a briefcase, then looked at his telephone, wondering whether to ring Father Lambert's room or to assume that he was resting and wait to see him at supper.

He decided to wait, and sat down to read at his desk. The light was weak, and he reached forward to switch on his lamp, glancing as he did so up and out of the window toward the window of Father Lambert's room in the other wing of the monastery; if the older priest was there, perhaps he too would have switched on his lamp. But no light was visible.

Andrew looked back at his book and was dazzled for a moment by the bright light reflected off the white paper; then, as his eyes focused on the print, his thoughts caught up with something he had seen when glancing toward Father Lambert's window. He looked again. His eyes, now accustomed to the brighter light, took a moment to adjust to the gloom of the cloudy summer evening. When they did, they confirmed what Andrew thought he had seen—an elongated shape like a canvas kitbag, apparently attached to the wall beneath Father Lambert's room. He stood and leaned out to get a better look, and then with a spasm of shock recognized the shape as a man's body, hanging from the window by a rope.

He ran wildly up the stairs, slithering on the polished wood. On the upper corridor he passed Father Thomas, one of the mathematicians, and gasped, "Quick, get help."

He reached the door of Father Lambert's room, out of habit raised his hand to knock before he entered, but then threw open the door and ran across the room toward the open window. The bed blocked his path; it had been moved in front of the window, and a line of blue plastic-coated cable, the kind sold for clotheslines, had been tied to a post at the foot and was stretched tautly over the sill. It was only by kneeling on the mattress that Andrew could look out of the window. He saw at once that the other end of the cable was tied around the neck of the suspended body and knew instantly from the texture of the close-cropped hair on the head that the body was that of Father Lambert.

In a frenzy Andrew grabbed the line and tried to haul the body back into the room, but its weight was so great that he could not lift it. Although reason told him that the man was dead, and that there was nothing he could do to revive him, he became unreasonably convinced that there was still breath in the body and that he could save his professor if only he could lift him back onto the bed. His weakness frustrated him and he began to sob and shout at the same time: "Wait, Father Lambert, wait . . . we're coming, we're here."

At that moment three others came into the room behind him— Father Godfrey, the prior; Father Thomas; and Gerry. Father Godfrey climbed onto the bed beside Andrew, peered over the sill, turned pale, and whispered "Dear Lord." He too took hold of the cable and with Andrew tried to lift the body, but given their awkward position on the bed, even their combined strength was inadequate.

"Leave it to Gerry," Father Godfrey said, as he always did when a fuse burned out or a door jammed. He moved back; so did Andrew, and it was the turn of the porter to crouch on the bed with Father Thomas. They pulled on the cable for a moment, but then Gerry came away from the window. "It will be best to bring him in from below."

The four men filed out of the cell, and while the porter went for some wire cutters, the three monks descended to the unused room immediately below Father Lambert's. It was locked. Father Thomas ran to get the key, while Andrew and his superior waited by the door. The younger monk, who had now mastered his sobbing, looked at the older one, not so much to ask a specific question as to search for some explanation in the expression on the other's face. The plump face of the Simonite prior, however, remained blank and severe, and he avoided looking into Andrew's eyes, as if knowing that his own had nothing to say.

When Father Thomas returned with the key he gave it to Father Godfrey, who opened the door. The furniture in the cell was the same as in all the others, but had a musty, airless smell. It was also dark, because the legs and torso of the body shut out much of the fading evening light. Father Godfrey undid the catch of the wide sash window and raised the lower half. Father Thomas, deferring to the greater strength of the younger man, let Andrew move up beside the prior. "Gerry wasn't sure if his cutters would cut the cable," he said. "He said he might have to use a hacksaw."

Father Godfrey nodded.

"He'll give a shout when he's ready," said Father Thomas.

Again Father Godfrey nodded. He reached out of the window to see where he could get a hold on the body. Standing on the floor, he could only reach the hip. "I hope he can lower him slowly," he said. He turned back to Father Thomas. "Go and tell Gerry to cut the cable near to the bed and then lower it slowly. Tell him not to let it drop suddenly."

Father Thomas left the room. Andrew stood beside his superior at the window. For a moment they were silent; then Andrew asked, "What can have happened?"

Father Godfrey opened his mouth to answer, but at that moment a cry of "Right!" came from the porter on the floor above. The two monks leaned out of the window and grabbed the body, guiding it through the window until, at the last moment, the two men above let go and the body fell to the floor.

Andrew had fallen with the weight of the corpse and now found that it lay half on his lap and half against the wall beneath the window. He shrank back, horrified to see a face he had revered already blackened and distorted, the tongue protruding between the teeth and the unfocused eyes bulging from their sockets.

"God forgive him," murmured Father Godfrey, whose face had gone a shade paler than before. Then he turned to Father Thomas who had returned, panting. "Quick, a stole and the chrism."

Father Thomas disappeared. The porter came in and looked astonished at the body on the floor. "Holy Mother of God," he muttered.

As if inspired by this pious ejaculation, Father Godfrey began to pray, but in a muttered whisper so that Andrew could not follow or join in. He floundered for a moment, searching in his mind for an appropriate prayer, then for something spontaneous to say to God, but the grotesque body in his lap seemed to drive out any other thoughts. No cry came from his heart and he could envisage no God to hear it.

Father Thomas returned with the paraphernalia of the last sacrament, and the familiar ritual enabled Andrew to escape from this moment of desolation. It was clear that Father Lambert was stone dead—no attempts had been made to revive him—and so when the four men lifted his body onto the mattress, it was as if onto a bier, not a bed. "He's been dead for a while, poor man," said Father Godfrey, as if voicing his own doubts, "but there's no knowing when the soul leaves the body, so we should anoint him all the same." He leaned forward and gently pulled the eyelids down over the bulging eyes, then placed the stole around his neck. Father Thomas opened the small silver box containing the chrism, the holy oil. Father Godfrey took some on his thumb and smeared it in the form of a cross on the eyelids he had just closed, saying, "By this holy unction, and by his most tender mercy, may the Lord forgive thee whatsoever sin has been committed by sight." He then did the same to Father Lambert's ears, nostrils, mouth, hands and feet, repeating the prayer each time with the words appropriate to each organ, and with a special emphasis when it came to the hands. "May the Lord forgive thee whatsoever sin thou hast committed by deed . . ."

When the ceremony was over, the four men stood still, either praying silently or simply wondering what to do next. As they did so the bell rang for the monks' supper. The sound seemed to make the prior suddenly less constrained, as if the situation could be saved by a return to routine.

"Will you take these back," he said to Father Thomas, handing him the stole and the chrism, "and tell the fathers to start supper without us."

"Should I say—" Father Thomas began.

"No, nothing at all."

The monk left the now darkened cell and Father Godfrey, with a last look at the corpse, went out after him and walked toward the stairs, followed by Andrew and the porter.

"Shall I ring the sisters?" asked Gerry, referring to the nursing nuns who customarily laid out the corpses of the dead monks.

"Yes," said Father Godfrey, "but first, perhaps . . ."

"The police?" asked Gerry, his voice taking on a respectful tone as it mentioned an institution that he revered almost as much as the Church.

The prior frowned. "I was thinking, rather, of Dr. O'Malley. I think we can leave it to him to bring in the police if he thinks it necessary."

"I think that in cases of this kind—" began the porter.

"I daresay," said Father Godfrey sharply, "but we'll let the doctor decide." He turned to Andrew. "Would you come with me, now, for a word?"

Andrew nodded in a dazed way and followed his superior down the stairs to the ground floor and past the refectory, from which came the sound of clattering cutlery and the voice of Father Wilfrid reading from de Joinville's *Life of St. Louis*, to the prior's study.

This too smelled of polish, but tinged with tobacco, for Father Godfrey occasionally smoked a pipe. In most other respects it was similar to the study of the headmaster of a public school: a large, half-private, half-public room with two old leather armchairs, a heavy oak stool, and in one corner a desk with two telephones, a dictating machine and a framed photograph of Father Godfrey's parents. On the wall behind the desk was a reproduction of a painting by Titian of St. Simon Doria, the order's founder, while over the mantel was a large crucifix which made it clear that the room's incumbent was a man of God.

Andrew, who had been in this room on many occasions without remarking on the figure on the cross, noticed it now for the first time as a graphic depiction of agony and death.

"Sit down," Father Godfrey said to him, pointing to an armchair on one side of the fireplace, and sat himself in the other.

Andrew did as he was asked, his eyes still fixed on the twisted Christ.

Father Godfrey followed his glance and for a moment said nothing, as if unwilling to interrupt a silent prayer. But Andrew was not praying; he was not even grieving for his dead friend. He returned his eyes to the face of his superior and wondered almost idly what he was going to say. He watched as Father Godfrey raised the fingers of both his hands to rub the shining skin of his bald temples, as if a massage might help clarify his thoughts. When he looked up, it was with the kind of official expression that always accompanied the announcement of some administrative decision. He started to speak, but suddenly seemed to appreciate who was with him, and a kinder look came into his eyes. "This is particularly terrible for you," he said.

Andrew shook his head as if to disown any selfish sorrow. "I don't understand what can have happened," he said.

Father Godfrey blushed as if caught out in an impious assumption. "It does seem," he said, "as if Father John killed himself."

"But that's impossible," said Andrew.

"What other . . . interpretation can there be?"

"It could have been an accident . . ." Andrew began, but his voice faltered, as if he realized that the suggestion was absurd. "Or murder," he blurted out, with a defiant look at his superior.

Father Godfrey hesitated, pretending to consider this last suggestion, but then with an ironic smile he asked, "Can you think of anyone . . . or rather, any reason why anyone would want to murder Father Lambert?"

Andrew shook his head. "No." He looked down at his clasped hands to hide the tears he now felt seeping into his eyes and blurring his vision. "But I can't think why he would want to kill himself, either."

Father Godfrey sighed. "It is a dreadful truth," he said, "but there are . . . occasional suicides among priests."

"Why?"

"Because the Devil tempts us with moments of despair—us above all, whom he loathes and envies because God has chosen us to be higher than the angels."

"But surely, after so many years—"

"If a priest's faith falters, it is precisely his age that deepens his despair, because he has given up so much—a wife, a family—all for a reward which he no longer believes will be his."

"I can't believe that Father Lambert ever wanted that kind of life," said Andrew fiercely.

Father Godfrey hesitated, choosing his words with some care. "He was an exceptional man, as you know, learned and holy, and he was already that way when you met him. But just as he only became learned after many years of study and concentration, so he only became holy after many trials and temptations."

Andrew lowered his head and mumbled, "Of course. I should have realized."

"I cannot believe," said the prior, "that almighty God will condemn him because he faltered in one moment of despair. Remember that Saint Paul said that, 'in Jesus, the Son of God, we have the supreme high priest who has felt our weaknesses with us—who has been tempted in all the same ways that we are, though he is without sin. Let us be confident, then, in approaching the throne of grace, that we shall have mercy from him'—and mercy, too, for Father Lambert."

"Yes." Andrew kept his head lowered, and for a moment the words of the older priest calmed his chaotic thoughts.

"Now," said the superior, reverting to the practical manner with which he clearly felt more at ease, "we must think of what is to be done."

"Dr. O'Malley will be on his way."

"Yes, and he may feel it necessary to call in the police. It is important, however, to make sure that no newspaper finds out what has happened. There are all too many enemies of the Church who take delight in reporting cases of this kind."

"But won't there be an inquest?"

"There will, yes, unless Dr. O'Malley decides that no good purpose could be served by calling in the police or specifying suicide as the cause of death."

"But we can hardly expect him to make out a false death certificate."

A small frown wrinkled Father Godfrey's bald brow and a trace of irritability crept into his voice. "It is not what we would expect of him, but what he would expect of himself. He is a good Catholic, after all, and he would not want to harm the Church."

Andrew said nothing, but his superior seemed to take his silence as a form of rebuke because he went on, rather tetchily, "As you will discover when you grow older, Andrew, we are often tested by choices not of good and evil but of the greater or the lesser evil. No doubt it would be wrong for Dr. O'Malley to say that Father Lambert had died from natural causes if he had not, but first of all we cannot be absolutely certain that some kind of embolism or brainstorm—perhaps a kind of sunstroke, from when he was in Israel—did not lead him to behave in this irrational way, and secondly we must weigh against the lesser evil of a small deception the certain and substantial evil that will result if it becomes known that Father Lambert, of all people, took his own life."

Again Andrew said nothing, but his silence was more hesitant and less sullen.

"It isn't just his fame as an archaeologist that matters, though this would make the story front-page news, it is his standing as a priest and a man of faith. Imagine the gloating of our detractors, and think of the demoralization of all those men and women who have looked on him as a heroic exponent of the Catholic religion. Think of our fellow priests, and the danger that this advertisement of a brief moment of despair might induce in one of them, perhaps inspiring him, too, to kill himself."

The prior argued with increasing agitation, as if to persuade himself as much as his listener, but Andrew, who had been gasping and struggling in his own mind not to be sucked under by the current of his despair ever since he had seen the body dangling from the upper window, could not help seeing the force of this argument. He looked up at his superior, and in his eyes there must have been a sign that he was persuaded, because now the prior sat back with a sigh, as if Andrew's concurrence was that of a whole committee.

There was a knock at the door, and Father Thomas walked in. "The doctor is on his way," he said.

"Good," said Father Godfrey. "Come in, please, and close the door."

Father Thomas did so and sat on the oak stool. Father Godfrey went to his desk, picked up one of the telephones and dialed a single number. "Gerry," he said, "would you come to my study at once, please."

"Father Gervase asked if you were coming to supper," said Father Thomas, in the voice of one terrified that he has done the wrong thing. "I said I thought not."

"Quite right."

Again there was a knock on the door and the porter entered. "Dr. O'Malley will be here in a jiffy," he said.

"Good. Thank you."

Gerry hovered near the door.

"Please sit down for a moment."

The old man crossed to the leather armchair the prior had vacated.

"We have all been the witness to a very tragic and shocking event," Father Godfrey began, leaning against his desk. "There is no escaping the fact that Father Lambert, in a moment of terrible despair, succumbed to the prompting of the Devil and took his own life."

"Indeed, indeed," muttered the porter.

"Now I have told Brother Andrew, and I will tell Dr. O'Malley, that if news of this reaches the wider world it will do incalculable damage to our holy mother, the Church."

"Of course," said Father Thomas.

"It is therefore incumbent upon us to make sure that it does not."

"Indeed," said Gerry again.

"I shall therefore propose to Dr. O'Malley that it be given out that Father Lambert died of a stroke."

"And no police?" asked Gerry.

"And no police. But clearly, if Dr. O'Malley is to risk his professional reputation for the greater good of the Church, then it is our duty to support him by saying the same thing."

"You can count on me," said Gerry.

"Even our brothers in the community?" asked Father Thomas.

"They must not know."

The old mathematician bowed his head. "Very well."

"I take it upon my own conscience," said Father Godfrey, "and as your superior I instruct you on pain of sin never to divulge to anyone how Father Lambert met his end."

2

Alone at his desk, his eyes closed, his face pressed against the palms of his hands, Father Godfrey awaited the arrival of the doctor. He too tried to pray, but the only words that came to him were those of Christ on the cross: "My God, my God, why hast thou forsaken me?" The suicide of Father Lambert appeared to undo everything he had achieved since the community had chosen him as their prior.

His election, seven years before, had marked the end of the long period of turmoil that had followed the Second Vatican Council. When the genial Pope John XXIII had summoned all bishops in communion with the Catholic Church to the Vatican in 1962, none among the London Simonites had envisaged the revolution this would bring about. Certainly the Church had become isolated, even aloof, from the outside world. Its light was hidden under a bushel of institutional conceit. The talent of a composer like Elgar, or a writer like Evelyn Waugh, was ascribed by the Simonites to their religion. Those outside the Church, even fellow Christians in the Church of England, were thought damned, if not for what they believed, then for what their forefathers had done to the Catholics in Elizabethan times. When all the Simonite monks were joined by the boys from their school and the lay people who belonged to the parish to sing the Credo in Latin, or a hymn like "Faith of Our Fathers," there was hardly a heart that did not swell with pride, or a face that did not flush with triumphal fervor.

All that changed because of the Council. First it was ordained that the Mass was to be said in English instead of Latin, then that the celebrant should not face God in the tabernacle but the people in their pews. The mystery of the consecration, once hidden by the bowed shoulders of the priest, now became a spectacle for all to see, like the feeding of animals at the zoo. Many of the old moral certainties, so painstakingly transcribed from parchment to parchment by the Simonites over the ages, were thrown aside. Sins were no longer either mortal or venial—or even sins at all, if they were committed with a comfortable conscience. The relics of the saints, once venerated, suddenly became so many bits of bone. Terms like "transubstantiation" and "consubstantiation" became meaningless distinctions, and the only difference in the eucharistic bread of the various Christian denominations was in the way it was baked.

Father Godfrey had not blamed the Council itself for what happened in its wake. It started and finished with the best of intentions, and nowhere in its promulgations could be found the texts and statements that would explain why tens of thousands of priests, friars, monks and nuns suddenly threw off their habits and abandoned their calling. Or more confusingly, threw off their habits without abandoning their calling. Or most confusingly of all, abandoned their calling without throwing off their habits, remaining as priests, friars, monks and nuns to reform the Church so radically from within that it bore no resemblance to what it had been before.

The English community of Simonites suffered the full force of this hurricane of change. In 1965 there were forty-seven monks in their monastery in London, forty-one priests and six novices; twenty years later there were twelve. Of the missing thirty-five, nine had died, five had been transferred to the American province, two had defected to the Dominicans, while the remaining seven had been laicized, six of them marrying, two of them to nuns.

The statistics alone, however, did not do justice to the terrible quarrels and conflicts of those twenty years. Rival camps were formed within the community whose mutual antipathy was so great that they would barely speak to one another. A strong prior might have prevented this degeneration of a community supposedly based upon love, but it was a tradition among the Simonites not to waste the talents of their eminent scholars on administration, and instead to elect as their superior a monk who had nothing better to do. In untroubled times, this arrangement worked well.

Most of the Simonites pursued their careers in secular universities, and the rule of the prior was a formality.

Suddenly, however, some of the younger monks began to behave in ways that outraged their older and more conservative brethren, discarding the gray habit that had been the uniform of the Simonites since the eleventh century, and even the black suit and clerical collar worn in the world outside, appearing first in suits with collars and ties, and later in jeans and open-neck shirts.

The prior of that period tried gently chiding these rebellious monks, only to be subjected to a counterblast of progressive theology—Karl Rahner, Hans Küng, and "the spirit of Vatican II." He would then retreat, only to find himself prodded in the rear by the indignation of the conservatives. The matter would be raised in Chapter, leading to painful debates in which insults were thrown from one side to the other, all couched in convoluted theological jargon. The Council had decided that the Church should be open to the world. How could the monks follow this teaching, the progressives argued, if they wore fancy dress dating from the Middle Ages? How could they keep themselves informed of what was happening in the world if they were not allowed television in their cells? Or stereos so that they could listen to the kind of music that was an integral part of contemporary culture?

The community capitulated on the question of clothes and television sets, but worse was to come. One of the progressive monks, a middle-aged man, was seen by one of the bretheren entering a restaurant with a nun—neither wearing habits, both in lay clothes, and not at midday, but at eight in the evening, and not a simple, honest restaurant, where two hungry people might go to get something to eat, but somewhere expensive and dimly lit, with pink tablecloths and the menu in French.

Then a second monk, who taught medieval history at Bedford College, began holding tutorials in his cell. Since his students were all girls, and it was an ancient rule that no women were allowed in the monastery, this aroused such indignation that the prior was forced to call a special meeting of the Chapter. The medievalist argued that the bar against women was the expression of the sexist, paternalist, misogynist, gynophobic prejudices of the Church, which were most emphatically at variance with the spirit of Vatican II. He was supported by the monk dating the nun, who, since he was not only the senior theologian in the community, but had also served as a theological adviser at the final session of the Council itself, persuaded a majority of the community that to bar women from entering the monastery was to disregard the promptings of the Holy Ghost.

It was decided that women should be admitted, but not after dark for fear of scandal. The medievalist continued to hold afternoon tutorials for his students, one of whom in particular seemed to need more supervising than the others. It was reported to the prior that music was heard from behind the door when she was there. The medievalist said it was a tape of Orff's *Carmina Burana*, which was relevant to the subject. Later still, some of the monks heard other sounds, this time of a kind they dared not interpret, but when the medievalist was laicized and then married the student it came to them as no surprise.

There were other sources of dissension, particularly when some of the young monks heard the call of the South American bishops to exercise a preferential option for the poor. Under their influence the community changed the school from a good grammar school to a bad comprehensive one, where monks who were authorities on the poetry of Catullus or the Theory of Relativity tried to teach math and English to the rough little ragamuffins who lived in neighboring council flats.

There was also the question of the order's endowments—bank deposits, stocks and shares, and some valuable paintings that had been bequeathed to the Simonites over the years. It was proposed in Chapter, and the motion was carried, that all these should be sold and the proceeds given to the poor; it was only through the deft and somewhat duplicitous transactions of the stubborn and conservative procurator that the English branch of the Simonites remained solvent.

This procurator had been Father Godfrey, who, together with Father Thomas and one or two others, made up the conservative faction. None of them, however, had the qualities that would have allowed them to wrest the moral initiative from the progressives. Father Thomas was shy, and could only see the hand of God in the formulae of higher mathematics. Father Godfrey was a good financier and administrator, but had a weakness for lunching with rich benefactors of the order, and knew rather too much about wine.

Their fortunes changed with the return of Father Lambert to Huntingdon College. He brought with him not just his prestige as an archaeologist, but also his distinction as a theologian and his reputation as a monk of an uncompromising kind. He was known to fast. He was seen to pray. He made a personal confession every week. Yet he accepted wholeheartedly the doctrines of the Council. He was open to the world, teaching at a secular institution. He was also ecumenical in spirit, with more friends than any of the other monks among Anglicans, Muslims and Jews.

Where Father Lambert differed from the progressives was on the question of what it meant to be holy. Their interpretation of the law of love led them to support famine relief, nuclear disarmament and the Sandinistas in Nicaragua. Father Lambert could see love in a kind word from a duchess to her servant, or in the prayer said by a general with nuclear missiles under his command. It was faith, not good works, which saved man from damnation. To those Simonites who dismissed the "cultic priesthood" in favor of helping the poor, he would say, like the Curé d'Ars, that welfare was merely the work of men, whereas Christ's sacrifice in the Mass was the work of God. It was not so much what he said, however, as the force of his example that won over the Simonite monks. Under his influence, they revived services such as Benediction, which had been abandoned after the Council. On his advice, they dismissed the ineffective headmaster of their school and appointed one of a sterner kind. When their prior died in 1981, many wanted Father Lambert to take his place. He asked not to be nominated because, if elected, he would have had to give up his post at Huntingdon College. The candidate he suggested was Father Godfrey, who was duly chosen.

3

As he left the prior's study, Andrew felt no appetite for supper; indeed, a nausea overwhelmed him when he smelled the aroma of sausages, cabbage and coffee from the refectory. He returned to his own room and to the desk where he had placed his books in what now seemed a different life. His window was still open and the lamp switched on, but he went neither to the window nor to his desk; instead, he knelt down by his bed and raised his eyes to the crucifix on the wall behind it. Neither prayers nor pious thoughts came to his mind. Instead, the tears, which for some time had been seeping into his eyes, flowed freely down his cheeks, and he began to sob with an abandon he had not known since childhood. The image of the leathery skin and smiling face of his beloved professor kept changing to the grotesque grimace of the strangled corpse. He buried his face in the cotton bedspread covering the blankets on his bed, not so much to muffle the sound of his sobbing or to soak up his tears as to shut out the light, as if darkness would obscure the reality of what had happened.

In time his weeping ran its course. He raised his eyes from the bed, though not to the crucifix, which he avoided because at that moment he felt far from God. Instead his thoughts turned to his older brother, Henry, who had always been his closest friend. He went to his desk and put his hand on the telephone, intending to call him and tell him what had happened. Then he remembered that the prior had forbidden it, and wondered if it would be worse to tell Henry half the truth rather than to tell him nothing at all. Yet the thought of not confiding in him, and so not receiving the kind of comfort his sardonic brother always provided, seemed to add to the already intolerable weight of his suffering. Though Henry was not a Catholic, and thought Andrew insane for wanting to become a priest, he had nonetheless witnessed the drama of his vocation, and so could hardly be excluded from knowing the present tragic turn of events.

As Andrew wondered what to do, he was distracted by a moth that had flown in through the open window and was throwing itself erratically at his desk lamp. He went over to close the window, and as he did so looked up to the spot where he had first seen the body hanging from the wall. A light shone in the room below—perhaps the doctor had arrived and was studying the body—and on the floor above, the window remained open. A reflex sense of responsibility for Father Lambert's affairs made him decide to go over and close it.

He passed no one as he climbed the stairs and walked the length of the long corridor to Father Lambert's cell. He opened the door, switched on the light and went to the window, squeezing between the wall and the bed, then pushing it back to its proper place. The end of the cable remained tied to the bedpost, a short length dangling at the point where the porter had cut it. Andrew worked the knot loose and dropped the line into the wastepaper basket.

He looked around the room, hoping to see something that might explain why Father Lambert had taken his own life. There was a crucifix on the wall, as there was in each of the cells; a narrow bed with posts of stained pine; the wardrobe, made of a heavier wood and decorated with the same kind of Gothic embellishments as the banisters of the stairs and the confessionals in the church. One of the white-painted walls was obscured by the books stacked against it from floor to ceiling. The other three were bare except for the crucifix. There was a sink in the corner of the room, with a small mirror above it; a chest of drawers, and a bedside table with a cabinet made to contain a chamberpot; a large desk against the book-lined wall, with a filing cabinet on either side, a lamp on one corner and at the other two telephones, one linked to the exchange at the porter's lodge, and the other a direct line.

Father Lambert had an office at Huntingdon College, but he had preferred to work here in his cell. The desk was piled with papers: issues of archaeological reviews from the U.S., France and Germany; articles sent by colleagues in different countries; theses sent for an opinion; and letters that were yet to be answered. These were spread out either on the desk or on a shelf behind it, which had been cleared of books.

Having acted as Father Lambert's secretary, Andrew knew the significance of every pile and glanced cursorily over them to see that each was in place. In the back of his mind was the thought that there might be something which would explain Father Lambert's state of mind. Andrew had not worked out quite what this clue could be, so he was not looking for anything in particular when it suddenly struck him that there was something odd about the arrangement of the papers on the desk. They were not displaced, but lay a little too neatly in their various piles. It was a difference no one would have noticed unless they were familiar with Father Lambert's habits. He had been orderly but not tidy, always able to find what he was looking for among the papers scattered on the desk and shelf.

Now, however, the piles were all neatly stacked, as if a cleaner had been dusting the room. He wondered for a moment whether the old Pole who cooked for the monks and polished the corridors might have broken the rule under which each monk had to clean his own cell, but by lowering his head at an angle to the light from the lamp, he could see that, although a thin film of dust had been disturbed around the piles of papers, it had not been wiped away.

The obvious supposition was that Father Lambert himself had rearranged his own papers before taking his life, but to Andrew's eye the neatness of their arrangement suggested someone else's hand. In any case, why would a man about to kill himself tidy a pile of back issues of the *American Journal of Archaeology* and the *Revue d'archéologie Biblique*? Yet why would anyone else have moved the magazines unless they were looking for something they had not found among his papers?

Andrew went to the desk and opened the drawers. His eyes fell upon familiar objects—paper, pens, ink, a magnifying glass, paperclips and postage stamps—and he stared at them for some time, unable to decide whether they had been moved or not. Once again it seemed as if they were all more neatly arranged than he had remembered them, but perhaps he was imagining it, imagining evidence to feed his suspicions. But suspicions of what? If he was searching for a note to confirm Father Lambert's suicide, he was hardly likely to find one; Father Lambert had considered himself answerable to God alone.

He took Father Lambert's diary from the top drawer of the desk. In it was written only the details of his flights to Tel Aviv and back again. He had not added anything to it since his precipitate return, and no appointments were entered for today, even though the porter had said that he had gone out. Nor were there any noted for the days he had spent in Jerusalem; he had clearly left his program to Dagan.

What interested Andrew was not the diary, but the canvas-covered notebook, in which Father Lambert always wrote down what was passing through his mind—observations from books he had been reading or discoveries made during an excavation. If Dagan had called him to Israel to witness some startling find, Lambert would almost certainly have written something about it. Andrew searched quickly through the drawers, and then in the briefcase beside the desk, but did not find it. Its absence, together with his suspicions that someone had been through Father Lambert's papers, suddenly made it seem possible that the scholar's death was not as straightforward as it seemed. The idea that perhaps, after all, he had not killed himself filled Andrew with great joy, and feeling that he must immediately share the good news with the prior, he rose and ran from the room, along the corridor and down the stairs to his superior's study, where, out of breath, he knocked and waited. He heard the word "Come" and entered to find Father Godfrey sitting at his desk. Dr. O'Malley had apparently left, and the prior looked up with relief on his face, as if Andrew had come at an opportune time.

"Yes, good. Come in."

"His notebook's gone," Andrew blurted out.

Father Godfrey frowned. "How do you mean?"

"His notebook, where he wrote everything down—it's gone."

The frown deepened. "What does that signify?"

"That someone took it from his room."

"Why would anyone take it?"

"I don't know, but I also noticed that everything had been neatly rearranged . . ."

"*Rearranged?*"

"Yes. As if someone had been through his papers."

"But you are the only one who . . . or Father Lambert, before he died."

"That's just the point," said Andrew, his agitation sounding a little like exasperation. "I'm almost certain that some third person has been through his papers and has stolen his notebook."

Father Godfrey sighed, a sigh that also had a touch of exasperation. "Who would want to do such a thing?"

"I don't know."

"And why?"

"I don't know that either. But there might have been some clue in the notebook as to why he . . . he died."

The prior looked wearily at the window, then back at Andrew. "I can understand," he said, "that you in particular should be upset by what has happened, and that consciously or unconsciously you have to search for some explanation of a rational kind. But you must accept that men act irrationally, even men like Father John, when they suffer inordinately or are tempted to the limits of their endurance."

"If someone was there . . ." Andrew interrupted as if he had been listening to his own thoughts, not his superior's advice.

"No one was there," said Father Godfrey.

". . . then we should call the police."

The prior lost patience. "We cannot call the police," he said irritably, "because Dr. O'Malley has signed a death certificate giving a stroke as the cause of death."

"I'm sure he was killed," said Andrew, tears returning to his eyes.

"Of course," said Father Godfrey, his tone kinder as he saw the younger man's reaction. "It is natural and noble of you to refuse to accept that Father Lambert succumbed to such a serious sin. But even if you are right, even if he *was* killed, you must see that the absence of his notebook, which he may well have left at the college or in Israel, and your sense that his papers were too neatly arranged would not constitute evidence worth showing to the police."

Andrew swallowed to control his tears. "No. Of course. I'm sorry."

Father Godfrey stood, and with a paternal hand on Andrew's shoulder guided him toward the door. "If anything else turns up— anything concrete—come to me again. I too would love to be able to believe that Father Lambert did not die by his own hand."

It was now about ten o'clock, a time when most of the monks went to work in their rooms. Andrew, however, returned to Father Lambert's to test his perception once more. He switched on the light, closed the door and sat on the edge of the bed looking at the desk from a distance, comparing the position of the books and the papers with how he remembered them from the week before. They still seemed a fraction too tidy, but nothing was out of place. Whether or not someone had been there, he recognized the force of the prior's argument; it would be absurd to suggest that Father Lambert had been murdered simply because his assistant sensed something odd in the arrangement of the papers on his desk or in the absence of his notebook.

The weakness of the evidence led to a collapse of the hypothesis in his own mind, and all at once he was overwhelmed by another wave of sadness. The idea that such a strong and vibrant man had so suddenly and totally fallen into despair that he had deliberately bought a clothesline, tied one end to his bedstead and the other around his neck, moved the bed to the window and then jumped out, conjured up in him both an oppressive sense of the power of evil and an acute feeling of pity. Since Father Lambert had been a much older man, his feelings for him had certainly been like those of a son, but sons can feel protective toward their fathers, particularly those who care for them in the way that Andrew, as his secretary, had cared for him, and with a certain bravado he now felt that he could have helped him if only Father Lambert had confided his despair.

Inadvertently Andrew started to pray. When he had tried earlier, no words had come to his lips and no image of God to his mind. Now, however, when he had not consciously intended to address his Creator, he found himself pleading for the soul of his dead friend, begging Christ to judge him not by the despair of his last moments but by the heroic virtue of his life.

These thoughts were interrupted by the ringing of one of the telephones on Father Lambert's desk. Andrew jumped up, startled not just by the sound itself but by the fact that a dead man's telephone should be ringing at all. It was the direct line. He watched it for a moment, wondering whether to answer; then, realizing that he remained in charge of Father Lambert's affairs, he picked it up and said, "Hello."

"John? Is that you?" asked the soft voice of a woman.

"This is his secretary, Brother Andrew."

"Ah. I had hoped to speak to Father Lambert."

"I'm afraid he . . . he's not here."

"I see." She paused, then asked, "Is he all right?"

"He's . . . he's . . ." Andrew could not bring himself to say that he was dead. "He's not well," he said.

"I see." She spoke as if she had expected him to say something of the kind.

"May I ask who is speaking?"

"Veronica Dunn. You don't know me. I am a friend of Father Lambert's. I saw him this afternoon and . . . he didn't seem well."

"You saw him today?"

"Yes. He came to lunch." She said this nonchalantly, as if he had been one among other guests.

"Where?" Andrew asked. "Where did he have lunch?"

"In my house. Why? Does he have food poisoning?" She asked this with a trace of humor.

"No, no," he said, "but I wonder . . ." He hesitated, uncertain how to go on.

"What?"

"Could I come and see you?"

"Tonight?"

"No. But perhaps tomorrow morning. I could tell you how he is."

"Of course. I live in Edwardes Square." She gave the address. "I'll expect you any time after ten."

Andrew was now exhausted, worn out from shock. This call itself was extraordinary. Andrew had been privy to Father Lambert's affairs for the last two years, but had never heard him mention a woman called Veronica Dunn; yet now she was ringing him on the line whose number he had kept secret from all but a very few. He picked up Father Lambert's address book, which lay next to his diary on the desk, and looked under the letter D. The name was not there, which suggested either that he had known her very well or hardly at all. If well, why had Andrew never heard of her? If little, why had he not only given her the number of his private line but also had lunch with her on a day he had expected to be in Jerusalem?

Tired as he was, Andrew was impatient to see the woman the next day. However, he first wanted to know something about her; he picked up the telephone and dialed his brother's number.

"Henry?"

"Yes."

He could hear *Newsnight* on the television in the background. "Is this a bad moment?"

"No. Wait a minute, I'll turn down the television."

"I thought you'd be out," Andrew said when his brother returned.

"I've just got back."

"Something dreadful has happened."

"What?"

"Father Lambert is dead."

There was a pause before Henry said, "I'm sorry."

"It has come as a most terrible shock, and there are various complications . . ." He longed to tell his brother how the priest had died, but remembering the command of his superior he let his voice tail off.

"What kind of complications?"

"I can't tell you just now. Perhaps we could meet tomorrow?"

"Do you want to have lunch?"

"Perhaps in the evening?"

"I'm out for supper, but come for a drink around six."

"At six. Fine. But there's another thing . . ."

"What?"

"Have you ever come across a woman called Veronica Dunn?"

"I've met her, yes. She was married to Tom Dunn."

"Who was he?"

"A businessman, the chairman of CDT."

"And now?"

"I don't know. They divorced and I think she got a degree from Birkbeck College."

"Is she a Catholic?"

"Yes. So was he."

"Were there children?"

"I daresay, but they'd be grown by now."

"So she's not young?"

"No. Why? Haven't you met her?"

"No. I'm going to tomorrow."

"I seem to remember she's fairly dreary."

"It's all very strange."

"What is?"

"I'll tell you tomorrow."

4

Andrew was awakened at six the next morning by a knock on the door of his cell and the shout of *"Benedicamus Domino,"* to which he mumbled *"Deo gratias"* in reply. He stumbled out of bed, his head aching after a restless night, sat dazed through matins and Mass, and at breakfast was glad of the rule of silence that prevented his fellow friars from discussing the death of Father Lambert. As he ate a bowl of cornflakes, he wondered whether or not to tell the prior about Mrs. Dunn, but remembering his irritability the night before, decided that it would be more charitable to spare him further complications.

He left the monastery at nine-thirty carrying his Air France bag as if to go to Huntingdon College, but instead of taking a bus to Bloomsbury caught one going to Kensington. He got off at the High Street and walked from there to Edwardes Square, arriving at the address he had been given at five minutes past ten.

The door was opened by a tall woman of around fifty with shoulder-length gray hair and kind blue eyes. She did not ask who he was or introduce herself, but invited him in; Andrew recognized her voice as that of the woman he had spoken to the night before.

"Go upstairs," she said, leading him into a narrow hallway. "I'll bring some coffee."

He went up to the drawing room on the first floor. It had two long windows looking out over the square, and was furnished with a deep sofa, and two yellow-covered armchairs with plump cushions. On the walls were two eighteenth-century paintings, dark canvases with fat gilt frames, and a Piranesi print. On the well-polished surfaces of an antique table were two silver-framed photographs, one of Veronica Dunn as a younger woman, the other of two grinning thirteen- or fourteen-year-old children.

There were footsteps on the stairs, and a moment later Mrs. Dunn came into the room carrying a silver coffee pot and two cups on a tray. She placed it on a low table and sat down, perched on the edge of the sofa. Her blue skirt and purple sweater, like the furniture in the room, were plain but elegant; there was a brooch pinned at her throat, and her carefully styled hair made a delicate frame for her melancholy face. Comparing her to the silver-framed photograph of her younger self, Andrew saw how her beauty had faded with age; yet when she smiled, he recognized the remnants of great feminine charm.

"I'm so glad to meet you," she said, handing him a cup of coffee. "John has talked about you from time to time."

Andrew blushed, not from modesty but to hide the confusion he felt that she knew about him when he knew so little about her. "It's kind of you to let me call on you . . ." he mumbled.

Mrs. Dunn smiled again. "How is he this morning?"

It was a sign of Andrew's confused state of mind that he had not prepared himself for this question. "I'm afraid," he said, "I'm afraid that he's . . ."

The smile left her lips. "Is he worse?"

"No. He's dead." The words came out abruptly only because he could think of no others.

Mrs. Dunn turned pale. "He's dead?" she repeated in a whisper.

"Yes."

"When? What was wrong with him?"

"I'm afraid that last night . . . I felt I couldn't tell you over the telephone. He wasn't ill. He was already dead. He died . . . in the afternoon."

"Dear God." She hid her face in her hands.

"I'm sorry. I'm terribly sorry."

For a moment they sat in silence; then she uncovered her face and looked up at him with an expression of horrified anxiety. "He didn't kill himself, did he?" she asked, her voice both pleading and emphatic.

"Yes, I'm afraid he did. He hanged himself."

He answered in this way only because he was so taken aback by her question that he forgot both his own suspicions that Father

Lambert had been murdered and his promise to his superior that he would tell no one the truth.

Veronica Dunn's face, already pale, became quite gray, and the features, which had seemed so bland and expressionless, took on a look of desperation. Her lips moved as if she was about to whisper, but no word came out. She glanced almost angrily at Andrew, stood up, went to the window and, her hands clenched, looked out over the square.

Feeling that it was his duty to console her, Andrew searched for something appropriate to say, but as he did so he realized that since she had suggested that Father Lambert might have killed himself, she might also know what had put him in a suicidal frame of mind.

"It was a terrible thing to have happened," he said awkwardly.

She said nothing.

"We feel, however—at least, our prior has decided—that it should not be known that he died in that way."

She turned to face him, her features more composed. "Of course," she said. "I shall tell no one." She came back to the armchair and sat down.

"I would be grateful," said Andrew, "because I was told to say that he had died from a stroke."

She turned to him, hesitated, then asked, "Did you find him . . . hanging?"

"Yes."

"How terrible for you." She glanced at him sympathetically.

"I loved him very much."

"So did I."

"May I ask . . . what made you suspect that he had killed himself?"

She looked grave again. "I was afraid that he might . . ."

"Why?"

"He came to lunch and behaved in a quite unusual way."

"How do you mean?"

Once again she looked intently at Andrew, as if trying to decide how much she should say. "I thought that perhaps he'd been affected by the sun in Israel."

"You knew that he'd been to Israel?"

"Yes. And something happened there to change him."

"To change him? How had he changed?"

"He no longer believed."

"In what?"

"In God. In Christ. In the Church. I don't know quite what it was. But he had changed. He was no longer calm or cheerful. Do you remember how calm and cheerful he always was?"

"Yes."

"There was a time—you won't remember, you're not old enough—but when he was younger he sometimes became agitated and morose. That calm and cheerfulness only came with time. But yesterday it was as if he wanted to return to the past, to go back and begin again."

"How could he?"

"Of course he couldn't, but he thought he could, and I . . ." She stopped, blushed and looked away. "He was worried about you."

"About me?"

"Yes. He thought that when you knew . . ."

"Knew what?"

"That he no longer believed—or *why* he no longer believed—you would suffer a dreadful disillusion."

"At least I have learned that my faith does not depend on his," Andrew said quietly.

"No. Nor does mine."

"Weren't you upset by what he said?"

"Yes, of course, but for him, not for me."

"You thought that he might kill himself?"

"Not at first, no, although for a man to abandon what he has lived for for so long . . . But after . . ."

"After?"

She looked down at her hands. "I knew . . . I told him that one can't go back and begin again."

Now, for the first time, a few tears ran down Mrs. Dunn's cheeks, but her grief was as reserved as the rest of her behavior.

"I don't really understand," said Andrew.

She looked at him kindly. "How could you? You are so young."

"I . . . I would like to," he said, "because it is important to me to know why Father Lambert took his life."

"But if I tell you . . . if I tell you everything . . ." Her voice faltered.

"What?"

"Then your memory of him . . ."

"That is secure."

"You are not a priest yet, are you?"

"No."

"But I can trust you as if you were?"

"Of course."

She sighed. It was the sigh of a child. "Some years ago, when my husband left me, I was very unhappy. I went to your church to speak to a priest. Quite by chance, it was John. I saw him from time to time and I ceased to be unhappy because—well, because I fell in love with him."

"But you were married," said Andrew.

She looked at him coolly. "Yes. My husband had left me for another woman, but in the eyes of the Church I was still married and had two children. Nevertheless, I fell in love with him and he . . . he fell in love with me."

"How terrible."

She smiled bitterly. "Yes, it *was* terrible. Terrible is just what it was for us both, because I was married and he was a priest. We could easily have become lovers, but we didn't. God triumphed over the Devil. We stopped seeing each other. We lived only a mile apart but we never met alone until nine or ten years later when we felt old enough and safe enough to be friends once again."

She paused and glanced at Andrew, but the young monk's face was hidden in his hands to conceal an expression not of disgust or disapproval, but of astonishment that Father Lambert had ever been tempted by a woman, particularly a woman as apparently conventional as Veronica Dunn. He looked up at her, then away, revealing the very thoughts he had hoped to conceal. "It must have been hard," he said lamely.

She smiled with the bitter understanding of a woman who is past her prime. "Other people's passions are always difficult to imagine," she said, "particularly when you are young and they are middle-aged."

"Not at all," he said chivalrously.

"They are even harder to remember," she said, "and as I told him, impossible to revive."

An unpleasant feeling overcame Andrew, similar to what he had felt the day before when he recognized the body hanging from the window. He became afraid that the woman in front of him was about to tell him something that he did not want to know, but as strong as his reluctance to listen was her urge to confess. "I told him yesterday," she went on, hesitating, blushing, but continuing inexorably all the same, "that we could not go back and relive the past in a different way, but he said that our love was now the most precious thing in his life and that he did not want to die with it unfulfilled."

Andrew looked at her appalled, but she was looking out of the window and did not see the expression in his eyes. "He was so agitated, so determined, and I felt, still . . . well, that if it mattered to him so much . . . The house was empty, so I agreed." She turned back and glanced involuntarily at the sofa upon which Andrew was sitting, then was silent.

Andrew also said nothing as he tried to digest the disgust he felt at the image she had conjured up—not just of a priest and a woman untrue to their vows, but of two aging bodies making love in the middle of the day.

"It was only a moment," she said quietly, "and I am afraid that he was dreadfully disappointed. He had imagined, I think, something altogether more magnificent."

"And did he show remorse?" asked Andrew.

"I don't know. He apologized . . ."

"For what he had done?"

She shrugged her shoulders. "Or for what he felt he had done . . . badly. He said it would take time, but I knew from the look in his eyes that it would never happen again, which was why I was afraid that after this second disillusion . . ."

"Yes, of course. It makes suicide more certain."

She looked at him, puzzled. "Why more certain? Was it ever *un*certain?"

"I thought that there was room for some slight doubt."

"Could it have been an accident?"

"No, not an accident, and at first sight he clearly seemed to have hanged himself, but I noticed—or thought I did—that his papers were too tidy. That is, they were always tidy, but yesterday they seemed tidy in an unusual way."

Mrs. Dunn frowned. "Are you suggesting that someone might have killed him?"

"No." Andrew's brow also wrinkled as he tried to think through the implications of what he was saying. "One can't really suggest that someone could have killed him and then tried to make it seem like suicide because one cannot think of any reason for it. But if someone *had* been there, going through his things . . ."

"Was anything missing?"

"Yes. His notebook."

"Stolen?"

"Not necessarily, no. He might have left it in Israel."

"Surely you should have called the police."

"The prior thought that the greater good was served by avoiding scandal."

"But if he was murdered . . ."

"It is very hard to think of a motive for murder, whereas suicide—well, you yourself felt that he may have had it in mind."

"I know, I know. So the mystery is not how he died, but how he lost his faith."

"Apparently there are priests who do."

"Of course. I know, and he did, too. So many of his friends abandoned the priesthood in the years after the Council; and John himself was sometimes pessimistic about the direction in which the Church seemed to be going."

"I know."

"That's why he placed so much hope in you. He told me that so many of the younger priests had been corrupted in the seminaries by the liberal theologians. They were no longer taught to believe in Hell, but without Hell the whole idea of salvation loses its meaning and there is no point in the suffering of Christ."

"*He* believed in Hell," said Andrew gravely.

"Until yesterday, yes, he believed in Hell, but then suddenly he behaved as if he knew for certain that there was nothing beyond the grave."

Andrew left Edwardes Square soon after eleven and, catching a bus which went toward the college, sat on the top deck trying hard to make sense of what he had just heard from Veronica Dunn. That Father Lambert had made love with her hours before he died was an appalling revelation, but it was only further evidence of the dreadful doubt and despair which had clearly overwhelmed him upon his return from Israel. More astonishing, and far harder to digest, was the discovery that nine or ten years before, shortly before Andrew had met him, he had been deeply in love with a woman.

Of course Andrew knew that many priests found celibacy an ordeal, and when considering the priesthood he himself had had misgivings on this account. He had instincts common to a man of his age, and novices were encouraged to be candid about their sexuality. Indeed his novice master, a veteran of Vatican II, had even expressed doubts about the Church's wisdom in insisting upon celibacy in its priests. It had been Father Lambert who had persuaded him that it had a value beyond the sacrifice of something pleasant for God, or the avoidance of the encumbrance of a wife and family, in order to dedicate oneself entirely to the Lord. In a priest, he had said, the man must transcend the male; holiness was incompatible with the qualities that women sought in their lovers. This was why Jesus had been celibate, and had asked those who would follow him all the way to make themselves eunuchs for the sake of the Kingdom of God.

Andrew had been readily persuaded. The only contrary opinion came from his brother Henry, whose cynicism about women had always made Andrew feel that it would be as well to leave them alone. There were times when he had wondered what it would be like to know the warmth and comfort of a woman's love; but by and large he had accepted that the reward for renouncing a wife and family of his own was the freedom to love both God and his neighbor in an entirely unstinting and unselfish way. Although called to serve God principally as an archaeologist, he had also worked as a stretcher-bearer at Lourdes, helped at a hostel for the homeless in Waterloo, and was always ready to listen to the troubles of his fellow students at the college when their love affairs went wrong or their parents let them down.

Now, sitting on the bus, and pondering what he had just learned about Father Lambert's passion for Veronica Dunn, he could not suppress the feeling that somehow he had been misled, if not actually deceived. He felt like a boy who had caught his teacher reading a pornographic book. Did it mean that the teacher was depraved? Or that the lewd passages were not as corrupting as he had been told? Was it possible that when Jesus had said that only the man who hates his life in this world will keep it in the next one, he had not meant it to be taken as literally as he had supposed? Was there some way, perhaps, in which a Christian could have his cake and eat it too?

5

Andrew got off the bus at Holborn still in some confusion, and walked through the elegant streets and squares of Bloomsbury to the ugly postwar buildings that housed Huntingdon College. There he went straight to the Master and told him that his professor of archaeology had just died from a stroke. Then he broke the news to those who worked in Father Lambert's department. One of the older lecturers blanched as if struck by the thought that it could easily have been he who had suddenly met his death, while the secretary sobbed quietly into a handkerchief.

Andrew went in search of Anna Dagan, and caught sight of her coming out of a seminar which he himself should have attended. From the way she greeted him and the cheerful look on her face, it was clear that she had not yet heard the news. They walked down the corridor to the canteen, where they picked up trays and helped themselves to lunch. It was only when they were seated at a table in the corner that he told her Father Lambert was dead.

Anna looked at him quizzically, as if he was making a bad joke, but seeing the grave expression on his face, she sank back shaken on the hard canteen chair. "But he always seemed so well," she said. "I can't believe he died just like that."

Andrew did not answer. He faced a dilemma. In obedience to his superior's instructions he had just told everyone at Huntingdon College that Father Lambert had died of a stroke. He was tempted to tell Anna the truth, not just because she was his friend, but because, as Michal Dagan's daughter, she was well placed to find out what had happened to Father Lambert in Israel. With the kind of quick casuistry which comes easily to the young, he decided that since the secret had inadvertently escaped him in the presence of Mrs. Dunn, it was really no longer a secret. Just as Father Godfrey in good conscience could decide that a greater good would be served by lying, so Andrew could equally well decide that a greater good would be served by telling the truth. Therefore he told her the whole story, and she, for the first time since he had known her, listened without interruption.

In normal circumstances, she would tease Andrew almost every time he opened his mouth. She made much of the fact that he was a Simonite monk, saying that she had been sent by God to test him. She was small, with short black hair cut in bangs over her forehead, sallow skin, brown eyes and an innocent, childlike face. She was often taken for sixteen instead of twenty-two, and part of her sharpness was undoubtedly meant to disabuse those who thought her as innocent as she seemed. She was clever, but also contrary, and had made life so difficult for her parents in Israel that they had sent her to study for a postgraduate degree with Father Lambert in London.

Here Andrew had befriended her, putting up with her relentless teasing and occasionally cruel moods because he was amused by her jokes and enlivened by her intelligence. He also felt sorry for her, sensing the uncertainty behind the shield of her caustic humor. He knew from Father Lambert that she got on badly with her family, particularly her brother Jake, as she called Ya'acov, and so he came to regard her as an adopted sister. As a result, it seemed entirely proper to tell her not only about the suicide and the possibility that someone had searched his room, but also about Father Lambert's fall from grace with Veronica Dunn.

Anna, who could not help smirking slightly when she heard this last piece of news, said, "Well, it's good to know he had it in him."

Andrew frowned. "That's a banal thing to say."

"You're right. I'm sorry."

Since Anna rarely apologized, her words dissipated his irritation. "What is odd, surely," he said, "is not that he fell in love with a woman—that can happen to any priest—but that he went back to her yesterday after ten years."

"You say she had gray hair?"

"Yes. She was really quite old."

"Well, some people just keep at it longer than you'd think."

Andrew blushed. "I don't think . . . I mean, she seemed to think it was . . . unusual. It was almost as if it was symbolic."

Anna wrinkled her nose. "Symbolic sex. Yuk."

"I do see that if he had lost his faith . . ."

"He'd want to lose his virginity?"

"He might want to know what it was he had missed—from curiosity as much as . . . desire."

"One of the things I can never understand about your creepy religion is why faith and sex are incompatible."

"They aren't."

"I know, I know," said Anna, in a tone of affected weariness. "A married couple with the blessing of the Church can do it so long as they bear in mind that it might lead to a baby and don't take any precautions to make sure that it won't. Great. That damns ninety-nine point nine per cent of all lovers. So my statement stands: the Catholic Church hates sex."

This was not one of Andrew's favorite topics of conversation. He sensed that Anna knew more about the subject than he did, but he preferred not to know the details. "You shouldn't see it as being *against* sex so much as *beyond* sex," he said. "The full Christian life, which is what a priest aspires to, transcends our natural condition . . ."

"Then why are you eating those sausages?"

"I have to keep alive."

"You could have had bread and water."

"One can legitimately take pleasure in God's creations."

"As the bishop said to the actress, or Father Lambert to Mrs. Dunn."

Andrew blushed. "Please don't."

She opened her mouth to say something more but shut it again before a word had escaped, and looked from under her bangs at Andrew to gauge whether he was genuinely upset. Seeing that he was undoubtedly in a vulnerable condition, she said in a much softer tone, "I really am sorry he's dead, you know. I loved him too."

"Of course."

"And I think, for your sake, we ought to try and find out why he suddenly threw all his eggs out of his one basket."

"I *would* like to know."

"Even psychologically it's interesting . . ."

"Yes."

"I'll call Dad and ask him what happened in Israel."

"Do you know why he wanted Father Lambert to come to Jerusalem?"

She shook her head. "Not exactly. It had something to do with the dig by the Western Wall."

"When will you call him?"

She looked at her watch. "We could try him now."

They left the canteen and went up to the Department of Archaeology, where the secretary, who was used to Andrew acting as Father Lambert's assistant, let them into his office. Anna picked up the telephone, dialed, and when she got through asked in halting Hebrew to speak to Professor Dagan. When he came on the line she reverted to English, and gave her father the news of John Lambert's death. Andrew heard her say that he had had a stroke, and then abruptly ask, "Can you tell us, Dad, if anything happened to him while he was in Israel? I mean, did he seem okay to you?"

There was a pause as she listened; then she said, "Sure, he's here," and held the phone out to Andrew. "He wants to talk to you."

Andrew heard the deep, gentle voice of Michal Dagan on an extraordinarily clear line. "Andrew, I am so sorry. This is terrible. I cannot believe it. But it is true?"

"Yes."

"He was a wonderful man. It is terrible, terrible, and for you especially. You were like his son, I know."

"We wondered—" Andrew began, uncertain about what to say—"we wondered whether anything might have happened to him in Israel?"

There was such a long silence that for a moment Andrew thought that he might have been disconnected. Then Michal Dagan asked cautiously, "Why do you ask?"

"The doctor thought that perhaps the sun, or a sudden shock of some kind . . ."

Again there was a pause and finally Dagan asked in a tone of voice even more cautious than before, "It was a stroke, was it? Are you sure?"

Andrew blushed as he lied. "Yes. They seem to think so."

"There is no question of foul play?"

"Foul play?" He repeated the odd, old-fashioned words, looking at Anna as he did so.

"It was only a thought," said Michal Dagan.

"Do you mean, was he killed?"

"No. It is far-fetched."

"Who would have wanted to kill him?"

Again there was a silence; then Dagan said, "Listen, Andrew, there are things I cannot talk about on the telephone."

"But should we tell the police that Father Lambert might have been murdered?"

"No, no. I should not have said it."

"His notebook is gone."

"*Ach.*" Another pause.

"Can he have left it in Jerusalem?"

"I don't know. Not here, certainly, but perhaps with the monks. You should call them. It should definitely be found, unless, of course, it has been taken . . ."

"I'll write to the prior," said Andrew.

"No. Better not. They may think that you know what is in it."

"I don't understand."

"There were many things. Many difficulties."

"About what?"

"I cannot tell you now. Perhaps Ya'acov, if you see him . . ."

"Is he in London?"

"He is, yes. Let me speak to Anna again."

Andrew gave the telephone to Anna, who after a few more words with her father hung up. She seemed melancholy, as she often did when reminded of home. "Apparently Jake's in London," she said.

"Did your father say why?"

"No. He sounded really confused."

"They were very good friends."

As they walked out through the gates of the college into the street, Anna asked, "What was all that about foul play?"

"He seemed to think that Father Lambert might have been murdered."

"Then something *did* happen in Israel."

"It would be wonderful, wouldn't it?"

"What?"

"If he *was* killed."

"*Wonderful?*"

Andrew blushed. "Not wonderful in itself, but wonderful that it wasn't suicide."

"Only he'd still be roasting in Hell, because he'd just jumped the old lady."

Andrew's blush grew deeper. "At least he would have had the chance to repent."

"I suppose. It doesn't sound as if it was much fun."

"Are you going home?"

"I guess so," she said. "Or I might go for a walk. Why don't you come?"

"I ought to go back to the monastery and sort out Father Lambert's affairs."

"You can do that later. It's such a lovely afternoon."

The clouds had cleared since the morning, and blue sky could be glimpsed above the buildings; as he looked up, Andrew suddenly longed to fly above the mist of fumes left by the traffic in the street. Thinking with an inward shudder of his dark cell and its morbid memories, he changed his mind and went with Anna on a bus to Chalk Farm. From there they walked to Primrose Hill. Other people were sitting on the benches or lolling on the grass, but they found a spot on the steep bank with its vast views over London. They sat facing the spires, steeples and glinting glass towers rising from the mauve mist of carbon monoxide. The ground was dry, the air warm, and Andrew, who had slept badly the night before, suddenly felt tired and sad. The fatigue undermined his control, and though he did not cry, he sat with a miserable look on his face.

At first Anna did not notice his dejection, but when she finally looked around and saw the expression on her friend's face, she said in an unusually gentle tone, "I guess it is really hard for you—his dying and you not knowing how or why."

He smiled gratefully. There were tears in his eyes. "We're trained to be detached," he said, "and taught to love God so much that we only love others for his sake, but it was always hard for me, with Father Lambert. He was such a wonderful man."

"Sure."

"He knew, of course, and so did the prior and the novice master, that I looked on him as an adopted father. Neither of them thought that wrong. After all, St. John loved Jesus in a special way. Of course I always knew that he would die, and I almost looked forward to the moment because I felt sure that he would die cheerfully and serenely. He was so sure of the life to come. What's difficult now is not so much that he's dead, as that his death was so ugly and his fate now . . . so uncertain."

"But can you really believe even for a moment that he might be in Hell?"

Andrew clasped his hands and kneaded them together as if the twisting fingers were mimicking his contorted thoughts. "Of course in a way I don't. I mean, I believe above all in the mercy of God, and Father Lambert was so sure of God and so loyal to Him for so long that it seems impossible that He would abandon him now."

"So doesn't that mean he's okay, scratching around in some archaeological happy hunting ground?"

"No. Because I also believe—I have to believe—in the power of the Devil to tempt us, and in the possibility that we might succumb to that temptation and fall."

"Why do you *have* to believe that?"

"If that *wasn't* possible, then we would have no choice, and without choice we would have no value."

Anna gave a little frown, unseen by Andrew, ready with some sarcastic rejoinder, but again held it back and said simply, "I don't know what's so great about choice if you end up roasting in Hell."

"Well, of course there are times," said Andrew, "when one would much rather not have that burden of living forever, and just settle down to the cosy life of an innocent beast. But having eaten the fruit of the knowledge of good and evil, we cannot escape what we know."

"Can't we live in blissful ignorance?"

"You can pretend to. You can even behave as if you do. But in the end even the atheist succumbs to original sin, and suffers the more because he can't recognize it for what it is."

"Give me an example."

"Well there's my brother, Henry. You met him that time . . ."

"I remember."

"He takes the line that man is no more than a superior baboon, and that any claims that he is anything more are pretentious nonsense. However, he himself doesn't behave like a superior baboon, but more like a fallen angel."

"In what way?"

Andrew hesitated. "I don't want to betray his confidence, but . . . Well, you don't know him, and in any case I don't think he'd mind. You see, he's made a lot of money, just as the baboon might amass a lot of bananas, and he has a series of beautiful girlfriends, just as the baboon might accumulate mates. But while the baboon goes on, in obedience to instinct, to procreate his species, Henry never marries or has children. His life is totally barren, and whenever it looks as if it might bear fruit in terms of a long-lasting love or a family, he abruptly alters course . . ."

"He ditches the girls?"

"Yes, even if he still likes them."

"Why?"

"Because they've come to the end of their three months."

She frowned again. "Their three months?"

"As soon as he starts up with a girl he sets a timer and when three months are up he ends the affair."

"Even if they're getting along?"

"*Especially* if they're getting along."

"Why?"

"So as not to become dependent upon another human being."

"He sounds like a cold fish."

"Of course he does, but what's so sad is that by nature he's affectionate and good."

"Some men simply don't want to get involved."

"I know. But Henry has made his philandering into a kind of religion and it hasn't really made him happy. And that's exactly the point I want to make—that the Christian hypothesis makes more sense of our moral condition."

"For Christians, perhaps."

"And for Jews. The whole story of the Fall, after all, comes from your religion."

"It's not my religion. I'm not that kind of Jew."

"I know. You don't believe it. Sometimes I envy people like you or Henry, who don't have to worry so much about whether what they are doing is right or wrong. But if you *do* believe—if you look at humanity and sense that there is much more to it than a herd of animals of a different species—if you see in it extremes of beauty and ugliness, virtue and vileness, such inhuman cruelty and at the same time such equally inhuman unselfishness and self-sacrifice, then one is bound at least to consider that there *is* more to our condition than the cosy life of an animal."

"Can't you think there *is* more, without accepting the idea of eternal damnation?"

"One could, yes, if one could explain away what Jesus had to say. If it wasn't for him, it would be much easier, but there he is. He said he died to save us from the consequences of our sins, and when you think *how* he died and what he suffered and how easily, even in human terms, he could have avoided it, then he must have felt that he was saving us from something unbearably dreadful."

"He may have thought so, but that doesn't mean his delusion has to become your delusion."

"But was it a delusion?" They had had discussions of this kind before, but now, since the fate of Father Lambert seemed to depend upon the conclusion they reached, Andrew spoke with an anguished urgency. "You see, with our knowledge of the human mind, it's easy enough to dismiss Jesus as a neurotic and an hysteric, with, perhaps, some kind of hypnotic power over his followers. That's certainly what Henry would do. But when you read the Gospels you realize that such a hypothesis won't stick, because what he said is so subtle and so convincing, and it is not only confirmed by miracles, which show an extraordinary power over nature, but by the final miracle of his resurrection from the dead."

"If you can swallow that, you can swallow the whole caboodle," Anna said.

"And if you can't swallow it, then clearly Jesus is no more than another Jewish prophet."

"I don't see what's wrong with living decently and hoping for the best in an afterlife, if there is one, without taking on board the whole paraphernalia of Heaven, Hell, judgment, resurrection and the Catholic Church."

"There's nothing wrong with it as far as it goes, and it is what most of us do, but fundamentally it's irrational, because it implies that if there is a God who has created us, he is either unable or unwilling to communicate with us. In other words, he is neither the jealous God of your Bible nor the loving God of ours, but a lazy or indifferent one who, having made us, leaves us to our own devices."

"In a way that seems safer," said Anna, "because whenever people do believe in a God who communicates his will, they start slaughtering the people who appear to defy it. Jews stoned the Christians, Christians burned the Jews, and the Muslims massacred everyone."

Andrew shook his head sadly. "I know, I know. But that doesn't mean that he isn't there, or that he doesn't wish us to know him and love him and go to him when we die."

"Or to the Devil."

"If we so choose."

They were back to where they had started—the death of Father Lambert—and the fact that they had come full circle deterred them from going on. It was also time for Andrew to make his way back toward Paddington. "I'd better go," he said, looking at his watch. "I've got to meet Henry."

"Don't forget your long spoon."

He looked puzzled. "My long spoon?"

"If you're supping with the Devil."

He laughed. "I'm only going for a drink. He's supping with someone else."

6

While Andrew traveled back toward the center of London, Anna returned to Belsize Park, where she lodged with her aunt, her father's sister, Miriam Lilien. Miriam lived in a substantial Victorian house she had bought after the war with the compensation paid by the German government to the children of those killed in the concentration camps. The Liliens had never occupied the whole house, having always rented the top floor, and now that Peter Lilien was dead and their two children had homes of their own, Miriam had retreated to the ground floor and basement. The entrance was still through the front door at the top of a flight of steps, but the main staircase now went up to the apartment above. A second door led into an inner hall, beyond which was the drawing room. This was sparsely furnished and rarely used, serving as a gallery for the modern paintings Anna's uncle, Peter Lilien, had collected in the 1960s. He had worked in the modern paintings department of Christie's, and seeing the rapid rise in the value of some contemporary painting, had backed his own judgment by buying the works of living artists. Unfortunately his judgment was not shared by the market, and the paintings he had bought were now uniformly worthless.

They were also, in the opinion of his widow, uniformly bad, but she could not bring herself to burn them or give them away, and having nowhere to hide them, had left them hanging on the walls of this large room, while she herself retreated to the kitchen on the floor below.

Here she concentrated all the *gemütlichkeit* of which her husband, when he was living, had disapproved: a plump sofa, an upright piano, a Welsh dresser with cups hanging from the hooks and a large library of paperback thrillers. The room next to the kitchen, once the dining room, was now her bedroom, and like the kitchen it looked out onto the garden. Anna had the bedroom on the floor above, which had been that of the Liliens' daughter, Rosie, now married and living in Bristol.

When Anna returned she came in at the front door at the top of the steps, left her books in her bedroom, then went down the stairs to find her aunt sitting at the kitchen table. A small, beetle-browed woman who looked quite unlike her brother Michal, she was now over sixty but in no way decrepit, and she followed Anna's life with as much interest as she had shown in the lives of her own children. Hearing Anna come in, she immediately made tea while Anna told her about the death of Father Lambert.

"The poor man," said Miriam. "Michal will be sorry."

"We called him from the college. He asked if he might have been *murdered*."

"Why should anyone want to murder him?" asked Miriam calmly.

Anna shrugged. "It seems crazy, but that's what he said to Andrew."

"It's because there's so much violence in Israel," Miriam said. "They can't imagine anyone dying of natural causes." She poured tea into a cup and gave it to Anna.

"Andrew actually hopes that he was murdered, because suicides go straight to Hell."

"Well, I wouldn't pay too much attention to *his* opinion."

Miriam Lilien had met Andrew on a number of occasions and disapproved of him, not because she disliked him or because he was a Catholic monk, but because she felt that his friendship distracted Anna from finding a man she could marry. In this way, she was somewhat old-fashioned, for she felt that a woman's destiny inevitably lay in a husband and a home. However, she knew her niece better than Anna knew herself, and understood that in her case this destiny might be difficult to achieve.

"Did Jake call?" Anna asked.

"No. Why should he?"

"Dad thought he might be in London."

Miriam shook her head. "I've heard nothing."

"Doesn't he usually stay here?"

"He prefers not to. It makes him feel uncomfortable."

"Why?"

"He doesn't feel it should be like this."

"Like what?"

"Like a home, here in England, with his aunt and his cousins all English. He doesn't like it. He's like a caged lion, pacing up and down. He's only happy in a kibbutz or a tent."

Anna smiled. "With a rifle under his bed."

Miriam nodded soberly. "You laugh, Anna, but the last time he came, he *had* a gun, not under his bed but in his bag in the wardrobe. I saw it when I was cleaning his room."

"He sees the PLO behind every lamppost."

"He frightens me, Anna."

"He frightens *me*. The whole country frightens me. That's why I left."

Miriam sighed. "But to do what, Anna?"

"A degree."

"Yes, a degree." She sighed again, as if passing judgment on higher education.

Anna smiled. "Just because you got married when you were twenty doesn't mean that we all have to do the same thing."

"It certainly won't happen to you if you spend all your time with that priest of yours."

"He's cute, and he's a good companion, *faute de mieux*."

"But how are you going to find the *mieux* if you're always with him?"

Anna took her aunt's hand and patted it fondly. "Don't worry, Auntie. I'll find a nice Englishman, just as you did. In fact I've got a date tonight."

Her aunt looked doubtful. "May I ask with whom?"

"You don't know him."

"Is he Jewish?"

"Does he have to be?"

"It would be better. My Peter was English but he was also Jewish, and that made many things much easier."

Anna laughed. "Thanks for the advice," she said, getting to her feet and kissing Aunt Miriam on the cheek before going upstairs to her room.

There, for a moment, she felt happy, as she always did after talking to her aunt, who was the only member of her family with whom she felt sympathetic. Like Miriam, Anna had rejected the Zionism the rest of her family espoused. This had not been just an expression of adolescent rebellion, but came from the confusion of her upbringing. Unlike her brother Jake, who had been brought up in Israel, Anna's childhood had been spent largely in the United States. She had been born in Israel, but at the age of four had gone to Princeton with her parents. Throughout the 1970s, when Michal Dagan held posts in different American universities, she had gone to American schools. Since her mother was originally American, English was spoken at home. She had never learned more than a smattering of Hebrew, and when Michal and Rachel went back to Israel, she had usually remained with her grandmother in New York.

After graduating from Brandeis, Anna's reassimilation into Israel might have been easier if there had been a more tolerant atmosphere in the Dagan household. Her father, who upon arriving in Israel in 1952 had espoused the old-fashioned, secular, socialistic Zionism of the founders of the Jewish state, changing his family name from Fischl to Dagan, now attended the synagogue every Sabbath and observed many of the precepts of Mosaic Law. Food that was considered unclean by the Law was banned from the kitchen, and to avoid the servile work of boiling a kettle on the Sabbath, water for making tea or coffee was kept simmering in an urn from sunset on Friday to sunset on Saturday.

All this, Anna knew, was because of the influence of her brother Jake. Six years older than Anna, he had been left with friends in Israel when the Dagans had gone to the United States. His first language was Hebrew, and just as Anna hardly knew Israel, he had little experience of the outside world. Raised on stories not just of Joshua's conquest of Jericho, or David's defeat of Goliath, but also of the assassination of British soldiers by the Irgun and the Stern Gang, Jake gloried in the military triumphs of his people, and never doubted their right to populate the territory that in antiquity God had given to the Jews. He supported the Likud under Begin and then Shamir, and the policy of Jewish settlement on the West Bank. He also believed in an inner commitment to the Jewish cause, and had persuaded his agnostic parents to call him Ya'acov, and to reintroduce the pious practices that had been unknown in their family for three generations.

If strict observance of this kind had always been part of the Dagans' way of life, Anna might have accepted it, but as she scornfully pointed out to her parents, the tradition of the family had been to play down the kind of scrupulous observance of the law of Moses that had so isolated the Jews in gentile societies. The atmosphere of her grandmother's flat in New York had been as much German as Jewish, and her father's original commitment to Israel had been as a homeland for his people, not as a colony of crazed fanatics like her brother Jake.

Michal Dagan had lamely defended himself to Anna on the grounds that a greater dedication to the Jewishness of Israel had become necessary "under pressure of events." His wife, Rachel, also seemed now to accept that observance had always been part of the faith of the Jews. Anna, however, not only ridiculed this Jewish fundamentalism, but also flaunted her own secularism in any way she could. She would make herself bacon sandwiches and cheeseburgers, and go to the movies on a Friday night just to exasperate Jake. The brother and sister had violent arguments, to the distress of their parents. Rachel Dagan would take her son aside to ask him to try to understand that after so many years in America, Anna was bound to have a different point of view, while Michal would explain yet again to Anna how Israel could only survive if the Jews deepened their sense of who they were by observing those laws and customs that had preserved their identity over the centuries of the Diaspora.

Neither child was convinced, and the arguments became so unpleasant that it was finally decided that Anna should study for a postgraduate degree abroad. If her grandmother had still been alive, she would have returned to New York; instead, she went to London to lodge with her Aunt Miriam and study under Father Lambert. She told herself that she was happy to go: she found Israel provincial and claustrophobic and had no intention of serving in the army, but all the same she felt that she had somehow been driven out of her home by her older brother, and that her parents had allowed it to happen because they loved her less than they loved him.

The room Anna had been given in her aunt's house was large and light, looking out over the garden to the backs of the houses in the adjacent street. Having been that of her cousin Rosie, it had a girlish look, with blue-and-white striped wallpaper and a shelf of china ornaments, but though her taste was different, Anna had done little to change the decor, substituting only a poster of a Bonnard exhibition she had seen in Paris for a picture of an English actor she did not know.

Now, with time to kill before she left for her date, she started the kind of puttering with which she always wasted an hour or so in the evening—arranging the work she meant to do rather than doing it; skimming through an article to see if she wanted to read it, but upon deciding that she did, putting it to one side, preferring to tidy the clothes draped over her chair or hanging out of open drawers. In doing this, she would come across some garment she had forgotten about, and would try it on to remind herself how she looked in it, turning first in profile and then to face the mirror in the corner of the room, looking less at the clothes that were her excuse for this narcissistic study than at her own childish face—the tiny nose, large eyes and black hair, and at her still-adolescent narrow hips, skinny legs and barely perceptible breasts. As always, she studied herself with alternating admiration and despair, at one moment thinking that she was really rather pretty in a waiflike way, and the next concluding that no man could possibly want someone so skinny and small. Of course she knew that this was not true. She had been to bed with half-a-dozen boys—fellow students in America, young soldiers in Israel and, most recently, Andrew's brother Henry, who was taking her to the opera that night.

This current affair had been complicated by Henry's insistence that it should be kept secret from Andrew, and by her own determination that it should also be hidden from her own family. This was why, until that evening, she had always pretended to her aunt that she went out with Andrew rather than Henry, and why she had listened to Andrew talk about his brother as if she hardly knew him. She disliked deceiving someone who would never deceive her, but, just as she knew that it would upset her aunt to know she had a gentile lover, so she accepted from Henry that Andrew would suffer if he thought she had been seduced by his degenerate brother. She also knew that Andrew would not understand how she could sleep with a man she did not love. If she had slept with him, he would assume that she must love him, when she knew that she did not. Since her adolescence, she had never considered herself to be in love. Few of her earlier affairs had been one-night stands, but none had lasted more than a couple of months. If Anna had let them, one or two of the young men she had slept with might have followed up the casual encounter with the kind of friendship that could have led to love, but invariably they had been dismissed, or had felt themselves to be dismissed, by the harsh things she said to them.

Anna was caught in the trap of desiring the kind of man she despised—someone physically large and mentally slow—as if the demands of natural selection obliged her to balance her own quick wit and small stature in the genes of the next generation. When Andrew had first introduced her to Henry, she had found him snobbish and affected. He was taller and better-looking than his younger brother, and in almost every way created a contrary impression. While Andrew was naïve, unkempt and cheerful, Henry was cold, secretive and demanding. He dressed so formally and fastidiously that he appeared almost foppish to Anna, and he always seemed on the brink of exasperation, as if expecting everyone and everything around him to fall short of the exacting standards he set for himself.

He was about thirty-three, but seemed older to Anna, partly because of the severity of his manner, partly because he was rich and so had all the appurtenances of the older generation, like a well-furnished flat and a silver BMW with a telephone and electric windows. He also wore suits and took her to restaurants where he never ordered the house wine, but chose some rare claret with a heady, musty flavor that doubled the already considerable bill.

Anna was not seduced by these luxuries—indeed, she found them unnecessary and absurd—but at first she had been pleased that a man of his kind should feel she merited his attention. Then she had become curious because he was English in the way she had expected Englishmen to be—not cheerful and casual like Andrew, but formal and reserved. Getting to know Henry better had seemed like going to see the Tower of London or a Shakespeare play at Stratford-on-Avon. The more she saw him, the more she felt drawn to him without quite knowing why. She could not say that she had become fond of him because he would not allow her to come close enough to feel affection. She could not say that she was attracted to him, at least not with the kind of straightforward lust she had felt for some of her previous lovers. Rather, she was fascinated, even challenged, by a man of a sort she had not come across before; while most of her earlier boyfriends had been wholly preoccupied with themselves, boring her with long, introspective monologues and demanding constant compliments to bolster their egos, Henry never spoke about himself or looked for reassurance. It was from Andrew that she knew about his unhappy childhood and successful career. If she herself put any question to him of a personal kind, it either returned like a boomerang or was simply ignored, as if she was a Delilah seeking the secret of his strength.

Yet Henry was constantly asking about her past life, not with the solicitude of a psychoanalyst or a confessor but with the cold curiosity of a scientist or a collector. This detachment did not offend her. Instead, it stimulated a desire in her to seem interesting enough to form part of his collection, to help prove or disprove whatever hypothesis about human nature was running through his mind. When she had first set foot in his apartment, she realized that there was more to him than an up-to-date version of the classic bowler-hatted English gentleman. Many of his books, for example, were in French, and by writers she had heard of but never read. The paintings, too, were strange, some large and colorful, others figurative and weird, and all quite unlike the dreary works in her parents' flat in Jerusalem or the restrained abstracts in her uncle's collection in Belsize Park.

All these manifestations of Henry's taste formed an image in her mind of an intriguing man whom in her turn she would like to intrigue. Sex seemed an obvious way to establish that she had succeeded. She was feminist enough to feel that a casual affair could be an adventure for a woman as well as for a man, and emancipated enough from Jewish ethics to discount any qualms she might have about going to bed with a man she hardly knew.

If Anna had hoped that by sleeping with Henry she would get to know him better, she was quickly disappointed; when they did make love, he remained as detached as before. He caressed her naked body as if he was repelled by what he desired and despised her for responding to his gestures of affection. Even while they made love he seemed removed, watching what they were doing with distaste, but far from offending Anna, this ambivalence enhanced her own pleasure, for she too felt the same blend of excitement and shame.

Since she was going to Covent Garden, that evening Anna chose her clothes with great care, changing back and forth two or three times, wanting to look elegant yet also to give Henry the impression that she had not gone to a lot of trouble. She made up her eyes in the same way, adding a barely perceptible touch of mascara to her already dark lashes and a small smudge of shadow. While she did this, she brooded about Henry's "three-month contracts" with women, but it was only when she was ready to leave that she went to her desk, looked at her diary and flicked back through the pages to find out if her time was up. She found the entry for their first dinner together at the beginning of February; she had written his name out in full. Then, on the pages that followed, there were increasingly abbreviated entries until the name had become simply "H." She also knew the date she had first slept with him; she had made an appointment to see a doctor two days later to get a new prescription for the pill. That had been at the beginning of March. Now it was early June. Her three months had run out last weekend.

7

Anna caught the tube at Belsize Park and emerged forty minutes later at Sloane Square. It was an area of London where she felt ill at ease. Hampstead had something cosmopolitan about it, while Belgravia, for all the foreign embassies, felt alien and English. Eaton Square in particular, with its classical façades of white stucco, seemed as cold and aloof as the lover who lived there.

When she reached the entrance to the building whose top floor formed Henry's flat, she rang the bell and waited for his voice to ask harshly who it was. When it did, she barked back, "Anna," regretting, as always, that the evening should begin by her shouting her name into a microphone embedded in a wall. When the buzzer sounded, she pushed the door and went up the carpeted stairs to the top floor. Henry was waiting by his door. She glanced at his thin face to assess his mood, but he greeted her as always with a mask of courtesy—an empty smile, a perfunctory kiss on the cheek—before guiding her into his living room, where the flames of a gas fire flickered soundlessly over asbestos logs. She sat down on one of the large sofas, while Henry crossed the room to pour her a drink. He was wearing, as he always did, a double-breasted, gray pin-striped suit, which suited his tall, slightly stooping figure.

"Have you heard about Father Lambert?" she asked.

He handed her a glass of white wine. "Yes. Andrew told me."

"Isn't it sad?"

"Particularly for Andrew." He filled his own glass with whisky and water.

"Did he tell you that it was suicide?"

"Yes. Or murder." He sat down on an armchair facing her.

"And about the woman?"

"Yes." He gave a sour smile.

She smiled too. "Poor Andrew."

"It had to happen sooner or later."

"What?"

"A crisis of this kind."

"Why?"

"Because sooner or later anyone in religious orders suffers a breakdown of some sort. With Lambert it came later, that's all."

"How can you be so sure?"

"Because a religious vocation is the symptom of a psychosis."

"Always?"

"What else can it be?"

Anna shrugged. "Well, *I* don't want to be a nun, but that doesn't mean that anyone who does is crazy."

He frowned. "By definition, isn't it demented to lead a life in which you suppress all your natural desires?"

She thought of the bed next door where they so often ended the evening, and acknowledged to herself that it did seem odd. Still, she was irritated by the confidence with which Henry passed judgment on others and said, "Perhaps you just don't have the imagination to envisage a life that is different from your own."

This appeared to irritate Henry. He swirled the ice in his whisky. "I can envisage a different life only too well," he said with a sidelong glance at Anna. "I can also envisage a different life for my brother."

"Well, so can I, I guess," said Anna.

"It's so patently obvious that after being deserted at a vulnerable age by our weak father, and then bullied in adolescence by our emasculating mother, Andrew found a psychological haven in the Catholic Church, with its strong but kindly God the Father and passive, patient and ever-loving mother in Mary. Add to that the personal influence of Father Lambert, who was determined to bring fresh blood into his decrepit order, and at the same time recruit a secretary without having to pay for one—"

"That's very unkind."

"I think he was unkind to bamboozle Andrew. Then, having

led him up the garden path, he confesses, if not in word, then in deed, that the whole thing was a grotesque fraud."

She sighed. "I really think he seems okay—Andrew, that is."

"For the time being, maybe. He's clinging to the idea, which your father seems to share, that Father Lambert did not kill himself but was murdered."

"I don't know why Dad thinks that."

"Andrew feels frustrated because he can't call on the police. He wants me to play the detective."

"And will you?"

"I'll do anything to help him."

"That's the . . ." She faltered. "It's one of the nicest things about you," she said.

"The only nice thing?" Henry asked, finishing her first sentence. He stood up before she could answer and moved toward the door.

They drove to Covent Garden to see Mozart's *La Clemenza di Tito*. She had been to the opera with Henry twice before, and on neither occasion had she enjoyed it, not because she had disliked the music or the production, but because she had felt he was uneasy at being seen with her in public. In the four months that she had known him, she had never met any of his friends. She knew that they existed because the telephone often rang when she was in his apartment, but it had soon become clear that he did not intend to introduce her into his circle. At first she had thought that this was because he wanted to keep her to himself, but later she decided that he was in some way ashamed of her, or at least embarrassed to be seen in her company. She wondered, without minding much, whether it was because she was Jewish or American or small, or whether he was conducting a parallel affair with some tall English rose who belonged to the group of his regular friends.

This idea did not upset her because she herself felt detached from Henry. She found him interesting and attractive, but entirely alien in a way that Andrew was not. She was fascinated by him, and flattered to be taken up by someone so rich, successful and decidedly grown up. She also appreciated the skill and style with which he made love to her. Yet once he had done so, she never felt close to him, or wanted to remain around. Once he had put on his cotton boxer shorts, his silk shirt and a grey pin-striped suit, once he had opened his mouth to speak in that sneering British drawl, once he had begun to move around in the stage set of his grandiose apartment, she felt estranged, and as inappropriate and out of place as the jeans, T-shirt, socks and sneakers she picked up off the carpeted floor.

It was the same this evening at Covent Garden. She had taken the trouble to dress as smartly as she could, but when she caught sight of herself in a mirror she saw just how preppy and teen-aged she looked, how dowdy, here in the long gallery where bankers, businessmen and their elegant wives waited for the next act.

Henry had bought her a glass of champagne, which she drank, even though she disliked it, while he asked her what she thought of the opera.

"It isn't quite what you expect from Mozart, is it?"

"It's apparently one of his last."

"You've never seen it before?"

"No."

"It's certainly interesting . . ."

"Why? To see that even a genius can be a bore?"

She laughed. "My father wouldn't like it."

"Why not?"

"Titus destroyed Jerusalem. He wasn't very clement to the Jews."

"Yet Berenice was Jewish and she loved him."

"Yes. Titus and one or two others."

"Who else?"

"His father, Vespasian. Three husbands. And her brother, Agrippa."

The bell rang for the second act.

"She also met St. Paul," said Anna, "but he was in chains so I suppose he was safe."

"How did she arrange that?" asked Henry, taking her empty glass.

"She and Agrippa were visiting Festus, the Roman procurator, in Caesarea. St. Paul was waiting to be sent off to Rome. Agrippa asked to hear him preach."

"How do you know all this?" asked Henry as they returned to their seats.

"From Father Lambert's lectures," said Anna. "It came into his course on Biblical Archaeology."

After the opera they drove back to Belgravia and had supper in Henry's flat. This was far from a simple bite. Instead of the glass of milk and peanut-butter sandwich that Anna, on her own, would have eaten in her Aunt Miriam's kitchen, Henry always arranged a three-course dinner, beginning with soup and ending with a sorbet, with smoked salmon, gravlax or game pie in between. He did not prepare it himself—someone else came in during the day—but he served it methodically by candlelight at the polished antique table in the corner of his living room.

There was always a half bottle of Meursault or Montrachet and a full bottle of some fancy claret, then a choice of liqueurs to drink with their coffee; while Anna at first found the formality of such suppers a little absurd, particularly after going to a film, they had the effect of arousing a pleasant anticipation of what was to follow in bed.

Before they reached this point, Henry always behaved as if it might not happen, or at least never referred to it with languorous looks or gestures. She sensed that for her to do so herself would offend his sense of decorum, like ogling the sorbet while sipping one's soup. Therefore she made conversation and, on this occasion, returned to the history behind the story of *La Clemenza di Tito*.

"I shall miss that course of Father Lambert's," she said.

"What was so special about it?"

"He made the whole ancient world come alive and make sense. I hadn't realized, for example, how tight that world was . . ."

"Tight?"

"Well, I'd always thought of Caesar and Cleopatra in one compartment, like History or Drama, and Herod the Great in another, like Scripture Studies. In fact Herod was a friend of Cleopatra's, and of both Julius and Octavius Caesar as well. He named the Antonia Fortress after Mark Antony. His son Antipas was deeply involved with John the Baptist, Salome and all that, and his great-grandchildren, Agrippa and Berenice, turn up listening to St. Paul."

"And what did they make of him?"

"Of St. Paul?"

"Yes."

"The procurator, Festus, thought he was crazy, but Agrippa was quite impressed. Father Lambert used to say that if you read between the lines, it looked as if Berenice dragged her brother away before he could be converted."

"I would have reacted in the same way as Festus."

"You've never been tempted to believe?"

66

"If I was, I would resist it."

"Why?"

"Because it degrades the mind to fall back on superstition."

"I don't believe either, but I don't think it's degrading. You can look on it as a kind of poetry, a way of letting something ancient and beautiful suffuse your being so that you are in fact ennobled by it."

"Like marinating a fish?" he sneered.

"If you like. We Jews, after all, are a people molded by our myths, and I don't have to believe that Moses heard God speak from a burning bush to be glad that I'm part of that tradition. And Andrew, whatever the reasons for his believing, gets something very beautiful from his faith. He really is gentler and kinder than anyone else I know."

"That's not thanks to Christ."

"To what, then?"

"His fear of life. He's like a monkey threatened by a stronger monkey, who lies down and proffers his genitals to deflect the other's aggression."

"That's a horrible thing to say."

"It doesn't help Andrew to shy away from an impartial analysis of his condition. Clearly his commitment to poverty, chastity and obedience is a way of saying, 'I won't compete for your money or your women, and I'll do anything you say.' "

"That's what makes him nice."

"It also makes him a victim."

"Of whom?"

"Of all those repressed pederasts and menopausal spinsters who run the Roman Catholic Church."

"He's nice to me too."

"But you don't sleep with him."

She blushed. "Liking and . . . loving are different."

"They are indeed. Different and probably incompatible."

"Why?"

"Because love is only a gloss on the crude instincts that ensure the survival of the species."

Anna looked down at her plate, wondering if this cynicism was meant to soften her up for the ending of their affair. "Can't you love and like people at the same time?"

He shrugged his shoulders. "Perhaps. But even liking, in my experience, has some ulterior motive behind it."

"Like what?"

"We choose our friends as we do our possessions, to enhance the image we want to present to others."

"You have a very low opinion of human beings."

"Vanity, vanity, all is vanity, as one of your prophets put it."

"Then why aren't you pleased that Andrew has climbed out of this cesspit?"

"Because you can't climb out. We are what we are—isolated individuals in relentless pursuit of gratification and power. The only way to be content is to own up to it and enjoy the chase."

"And *do* you enjoy the chase?"

He looked at her briefly as if assessing his prey. "Do I? Yes, I do. The fittest are always happy to survive."

"Whereas your unfit brother is unhappy?"

"Yes, because of Lambert."

"But in general?"

"The general and the particular are linked. That's the point I'm trying to make. Andrew imagined that he had escaped the struggle by joining the Simonite order. Sooner or later he was bound to discover that you can neither change human nature nor deny it; you can simply pervert it. Most dangerous of all is the celibacy of priests, because all that energy which should be dissipated in sex is obliged to find other outlets like pride, ambition and the sinister pleasure priests take in exploiting and manipulating the weakness and uncertainty of others."

"Do you say this to Andrew?"

"No. It would upset him. But you . . . well, I should have thought that you would sympathize with my point of view."

"Because I'm a Jew?"

"Yes." He answered at once, but she could tell from his slight confusion that he would rather not have been caught labeling her in this way.

"My brother would agree," she said, "but the only Catholic I have ever known besides Andrew was Father Lambert, and he always seemed to me to be kind, cheerful and completely unselfish."

"But now you know you were wrong."

"How?"

"Because suicide is at the apex of egoism."

"Perhaps he didn't kill himself," Anna said. "Perhaps he was killed."

"Even if he was killed, he had sex with that woman before he died."

"That—well, in a way it's kind of romantic, and it also proves your theory wrong."

"How?"

"You can hardly say that he did it to improve the species."

"No. He was probably just curious to know what he'd been missing all those years."

"And had he been missing much?" she asked, attempting the kind of ironic smile that she saw so often on Henry's face.

"By definition," he said.

"Why by definition?"

"Because if our genes are programmed for survival, not just as an individual but as a species too, then those things which ensure our survival must be pleasurable."

"Like eating?"

"Yes."

"And screwing?"

"Yes, except that that is complicated by psychological factors."

"Like love?"

"Love, yes. Or the lack of it." He looked at her sadly.

"It's a pity," she said.

"What?"

"That I don't inspire love."

"And do I?"

"No." She lowered her head to hide the tears in her eyes.

"It's better, don't you think?" he asked.

"What?" She understood what he meant but wanted him to say it.

"That we stop."

"Don't you like it any more?"

"It's not as simple as that."

"It seemed perfectly simple up to now."

"For the body, perhaps, but not for the mind."

"You shouldn't take it so seriously."

"Perhaps not."

"It's just sex, for God's sake."

He looked at her from across the table expressionlessly. "I'm sorry if you feel let down."

"No." She turned away. "I always knew that there were no strings."

Henry stood up and went to the kitchen to fetch the coffee. When he returned, she asked, "Is it true that you always end affairs after three months?"

He frowned. "Who told you that?"

"Is it true?"

"In my experience, it's always wise to quit while one's ahead."

"Why?"

"Because familiarity breeds contempt."

"Always?"

"Always. But I wish . . ."

"What?"

"That it didn't."

Anna sniffed and stood up. "I guess it's good for me to get dumped once in a while, since it's usually me who does the dumping." She moved toward the door.

"Don't you want any coffee?"

"I'd rather get home."

"Are you sure?"

She nodded. "Yes."

"I'll call a cab."

"I can find one in the street."

"No, wait." He went to the telephone. "If I book it from here, you can charge it to my company account."

8

After he had seen Anna into a cab, Henry Nash returned to his flat, where he refilled his glass with whisky and water and sat down on the sofa facing the blank screen of his television. He remained like this for some time, a man in a suit, now crumpled, with tired features and bloodshot eyes. Occasionally his head would turn and he would look at the fabrics and artifacts that decorated his flat, and at the beige walls with olive-green borders that matched the somber pattern of the heavy curtains. To Anna it had seemed grand. To Henry it was meant to seem grand, even aristocratic. After all, he had paid a designer to create such an effect. In the four years since he had moved in, there had been, he knew, many who had been convinced, and not all of them were as impressionable as Anna. However, he had never been convinced himself, any more than an actor who plays Hamlet on a stage set of Elsinore believes that he is a prince of Denmark.

He intended to replay the tape of *Newsnight* that had been recorded automatically earlier in the evening, but he did not reach for the controls. Instead, he sat in quiet obeisance before the dead set as if praying before his household god. It was a fine god—a Bang & Olufsen: its colors outshone the flames of the gas log fire. The video recorder was also the best of its kind, slim and gray like a revolver, with twinkling numbers and symbols waiting to obey those invisible rays that emanated from the small box Henry held in his hand.

That box was not the only magic wand in his possession. There was another for the television, and a third for the stereo, which, again at the touch of a button, would instantly bring into his living room the finest choirs and orchestras. In his gleaming silver-gray BMW 635 CSi, he would listen to the same tapes and, like the fine lady riding to Banbury Cross, could have music wherever he went. From his car, or in a restaurant, he could speak on his portable telephone to anyone anywhere in the world. There was no invention of modern man he did not exploit to wash his clothes or his dishes, to clean his flat or his car, to transpose his thoughts into words, his words onto disks, then back onto paper, and from paper, by telephone to another sheet of paper at the other end of the line.

Henry's clothes, too, were the best—cashmere sweaters, cotton or silk shirts, handmade shoes. Nothing he touched was cheap; even the women before Anna had worn exquisite dresses from the great fashion houses of France, and beneath them silken, lace-edged lingerie, smelling sweetly of heady scents that mingled luxuriously with the musks of nature. Now, when he thought of Anna's childish underclothes, and how touching her small, tanned body had looked on the white sheets of his large bed, he felt a sense of regret that joined, but did not supplant, the relief he had felt at seeing her leave. Indeed, the question he asked himself was not why he had dropped her, but why he had taken up with her in the first place. He remembered how, when he had met her with Andrew, he had, as always when meeting a woman, appraised her for her sexual potential, and that he had disqualified her, as he disqualified most of them, not because she was ugly—her face was unquestionably pretty—but because she was socially irrelevant and physically out of scale.

It was not snobbery that led him to consider her irrelevant, but rather the culture that spoke through his flickering, multicolored 24-inch screen, and valued only long-legged, well-dressed, upper-class girls. Her size also put him off, not because she was squat or built in inelegant proportions, but because she seemed too fragile and childlike to be eligible for a grown man's bed. Certainly he had been amused by the way she had tormented his pious brother with her sharp answers and the kind of casual obscenities with which young Americans spice their speech, but the only reason why he asked where she lived, and had later asked her to lunch, was because he had learned from Andrew that her brother

Jake worked for military counterintelligence in Israel's army, the Israeli Defence Force.

Henry owned and edited a series of newsletters providing inside information on business and trade. At the time he had been preparing an issue on the arms industry, and he knew that Israel had one of the largest arms budgets in the world. He already had contacts in Tel Aviv, but another would be useful, so it had seemed worthwhile to try and find out from the sister what her brother might know.

It quickly became apparent that Anna could not help him but she had amused him sufficiently for Henry to ask her out again, once to the theater, then to the opera and finally to the kind of restaurant where the expense was a compliment and the atmosphere enticing. When, a month after meeting her, he had asked her back to his apartment, he still did not fancy her in the usual way, but was partly curious to know what she would be like in bed, and partly conscious that it would be almost insulting if their candlelit dinners did not end in this way.

From the start it had been a shallow commitment. Henry's chief concern was to keep the affair a secret from Andrew, fearing that if he learned about it, he would blame himself for leading Anna into sin. He loved his brother and wanted to protect him from the coarse realities of life. He also pitied him profoundly, having seen what he had suffered as a child. It was not so much the divorce that had hurt him as the humiliation they both had witnessed, during the years that led up to it, of their weak father by their embittered mother.

James Nash had been an officer in the Royal Navy, and, in their infancy, both boys had seen him as a hero. Failing in middle age to gain the promotion he felt was his due, he had retired from the Navy to work as a management consultant. This was intended to make him rich, but he was no more successful on land than he had been at sea. Having suffered from the sneers of the naval wives whose husbands had risen faster than hers, his wife now languished in genteel poverty in a villa in the suburbs of London. Doubtless, there was sexual dissatisfaction too, but the complaints Henry remembered being shrieked at his father by his mother were more about the career she had sacrificed to marry him and the drudgery of domestic life. How he had longed for his father to answer her charges; instead, he had stayed silent, and to escape his wife's nagging went to sleep on a narrow bed in the attic.

At the age of thirteen, Henry had been sent to a boarding school that was both cheap and second-rate. Andrew had joined him three years later. It was here they learned that their father had gone to live with his secretary, whom he later married. They now saw him only on odd weekends, and for a fortnight in the summer when he took them camping in Wales.

His departure exacerbated their mother's discontent. She took a job as a receptionist in a doctor's office, but this only reminded her of the career she might have had if she had gone to university instead of marrying and raising a family. With no husband to blame for her condition, she turned instead upon her two sons, making clear how much she resented having to cook their supper and wash their clothes. Her social circle contracted to a few other embittered single women, and the boys themselves, since going to boarding school, no longer had friends in the neighborhood. As a result, the holidays in Wimbledon became tedious and tormenting. They were no happier with their father and stepmother in their cramped apartment, and they both came to look forward to going back to school, which most of the other pupils found grim.

It was at school that the boys had their friends, and there were also some inspiring teachers. As a result, they did well, Henry going on to study economics at Leeds University, and Andrew, four years later, archaeology at Huntingdon College in London. While they were at university, there was nothing in particular to tell them apart from students from happier homes. Certainly as he started out in life, the qualities Henry was aware of in himself did not appear as either strengths or weaknesses, but simply as features of an interior physiognomy. For example, he did not feel that he loved Andrew because he pitied him, but only because brothers always loved brothers; in any case, Andrew was a patently lovable young man. Nor did Henry ascribe his own determination to make money to the humiliation he had suffered in witnessing his father's penury; rather, he felt that it was a normal enough ambition in a young man at the time.

His attitude toward women also seemed not the fruit of a neurosis but the application of common sense to relations between the sexes. After all, desire was a given factor. Not only the promptings of his own instincts, but also the propaganda implicit in every book, magazine, film and advertisement on television confirmed the view that nothing equaled the delights of sexual love. If on the first few occasions the nervous fumbling in student hostels or shared flats in Leeds had not quite matched the ecstasy he had imagined, it did not deter him from continuing his pursuit of girls; seducing them brought about a catharsis that satisfied more than his senses.

In the isolation of his own ego, it did not occur to Henry that others found sexual encounters simple and fun. Just as nakedness was shameful, so copulation was degrading. It was the defiling of women that excited him, and led him to prefer those who were reluctant to sleep with him. To shift the source of a woman's will from her mind to her groin, and to see her shed the pose of an intelligent being to rut like a beast, filled him with a dour satisfaction. He did not feel that he himself was degraded as the other half of the copulating couple; he remained detached, not merely from what he was doing but from the very part of his body that was ramming home the resentment he felt against the whole female sex.

After graduating from Leeds, Henry worked as a financial journalist and researcher, first for the *Investor's Chronicle*, then for *The Economist*, and finally for *The Economist* intelligence unit, before leaving with a colleague to start a series of newsletters. These picked the brains of dons, diplomats and international civil servants to provide both legal and technical data about world trade. At first the enterprise had gone badly; it was too limited in its application and was inadequately financed. Understanding this, Henry persuaded his partner to sell him his shares, which he bought with borrowed money. He then borrowed more to buy the lease on an office in Soho. He expanded the range of the newsletters, and took them to the limits of the laws on official secrets and industrial espionage. As a result, his newsletters became essential reading for investment analysts and export managers wanting to know, for example, what standards were required for electrical equipment in South Korea, what products were being prepared by rivals in Singapore, or what bribes should be paid, and to whom, to get goods through customs in Ghana. As the newsletters grew in size and scope, Henry increased both the number of subscribers and the cost of the subscription. After two years, he was making a profit, after four he had paid off his loans, and by the age of thirty he was a rich man.

This success had enabled him to acquire all the material appurtenances of a pleasant life, including the apartment in London and a house in France, but it meant that he lost some of his oldest friends, who began to envy him. He made others, but of a more superficial kind: men who had also made money, usually in the City, and who were ambitious and selfish in the same way. It also enabled Henry to extend the range of his philandering into circles that had hitherto been out of his league, but to his disappointment he found that one woman's body was much like another's, and their minds not much different, either. It was then that he decided all love affairs should end after three months; prolonging them invariably led to ragged and painful endings. As the length of each liaison was limited, the period between them grew longer. He grew bored by love, just as he had grown bored by business, and looked for something new to engage his interest. For a while he considered a career as a Conservative politician. Since he had grown rich as a result of his own initiative and hard work, he believed strongly in the Darwinian ethos of the government of the day. He joined the local Conservative association, went to one or two meetings and canvassed at a local election, but soon realized that he was too easily exasperated to listen patiently to a constituent's complaints, or to spend a lifetime trimming his opinions and kowtowing to people he despised, all for the remote chance that in due course he might exercise political power.

What was left? More money? To build his business into an empire? To fatten his fortune into twenty or even two hundred million pounds? For what? He was content with his London apartment, but found his house in France a time-consuming encumbrance. He had more clothes than he could fit into his wardrobe, and traveled whenever and wherever he liked. He liked painting and sculpture and bought one or two works of art. He also liked reading, as Anna had noticed from the books on his shelves, and had taught himself French because its literature appealed to him— or had when he was in his twenties and could relate his own experience to the escapades of the young heroes of Stendhal or Flaubert.

But as Henry grow older, he found that he had more in common with the nihilistic and pessimistic characters in the novels of Sartre or Céline. However, the more he became absorbed in a novel, the more he suffered from the banality of his own life. Films frustrated him in the same way; he felt he was watching life from the auditorium when he should be onstage. He was sure there must be more to achieve than what he already had. At times, a sense of destiny convinced him that something glorious and extraordinary lay ahead, but even as he felt this, the voice of common sense would remind him that man was no more than an evolved baboon.

This conflict between the vague but grand aspirations of what was poetic and romantic in his nature and the prosaic expectations of the realist came to torment him. He was determined that a man equipped with reason should be able to master his own mind, and refused to believe that people are all subject to the dictates of their subconscious. Such a hypothesis seemed to undermine the foundation upon which all science and philosophy depended; yet he had read the works of psychoanalysts and felt he understood quite clearly what had driven Andrew to become a priest. He was obliged to recognize that if Andrew had been conditioned by his childhood, he too must have been affected—that his vengeful feelings toward women, for example, and his reluctance to commit himself in love, came not from an impartial assessment of the character of women or the drawbacks of marriage, but from the harm done by his mother.

His affair with Anna might have been his salvation, or at least might have marked a change of direction, because she was so different from the girls he had gone out with before—different in size, different in style, simpler, funnier, cleverer and more serious-minded. For the first time in his life he had slept with a girl whose views he respected, not just on history or archaeology, but on general matters like politics and art. Her vocabulary was limited, and it irritated him that she so often expressed herself in college-girl slang, but her opinions were original, her judgments sound and her gibes often painful to his self-esteem.

However, the very qualities that made him like her also made loving her out of the question. If courtesy and curiosity had led him to sleep with her in the first place, he had persisted only because it seemed the proper thing to do. The sex itself had apparently been to her satisfaction; he had found that for all her delicate proportions, she had the appetites and attributes of a mature woman. Still, she lacked the voluptuousness that he needed to arouse his lust. Anna was too likable and intelligent to be credible as an object of resentment and contempt, and when sex did not express his vengeful passion for women, it became nothing more than a banal routine.

That he might love her despite this absence of desire was inconceivable; it went radically against the teaching of that religion preached not by priests from a pulpit, but by advertising copywriters over the TV screen. Love was an appetite that, once satisfied, came to an end. That was why it never lasted, why most of his married friends were unfaithful and unhappy, their children millstones around their necks. Yet the more Henry raged against love, marriage and family life, the more he longed to love someone other than himself. He began to imagine a love that went beyond the tempestuous egoism of sexual passion—something like the idealism that had led patriots to die for their country or revolutionaries to fall at the barricades. But he was trapped by the disillusion of his generation, which found idealism impractical and patriotism absurd. His yearning had no object; he had to live with it unfulfilled.

PART
II

9

Anna Dagan had a friend from Brandeis called Naomi Sherz, who was writing a thesis on Brancusi at the Courtauld Institute of Art. She was the closest thing to a confidante Anna had in London, or indeed anywhere else in the world, and, though she did not know the identity of Anna's mysterious lover, she at least knew that he existed.

Waking the morning after the opera feeling quite miserable, Anna telephoned Naomi and arranged to meet for lunch. She liked the idea of telling her friend how she had lost both her lover and her professor in the space of a single day, and though judging from the mess Naomi had made of her own life she did not expect any valuable advice, she knew she could count on some sympathy in return for that which she had shown Naomi on many occasions following the breakup of her own affairs.

She spent the morning at Huntingdon College, hoping to see Andrew, but he did not come in. At noon she took a bus to the Courtauld. Reaching Oxford Street early, she went into Selfridges to kill time, wondering wistfully whether Henry might have kept her on if she had worn more elegant clothes. Finally she went up to the book department to look for a paperback. Even when strolling between the racks of dresses, she had felt she was being watched. Now, as she scanned the bookshelves, she sensed that a man was hovering a short distance away from her. She turned, but there was no one, or whoever was following her had ducked behind a stack of books. She looked at her watch; she had ten minutes to kill. She continued to browse, still with the odd sensation that she was being observed.

When it was time to meet Naomi, she picked up Jean-Paul Sartre's *The Words* almost at random and went to the cash desk. As she stood there, she remained aware that someone's eyes were on her, and the feeling grew until she was certain that whoever it was stood directly behind her in line. Suddenly angry at being pestered in this shadowy way, she turned abruptly and found herself face to face with her brother Jake.

"Hi," he said, with an amused look in his eye.

"What are you doing here?"

"Buying a book." He showed her the paperback he was holding.

Anna made her purchase, then stepped back to let him get to the cash desk and waited for him. As they walked out of the department store and into the street leading to Portman Square, she asked, "But what are you doing in London?"

"I came to see you."

"Huh?"

"Let's say I was offered the trip and thought how nice it would be to see my sister."

"Why didn't you call?"

"I was busy."

"And Aunt Miriam? She thought you might stay."

"She knew I was here?"

"Dad told us yesterday."

Jake nodded. "Shall we go eat?"

"I'm having lunch with a friend."

"Couldn't you cancel it?"

She frowned because her brother had always taken it for granted that he would get his own way. "I could, I suppose," she said, "but I'm not sure that I want to."

"I fly back this evening."

"So?"

He smiled wryly, acknowledging that there was little affection between them. "There are things to talk about," he said.

"Like what?"

"Like the death of Father Lambert."

"You heard?"

"Yes."

"Do you know what happened in Israel?"

"I know, yes."

"Okay," said Anna. "I'll go tell Naomi that I can't make it."

At the Courtauld Institute Anna left a message at the desk rather than wait, then rejoined Jake outside and walked with him toward Baker Street. She felt ill at ease, as she always did when she found herself alone with her brother. She was particularly suspicious when he was friendly, as he seemed to be now, because she knew from experience that it meant he wanted something from her. His usual manner was that of the sneering older brother who had resented her presence in the Dagan family ever since she was born. When they were young he had bossed and bullied her in the ways boys often do, but maturity had not mellowed his behavior. When they were apart—Anna in the United States, Jake in Israel—each had envied the other the company of their parents. Every time Anna had returned to Israel, Jake's disdain for his younger sister had become ideologically more explicit. She had grown into an easygoing American, he into a determined Israeli, but it was not until he had joined the army that she had actually come to fear him.

He had always been older, taller and stronger than she was, and had dominated her when they were children with his greater aggression and superior strength. As a recruit in the IDF, he had learned to use this strength and aggression in a lethal way. He was trained in the use of weapons and came home on leave with a machine gun, which he left hanging over the back of a chair in the kitchen; all of this was normal enough in Israel, but it was alarming to a girl raised largely on the east coast of the United States.

More disturbing to Anna than Jake's familiarity with guns was the training his mind had received. He had chosen to serve for four years, and thereby gained a commission. She and her parents had witnessed his induction as an officer in the Armored Corps in a torchlight ceremony held in the ruins of the fortress of Masada. When she had heard him take the oath that "Masada will not fall again," she could imagine him as El'azar, the leader of the resistance to the Romans, killing the whole of his family and then himself rather than surrender an inch of the land of Israel to the Arabs.

Later Jake had gone to the Lebanon and fought in the siege of Beirut. Once, when she had asked what he knew about the massacre of Palestinians in the Sabra and Chatila camps, he had first answered that it was nothing to do with the Israeli army, and then had added with a cold smile, "And where would Israel be without

Deir Yassin?" This massacre of Arabs by the Irgun and the Stern Gang in 1948, which had led to an exodus of refugees, was defended by Jake as the only way to get Palestinians off the land that God had given to the Jews. Anna had talked about self-determination and human rights, but always came up against her brother's unshakable conviction that no human concept of justice could override a divine gift to a chosen people.

She had appealed to her father and mother, but they had given her little support. They had been less happy than Jake to relish the triumphs of modern Israel, and they expressed their opinions in a gentler way, but they too believed that the land, like the Law, was the birthright of the Jewish people.

These arguments had been largely academic until the *intifada*, during which stories appeared daily in the *Jerusalem Post* about Arab rioters being shot dead by the IDF; there were pictures on television of soldiers using rocks to break the bones of their young Palestinian prisoners, and of the razing of houses of those active in the uprising; the Arab schools and universities were closed, and the refugees in Gaza were confined by curfew to their wretched shacks in the burning heat. In this atmosphere the arguments between brother and sister had become less theoretical and so impassioned that the atmosphere in the Dagans' home became impossible for them all. When Anna announced that she was going to refuse to serve in the army because of what it was doing to the Palestinians, her father at once applied for a deferment, and then had called Father Lambert and his sister Miriam to arrange for his daughter to go to London.

It was now almost a year since she had seen Jake, but neither the time nor the distance that had separated them had lessened his ability to irritate her. She acknowledged to herself that if, as everyone suspected, he still worked for Mossad or Shin Bet, he had reasons to be secretive about his movements, but why had he followed her into Selfridges instead of telephoning her at Aunt Miriam's? And why did he have to walk along Baker Street as if he was on patrol in Gaza or East Jerusalem? She was even annoyed that he knew that there was a kosher sandwich bar on the corner of George Street where he could eat lunch without being defiled.

As they went in, she intercepted the look of a girl at the counter and recognized reluctantly that her brother was handsome, almost heroic. Even here in London, wearing beige chinos, a check shirt and sneakers, no one could mistake him for an off-duty accountant from Golders Green. His eyes were too quick and their expression too hard; his body was too fit and its movements too controlled, and there was something indefinable in his bearing suggesting a man who knew neither scruple nor fear.

"So how did Lambert die?" he asked Anna, as he sat down with a salt-beef sandwich.

"Officially?"

"I know. A stroke."

"He hanged himself."

"He *hanged* himself?"

She nodded.

"Who found him?"

"Andrew."

"Was it suicide?"

"Yes, though for a while Andrew thought he might have been murdered."

"Why?"

"He couldn't find his notebook."

"He might have left it in Israel."

"Of course. But he also noticed, or thought he did, that Father Lambert's papers were too tidy."

"Did he call the police?"

"No."

"Why not?"

"The prior wanted to avoid a scandal."

"But if Andrew thinks he was murdered . . ."

"He doesn't now."

"Why did he change his mind?"

"Because . . . Well, he discovered that just before he died, Father Lambert did something that seemed to prove he had lost his faith."

"Did what?"

"Never mind. But it was more than enough to convince Andrew that he was in a real state of despair."

Jake put down his sandwich, licked his fingers, then said nonchalantly, "I think it's quite possible that he *was* murdered."

"Why would anyone want to murder him?"

"To silence him."

"To silence him?"

"To stop him speaking at the Congress."

"Why? What was he going to say?"

"That Dad's dug up the body of Jesus."

She looked at him oddly. "Why should he want to say that?"

"Because he has."

"Dug up *Jesus*?"

He put a finger to his lips. "Not so loud."

"How can Dad have dug up Jesus?" she whispered, half giggling.

He went on munching. "We found him in a cistern under the Temple Mount."

"Jesus? Jesus Christ?"

"Sure." He took another bite.

"You mean the remains of a crucified man?"

"As described in the Gospels."

"There are marks?"

"Yes. On the wrists, the ribs, the skull. And a long nail through the ankles."

"What kind of marks on the skull?"

"Scratches."

"The crown of thorns?"

He shrugged. "I guess so."

"But this is ridiculous," said Anna. "Even if you've dug up the skeleton of a crucified man, how can you possibly know that it's Jesus?"

"Because of the Codex."

"What Codex?"

"Four or five years ago, they found a fragment in Lithuania of the Slavonic version of Josephus's *Jewish War*."

Anna frowned. "I remember Father Lambert telling us something about it."

"It contained a passage not found in any of the other editions, to the effect that the Romans might have smuggled the body of Jesus out of the tomb hidden in a storage jar and then built it into a cistern beneath the Temple."

"And Dad found the cistern?"

"We've known it was there since they dug along the side of the Western Wall. The wall cuts right through it. What we've never dared do until now is go through the wall into the other half of the cistern."

"And when you did, you found the jar?"

"Yes. With the body inside."

Anna shook her head. "I don't understand. I thought you were excavating beside the Western Wall, not under the Temple Mount."

"Of course. We had to say that because the Muslims would go berserk if they thought we were digging under the Haram, the

Temple Mount. But once the Department of Religious Affairs had dug their passage alongside the Western Wall, and linked up with the cisterns under the Via Dolorosa, Dad had always wanted to go through Herod's Western Wall and see what there was between that and the retaining wall built by Zerubbabel and Solomon."

"But who sanctioned it?"

"Certainly not the Department of Antiquities."

"Religious Affairs?"

He shook his head. "No. To them it would be desecrating the Temple. It was authorized on the grounds of national security."

"And who did that?"

Jake grinned. "Let's just say there was a common interest between those who wanted to listen to what was being said by the Arabs on the Temple Mount and those who wanted to know what was on the other side of the Western Wall."

This irritated Anna, but not enough to smother her curiosity. She was, after all, the daughter of Michal Dagan and an archaeologist in her own right. "But isn't it just bedrock?" she asked.

"In parts, yes. By Warren's Shaft, bedrock. By Wilson's Arch, probably infill. By Robinson's Arch, infill and the stables of Solomon. What had always interested Dad was the northern corner, at the very end of the new tunnel."

"Why?"

"Did you ever go down there?"

She shook her head. "No."

"Herod built the Antonia Fortress overlooking the Temple, right?"

She nodded.

"He built it on the site of a Maccabean fortress that had stood on bedrock. Some of that had to be cut away for the Western Wall of the Temple."

"So what was the point of going through the wall into bedrock?"

"No point at all. But at the very end of the wall there is a break in the bedrock where the wall cuts through the old cistern."

"Fed from where?"

"The same source as the cisterns beneath the Via Dolorosa— the water that ran down from the Damascus Gate to the Antonia and the Temple until it was blocked off by the Western Wall."

"So the other half of the cistern . . ."

"Must link up to the entire network of cisterns serving the Temple."

"But how did they fill them after the building of the Wall?"

"We don't know. Possibly with water collected from the Temple precincts themselves. But those on the higher level—certainly the other half of the cistern cut in half by the wall—would be dry."

"And it was there that you found the body?"

"Yes."

"In an ossuary?"

"In a jar."

"What kind of jar?"

"An ordinary storage jar, for olives or grain."

"From what period?"

"Early first century."

Anna sat back, her face flushed with excitement. "But that's . . . that's fantastic. I mean, if it really is . . . if it can be shown to be the skeleton of Jesus, it beats the mask of Agamemnon or the tomb of Tutankhamen."

"Of course it's fantastic," said Jake, "but it's also kind of awkward."

"Why?"

"Think about it."

"My God! Of course! Father Lambert. Dad showed it to him and he believed it."

"He had to believe it."

"So he came back and . . . of course, now it all makes sense."

"It was really very unfortunate for Dad," said Jake, "because he not only liked Father Lambert, but counted on him to break the news."

"He said he would?"

"Yes. At the Congress at Oxford."

"Why can't Dad announce it himself now in Jerusalem?"

"Because Christians won't believe a Jew."

"They'll think Dad faked it?"

"What do you think?"

"I guess they would."

"It's got to be announced by a Christian, and not just by any Christian, because half of them don't believe in the Resurrection anyway. It has to be a hard-line, old-fashioned Catholic like Father Lambert."

"And he was definitely going to announce it?" Anna asked again.

"Yes. That's why we think he might have been killed."

"Who could have killed him?"

"Catholics."

"One of their own priests?"

He laughed. "They've done as much before."

"Who?"

"The Jesuits, the Dominicans, the Franciscans. They've always believed that the end justifies the means. Or one of these new groups of fanatics like Opus Dei or the Society of Pius X. If they got wind of what Lambert was going to do, they could well have decided to stop him."

Anna shook her head. "If you knew what I knew," she said to Jake, delighted to be able to remind him that he did not know everything, "I think you'd come to the conclusion that he took his own life."

"Perhaps." He did not seem irritated to have his opinion contradicted. "But it leaves us with a problem."

"You've got to find someone else?"

"Precisely. And that's where you come in."

"Me?"

"We don't know who to approach."

"The Vatican, I suppose."

"But who in the Vatican?"

"I don't know."

"But Andrew would."

"Sure, he'd know. Do you want me to ask him?"

"Yes. Tell him it's got to be someone like Lambert, who is known to believe in the actual Resurrection of Christ but who has the integrity to accept the implications of what we've found."

"Okay, I'll see what he says."

"Take care . . ."

"Why?"

"We don't want anyone else found hanging out of a window."

10

Anna returned to Huntingdon College, hoping to find Andrew in Father Lambert's office. He was not there, but the secretary said that he had telephoned to say he was on his way.

To prepare for his arrival, she went down into the library of the Department of Archaeology to check the references to the Vilnius Codex. She first looked through the back numbers of the *Review of Slavonic Studies*, then the *Cahiers d'études d'archéologie Biblique* and finally the *Soviet Archaeological Review*. Here she found what she wanted, the translation into English of the original article by Natalija Vesoulis of the Lithuanian State Archives in Vilnius. Taking it to a desk by the window, she went through what she had read the year before for a seminar on the literary verification of archaeological data. Now she remembered the whole controversy about the Slavonic additions to Josephus's *Jewish War*, those which mention both Christ and John the Baptist, and were said by some to be forgeries by Byzantine monks, and by others to be part of the first draft of Josephus's *Jewish War*, which was later censored at a time of Christian persecution.

Father Lambert had mentioned the later "addition to the additions" only as an instance of how fragments like this, or the Dead Sea Scrolls, could turn up even in our own time. He had certainly accepted that the Slavonic additions were genuine, but had not considered that the rumor in the later addition could be true. Nor, when it was discovered, had anyone else, because no one had any reason to envisage finding in a cistern a jar containing the remains of a crucified man.

Anna photocopied the article in order to show it to Andrew, but she suddenly wondered how he would react when told of her father's find. Until that moment, elation had overwhelmed any misgivings, but now she remembered the effect the news had had on Father Lambert. Andrew might react in an equally dreadful way. Only the day before, on Primrose Hill, had he not told her that the Resurrection was the cornerstone of his religious belief, and hadn't Henry explained that his brother's religious beliefs were what saved him from the consequences of a miserable childhood? She quickly folded the pages of the article as they emerged from the copier, as if afraid Andrew might come up and read them over her shoulder. Then she hurriedly put the *Soviet Archaeological Review* back onto the shelves and went up the stairs toward the faculty offices uncertain about what to do. She had promised Jake to ask Andrew who could replace Father Lambert as the herald of her father's momentous find, but if she did so she risked destroying the illusion upon which his peace of mind depended.

Only one man could advise her how to deal with this dilemma: Henry. She did not want him to think she had seized upon the first possible pretext to see him again, but her anxiety about Andrew overcame her embarrassment and she went to the public telephone in the passage and called him at his office.

He was not there, so she tried his flat. When he answered, she told him briefly that she had to see him at once, and added, to reassure him, "It's not about us, it's about Andrew."

Henry was neither friendly nor unfriendly when he opened the door, greeting her, as always, with a kiss on the cheek. He had been working, and his eyes were glazed from focusing for hours on the screen of his word processor, as well as on the papers and reports that covered the desk and the table in front of the sofa.

"I'm sorry," she said. "I guess you were working."

"I needed a break. Would you like some coffee?"

"Only if you want some."

"I do."

She followed him into his small kitchen overlooking Eaton

Square and sat down on one of the high stools at the counter while Henry filled the electric kettle.

"Jake's in town," she said.

"When did he arrive?"

"I don't know. Yesterday or the day before."

"Have you seen him?"

"Yes. We had lunch."

"Did he know about Lambert?"

"Yes. Dad must have told him."

"What did he say?"

"It's all kind of unbelievable . . ."

"What is?"

"In a nutshell, Dad's found the body of Christ."

For a moment Henry hesitated, his hand holding the packet of Colombian coffee. Then he frowned and said, "You mean he's dug up the body of a crucified man?"

"They know that it's Jesus."

His frown deepened. "How can they know?"

"It's a long story."

He put measured out the coffee. "Tell me."

"Do you know who I mean by Josephus?" Anna asked.

"The historian? Flavius Josephus?"

"Yes."

"Not much. Wasn't he a Jew who changed sides in the middle of the revolt against the Romans?"

"Precisely. He was an aristocratic Jew, Joseph ben Matthias, born around forty years after Jesus. During the revolt against the Romans, he was sent to organize the resistance in Galilee. At the battle of Jotapata he changed sides, surrendered to the Romans and became a big-time collaborator. He helped Vespasian with the siege of Jerusalem, and after its fall, while the Jews were either slaughtered in the arena or led off as slaves, he retired to Rome on a pension to write the histories in which he tried to justify what the Romans had done."

"Did the Romans themselves have doubts?" asked Henry, pouring boiling water onto the coffee.

"That's just the point. The Romans didn't need convincing, but there were large numbers of Jews who lived under the Parthians in Babylon, so his first draft was not written in Latin or even in Greek, but in Aramaic. However, the version of Josephus's *Jewish War* became known in the West was not this original draft, but a later edition, written in Greek some twenty years later under the Emperor Domitian. It wasn't until the end of the nineteenth century that some German working in Latvia, then ruled by Russia, discovered a version of the *Jewish War* written in old Slavonic, which looked like a translation of that first Aramaic edition. It lacked passages from the later version, and was written in a more primitive style, but it had seven passages not found in the later edition which refer to John the Baptist and Jesus Christ."

"What did they say?" asked Henry, taking a tray with the coffee into the living room.

"Nothing very extraordinary, but if they are genuine they confirm that Jesus and John the Baptist actually existed."

"*Are* they genuine?"

She sat down. "Who knows? You see, there were already two passages of the same kind in Josephus's *Antiquities of the Jews*, which some scholars thought had been inserted by pious monks in the Middle Ages, so the same was said of these Slavonic additions to his *Jewish War*. But the evidence that they are genuine is strong. They are very much in the style of Josephus, and they mention both Jesus and John from the standpoint of a sceptic."

"Perhaps they were just being cunning?"

"But the only reason for doing that would be to prove that Jesus and John really existed, which at that time no one doubted."

"Then why," asked Henry, "were there no similar passages in the Greek version of the *Jewish War*?"

"That's easier to explain. By the time Josephus wrote his second edition, under the Emperor Domitian, the Christians were regarded as enemies of the state. It would have been crazy for Josephus, still living on an imperial pension, to refer to the founder of their religion as a miracle worker and demigod who was executed unjustly by a Roman official in exchange for a bribe."

"But what has all this to do with the death of Father Lambert?" asked Henry, handing her a cup of coffee.

"Wait. I'll tell you," said Anna, taking a sip of her coffee. "This German scholar, Alexander Berendts, who had pieced together the Slavonic edition of Josephus from several different manuscripts, published his preliminary findings in 1911, but his work was not complete when he died the following year. He had got hold of bits of manuscript from monasteries and museums in Russia, and after his death his work was continued by a colleague called Konrad Grass. The First World War put a stop to Grass's researches. Then came the Russian Revolution, the German invasion of the Baltic states, and the loss of some of the old Slavonic texts—in particular, a certain Codex 109, in which parts of Josephus's *Jewish War* were mixed with bits of the Gospels and various apocrypha. This Codex was thought to have been taken to the public library in Leningrad by the retreating Russians, and supposedly lost in the fire of 1919.

"Three or four years ago, it was discovered in Lithuania—or, more exactly, it turned up among other manuscripts given to the State Library in Vilnius by some Orthodox monks. A woman working at the library who knew old Slavonic noticed almost at once that this Codex differed in one small way from the others from which Berendts's translation of the Slavonic version had been made. There was, as it were, an 'addition to the additions,' to the sixth one, which dealt with the rending of the veil in the Temple."

"What did it say?" asked Henry.

"You can read it yourself." Anna took the copy of the article from her bag. "This is a translation of the article by Natalija Vesoulis, which was published in a Soviet archaeological review. It was Father Lambert who first showed it to me."

"Must I read it all?"

"No. Just the passage from Josephus. The words in italics are those found in the new Codex."

Henry took the article and read the text under the title "The Rending of the Veil":

In the days of our pious fathers this curtain was intact, but in our own generation it was a sorry sight, for it had been suddenly rent from top to bottom at the time when by bribery they had secured the execution of the benefactor of men—the one who by his actions had proved that he was no mere man. Many other awe-inspiring "signs" happened at the same moment. It is also stated that after his execution and entombment he disappeared entirely. Some people actually assert that he had risen; others that his friends stole him away; *and others still that Pilate himself had his body taken from the tomb in a jar and then hidden in a cistern under the Antonia.* I for one cannot decide where the truth lies. A dead man cannot rise by his own power; but he might rise if aided by the prayer of another righteous man. Again, if an angel or other heavenly being, or God Himself, takes human form to fulfil his purpose, and after living among men dies and is buried, he can rise again at will. Moreover it is stated that he could not have been stolen away, as guards were posted around his tomb, 30 Romans and 1,000 Jews.

Henry looked at Anna. "And your father has really found the body of a crucified man in a jar in a cistern under the Antonia?"

Anna nodded. "Yes. Or, to be more precise, under the Haram, which at its northwest corner was connected to the Antonia. Two weeks ago they broke through the wall of an old cistern and found this jar containing the skeleton of a crucified man."

"From what period?"

"The first century A.D."

"But thousands were crucified at that time."

"Of course. But on the skull of this skeleton are marks consistent with those that would be left by a crown of thorns, and on one of the ribs on the right side there is a mark that could have been made by a sword or a spear."

"And they showed all that to Father Lambert?"

"Yes, and apparently he realized at once that what Josephus had suggested in the Vilnius Codex was true."

He frowned. "One would have thought he would wait before jumping to any conclusions."

Anna was irritated that Henry should seem to doubt the veracity of her father's momentous find. "He didn't jump to any conclusions. He had the evidence."

"It still seems . . . improbable."

"Father Lambert didn't think so."

"No, that's true. And it explains his suicide."

"Or his murder."

"How . . . his murder?"

"He was going to announce the find at the Congress."

"Why him? Why not your father?"

"They thought it should come from a Catholic."

"Of course."

"But Jake thinks that some of Father Lambert's fellow Catholics may have got wind of what was going on, and may have killed him to shut him up."

Henry put down his cup. "Killing Father Lambert could hardly prevent the find from becoming known."

"No, but it would make it less likely that people would believe it."

"Why?"

"Because if Dad or any other Jew breaks the news to the world, then everyone is going to say it's a forgery."

"Why should your father pretend to dig up the body of Christ?"

She shrugged. "To subvert Christians, I suppose."

"So they called in Father Lambert, who was not just a distinguished archaeologist but a Catholic priest of a most conservative kind?"

"Exactly. And now that he's dead, they want me to ask Andrew who they can get in his place."

"Wouldn't your father know better than Andrew?"

"About the archaeology, yes, but not about the theology."

Henry smiled. "No. I can see where it would be no use asking a liberal theologian."

"Why not?"

"They don't believe in the empty tomb. But Andrew does, so you must be careful how you break it to him."

"That's what I wanted to ask you. How do you think I should tell him?"

"Try to seem a little less pleased."

Anna blushed. "I'm not pleased—I mean, not that it's Jesus, but you've got to agree that it's great for Dad."

"It will certainly make his name," said Henry, offering her more coffee.

"It's very hard for me to imagine how the news will affect someone who really believes that Jesus literally rose from the dead."

"It will be painful."

"I'm also afraid Andrew will hate me for telling him, whether he believes it or not."

"No one likes the bringer of bad news."

"And I know that he'll think I'm pleased because I'm a Jew, even though I couldn't care less about being a Jew and that it's only because of Dad that I'm a little excited."

"Would you like me to tell him?"

"Then he might hate *you*, and he'll think you're pleased because you've always said it was nonsense."

"I hope it would take more than that to turn Andrew against me."

"You mean he'd take it from you but not from me?"

"I've known him longer."

"But if I leave it to you, he'll know that I've ducked out of telling him and may decide that I don't trust him."

"Perhaps."

"So if you don't mind, I think *I'll* tell him."

"As you like."

She looked at her watch. "He'll probably be at Huntingdon. I'll catch him there."

11

When Anna left, Henry returned to his desk. His eyes fell on the columns of print from which he was drawing up an abstract on the regulations governing the import of canned meat into the United Arab Emirates, but his mind, normally able to concentrate at his command, remained preoccupied with what Anna had just told him.

When she had telephoned, he had assumed, despite her assurance to the contrary, that she was coming around to try to repair the rupture of the night before. How many times had his girlfriends contrived to reappear in a sexy dress or with their hair done in a different way, as if the glimpse of a breast or a cascade of tinted curls could reanimate a dead affection? The very crudity of these assaults upon his senses only exacerbated the revulsion he felt for the body that had once inspired desire. But as soon as Anna had entered his flat, Henry had known his assumption was wrong. Not only had she taken no trouble with her appearance, but she hardly looked him in the eye, and when she did, it was not with any lingering innuendo, but with a strange, mixed expression of anxiety and triumph. He wondered whether perhaps she thought she had done something that might impress him, but as she told him about her father's find she had showed none of the conceit girls sometimes feel because of their father's celebrity or their family's distinction.

She was excited, of course, and proud on her father's behalf and undoubtedly if Dagan had discovered the skeleton of Christ and could prove it, it was momentous news. There remained enough of the journalist in Henry to be intrigued by such a sensational story. He was also amused by imagining the effect the news would have on the clergy up and down England—the sermons that would be preached, the articles written and the learned correspondence in the columns of *The Times*. All the same, he too was anxious about the effect the discovery would have on his brother. However convinced he was that Andrew's beliefs were false, and however contemptuous he was of the Catholic Church, he saw the value to his brother of his religious convictions.

Henry had always known that sooner or later Andrew would discover that his faith was no more than a means of avoiding unpleasant truths about human nature, but he had hoped he would be eased into this understanding when he was more mature. Andrew might be twenty-eight years old, but monasticism had protected him from the coarse realities of life. To the monks, his naïveté might be evidence of spiritual strength; to Henry, it was the sign of someone fragile, someone who, upon being obliged to admit that his beliefs were bogus, might retreat into insanity.

Eventually, he forced himself to return to work on the digest of trade regulations. Sometimes he called his office to check a fact, or answered the telephone when it rang, but he kept the calls short, wanting to leave the line open in case Andrew tried to reach him. Toward six, his head tight from prolonged concentration and his eyes bleary, he longed to leave his flat and go for a walk before it became too dark, but his anxiety about Andrew took precedence over his desire for fresh air, so he went to the window and leaned out, his folded arms resting on the sill.

At eight, Henry called the friends who were expecting him for dinner to say that he could not come. At nine, he ordered a pizza to be delivered to his flat. Soon after, Andrew rang, as Henry had known he would, and asked if he could come around at once.

He arrived at the same time as the pizza, his tousled appearance and distraught expression contrasting with the neat, bored look of the uniformed delivery boy who stepped aside to let him in. Henry bribed the boy to give him a second pizza from the box on the back of his bike, and then took both of them into his living room, along with a bottle of wine and two glasses.

Andrew turned as he came in. "You can't imagine what has happened," he blurted out at once. "Really, things have been said which . . . well, if anyone else had said them, or they'd been said without my knowing . . . without my having *seen* what had happened to Father Lambert . . . well, if it hadn't been for that, I would simply have thought them a joke in poor taste, or not even a joke—more a kind of silly science-fiction fantasy . . ."

Henry sat down with the wine and the pizzas, wondering how convincing he could make his pretense that he had not already heard what Andrew was telling him. Then he saw that his brother was oblivious to his reactions; he was gazing wildly into midair and talking in an unusually loud voice, not as if addressing an audience but as if he wished to shout down other voices that were attempting to interrupt him.

"You see, everything that is incredible in itself is proof of the next incredible thing, which in turn proves another, until you have a complex circle of facts that are established, which cannot be discounted, at least not by me who saw with my own eyes his dead body and heard with my own ears Mrs. Dunn's confession."

"What have you learned now?" asked Henry.

"It seems—it will seem absurd to you if I tell you just like this, but there's no other way—it seems that Father Lambert killed himself because he saw the body of Our Lord—a skeleton, I mean, which he believed to be that of Our Lord, not just because it had a nail through the feet and the marks of thorns on the skull, and that of a spear on the ribs, but because it was found in a storage jar just like that described by Josephus in the old Slavonic version of his *Jewish War*."

Henry was ready to ask for more details of this revelation, as he would have if he had not known them already, but again it was quite clear that Andrew was beyond suspicions of any kind, so he simply allowed him to continue talking.

"Of course, no one thought the new addition in Josephus particularly significant at the time. I remember Father Lambert mentioning it, and I think he referred me to the articles that described it, but I never read them because it never occurred to anyone that the body of a crucified man would be found in a jar in a cistern. But now it *has* been found, and it seems quite plausible that Josephus should have known about it, because he had access to all the imperial records in Rome, and it is accepted that procurators like Pilate reported what they were doing in great detail. He would certainly have seen the records of the period—he might even have known old men who had served under Pilate in Palestine when they were young officers in the Roman army."

"But Josephus mentioned other possibilities," said Henry, "even that Christ did rise from the dead."

"Yes I know, which is why until now it didn't occur to anyone to take this new addition seriously. But if they have found a skeleton with those marks in a cistern just like the one described by Josephus—well, it's difficult to know what to think. I have been trying to come up with reasons why it could *not* be the body of Our Lord, but just that of an ordinary criminal. But why would an ordinary criminal have been buried in such an obscure place?"

"Both could be forgeries."

Andrew frowned. "But how? That would presuppose collusion between Professor Dagan and Russian Orthodox monks in Lithuania, and even if that is theoretically possible, it is extremely improbable to anyone who knows Professor Dagan."

"Which is presumably why Father Lambert accepted it."

"Yes. That is the most telling evidence, because if Father Lambert had had any excuse to doubt the validity of the find, he would surely have grabbed at it; instead, he returned feeling that everything he had done and sacrificed, everything he had stood for, was in vain."

"Do you feel that?"

Andrew laughed. "I haven't really had time to be affected one way or the other. Anna gave me the news at Huntingdon. Then we rang her father again in Jerusalem. He couldn't say much over the telephone, but he seemed very upset about Father Lambert, and is in something of a quandary about his find. Naturally, the archaeologist in him is very excited—one can hardly blame him for that—but the death of Father Lambert, whether it was murder or suicide . . ."

"Doesn't this prove it was suicide?"

"Jake apparently thinks he may have been murdered by some Jesuit, but that's very improbable. Anyway, whether he killed himself or was murdered, he was the first Christian to be told. Naturally Professor Dagan is alarmed by what will happen when the discovery is announced to the world. He even wonders whether it *should* be told, and asked me to advise him."

"What did you suggest?"

"How could I advise him? I'm not even a priest. Instead I asked him if I could tell my superior."

"Did he agree?"

"In the end, yes. So I went back to the monastery and told Father Godfrey. At first he thought it was a joke, but he too had to face the fact of Father Lambert's death and all that it implied, so he thought for a moment and then said, as I had, that *he* couldn't decide what should or should not be done, and that he would have to consult the papal nuncio or Cardinal Hume, and he picked up the telephone to ring one or the other. Then he realized how absurd it would sound just to blurt out that some Israelis had dug up the body of Christ, particularly since the only thing that made *us* take it seriously was that Father Lambert, whom we knew, had taken it seriously enough to hang himself. Neither Cardinal Hume nor the nuncio know that Father Lambert hanged himself, because Father Godfrey announced that he had died of a stroke, and he is reluctant now to change his story."

While Andrew was talking, Henry pushed the pizza plate toward him; he took a slice, but instead of biting into it, he used it like a conductor's baton to gesticulate while he talked.

"Father Godfrey therefore decided to call Cardinal Memel in Rome."

"Who is Cardinal Memel?"

"The head of our order."

"Is he a German?"

"No, an American. He was the rector of Pater Noster University for ten or fifteen years. Father Lambert didn't think much of him, but he is our General, and I suspect that Father Godfrey had already told him about Father Lambert's suicide. He got on to Memel almost immediately and told him what had happened. Then he handed me the telephone, and I had to repeat the whole story again. Then when the cardinal said, 'You think there's something in this?' I had to say yes. He hesitated for a moment, then told me that I was to go to Jerusalem at once and that he would fly out to meet me there."

Andrew finally bit into the slice of cold pizza, and drank his glass of wine in one gulp. Henry realized with some relief that his brother had been saved from the full shock of what the news implied by being swept into the center of such momentous events.

"Is Cardinal Memel an archaeologist?" he asked, filling Andrew's glass.

"No, he's a biblical scholar."

"Then how will he be able to form an opinion about the find?"

"I daresay he'll bring in a team from the Pontifical Biblical Institute, which will carbon-date the skeleton and all that kind of thing." Andrew drank from his glass of wine. "The difficulty, of course, will be to prevent the news from getting out before the tests have been done. In fact it won't be possible, and that's why Professor Dagan thinks that if it *is* to be announced, someone should do it at the Congress in July."

"Cardinal Memel, perhaps."

"Yes."

"Inevitably there will be people who won't believe it."

"I know. All those fundamentalists in America, and even Catholics . . ."

"Wouldn't they have to accept a ruling by the pope?"

"Not people like Archbishop Lefebvre, particularly not if such a ruling was made on the advice of Cardinal Memel."

"Why not?"

"He's very liberal and ecumenical."

"Is that why Father Lambert didn't like him?"

"Yes." He emptied his glass again and Henry filled it, noticing that rather than making Andrew cheerful, the wine was changing his mood from elation to anxiety. "It's so difficult to know," he said, "what effect it will have on the church if it *is* established that the skeleton is that of Christ. Clearly those theologians who presumed a purely spiritual Resurrection will be delighted, and even those of us who believed in a more literal way . . . Well, it's not the only article of faith in the Christian religion."

"No."

"There are still the many sayings of Our Lord, which I would have thought have an intrinsic value, and so people will still be able to model themselves upon him."

"Of course."

"But it would seem to suggest that despite the inherent moral values in what Jesus said about loving one's neighbor and all that kind of thing, he did have illusions about himself and his immortality, and about his kingdom in another world."

"Yes," said Henry carefully, "but perhaps that aspect of his teaching will turn out to have been less important than has been imagined."

"But there are several aspects, not of Christian teaching but of the practice of the Church, particularly the Catholic Church, which in the end do depend upon Jesus being the Son of God, who speaks with the authority of God."

"You mean the Eucharist?"

"Yes. Clearly an ordinary man, however wise and good, cannot turn bread into his body, or wine into his blood."

"No."

"And the same goes for the forgiveness of sins. We cannot presume, as we have up to now, that the priest in the confessional can forgive sins in the name of God if Jesus himself had no power to do so, because it was he who delegated that power to the apostles and through them to the clergy today."

"It would be a pity to abandon a practice that serves a therapeutic purpose," said Henry.

"But will it serve a therapeutic purpose if the penitent no longer believes that it is God, through the priest, who is forgiving his sins?"

"I don't know. I have never been to confession."

"No, of course not." Andrew blushed and looked apologetically at his brother, as if realizing suddenly that he was not talking to himself.

"But I can see its value," said Henry, "and I sometimes wish . . ."

"What?"

"That there was some equivalent for nonbelievers."

Andrew smiled. "I may soon be looking for something of the sort myself."

"Have you ceased to believe already?"

"No, no, certainly not. At least not in Jesus or his teaching or in the value of his suffering and death. But I suppose that the finding of this skeleton, and the possibility that it might be his, has made me wonder whether there is much point in being a priest."

"That seems to be the effect it had on Father Lambert."

"Yes. But for him it was too late, whereas I am young enough to change the direction of my life."

Henry emptied the last of the wine into their glasses. "You know," he said, again choosing his words carefully, "that because I didn't accept the premise upon which it was based, I never saw much point to your life as a monk. All the same, I'd be cautious about making any sudden decisions. Give yourself time to take it all in."

"I will. I don't intend to leave the order tomorrow. Quite apart from anything else, it will pay for my ticket to Tel Aviv. But I am glad, all the same, that I have my academic qualifications to fall back on. Think of all those poor priests who have never done anything but administer the sacraments and preach the gospel of the risen lord."

12

The next morning Andrew called Anna and asked her to go with him to Israel. At first she was reluctant—she still felt some resentment toward her parents and was afraid she might be in trouble for avoiding the draft—but Andrew argued that as an archaeologist she should grab the chance to study her father's find, and that he would find it very useful to have a second opinion from someone he could trust. When she still hesitated, he said that her company was important to him; it would help should he be affected in the same way as Father Lambert. "I'm sure I'll be all right," he said, "but Henry thinks I should have a chaperone, and he's offered to pay for your ticket."

She agreed to go, and on the El Al flight to Tel Aviv chatted cheerfully to Andrew as if they were going on holiday to the Red Sea. Her mood changed as soon as they arrived at Lod Airport and were met by Michal and Jake Dagan, for though her father greeted her with all the conventional gestures of affection, it was apparent even to Andrew that there was a certain reticence and artificiality in both his kiss and his embrace.

Like Jake, Michal Dagan was a slim man of medium height with brown eyes. His hair, once black, had thinned at the temples and turned gray. Unlike those of his son, his features were small and precise, almost feminine, and his expression alternated between a look of petulance and a youthful, roguish smile. Andrew had heard him lecture, and knew he could look distinguished on a dais, but his eyes avoided those of others, as if he was afraid that something might be read in his expression that he did not want known.

Professor Dagan also hid whatever thoughts might be passing through his mind behind a patina of irony, one that Anna had either inherited or learned to imitate as a child. It was this that made his kiss less than a kiss and his embrace a false one—as if he were saying to Anna even as he welcomed her, "Isn't this how fathers greet their daughters? Isn't this the way it's meant to be done?" Knowing how behind the same ironic manner Anna herself longed to be enveloped in an instinctive, unselfconscious hug, Andrew winced as he witnessed her disappointment and anticipated her disgruntled mood.

Professor Dagan was more friendly toward Andrew than he was toward his own daughter—not, Andrew recognized, because he was fond of him, but because he was the protégé of one of his closest friends. Yet it was Father Lambert who had once described Dagan as the archetypal Wandering Jew, part German, part American, part Israeli, eminent in all these countries but at home in none, dreaming of a homeland that could only exist if central Europe were to be re-created in the Middle East.

As they left the airport, Professor Dagan said no more about the death of his friend than he had over the telephone to London. He led Andrew and Anna to a white Volvo, where a swarthy man who might have been either an Arab or a Jew sat waiting in the driver's seat. Jake sat next to him in the front, while the others got in behind. The car was air-conditioned, but outside it was so hot that soon the driver was looking anxiously at the temperature gauge. Jake talked to him in Hebrew, which Andrew did not understand, but because of his presence and because Dagan himself did not bring the subject up, he felt unable to discuss either Father Lambert's death or Professor Dagan's find. He sat in silence as the car followed the motorway across the coastal plain toward Latrun, then curved up into the Judaean Hills toward Jerusalem. As they passed the burned wrecks of armored cars, which had been preserved as memorials to the battle for the city, Anna asked, scowling, "Why don't they clear those hulks away?"

"Why should they?" asked Professor Dagan.

"They spoil the landscape."

"People want to remember."

"What? How they clobbered the Arabs?"

"What they sacrificed to recover Jerusalem."

When they reached the outskirts of the city, Jake directed the driver toward East Jerusalem, and all at once Andrew caught sight of the domes, spires and minarets of the old walled city and was moved, as he always was, by the sight of this paradigm of Heaven. It did not matter that the walls had been built by a Turkish sultan, not a Jewish king, or that the breach in the wall by the Jaffa Gate was made not by the legions of Titus storming the city, but by Turkish caliphs to enable Kaiser Wilhelm to enter in his landau. The city's setting was as dramatic now as it had been when King David had chosen it for his capital three thousand years before, and the jumble of churches, mosques and white, flat-roofed houses brought to mind not just scenes from the Gospels but also exotic figures such as Sindbad and Ali Baba.

It was difficult for the car to enter the narrow streets of the Christian quarter, so at Andrew's suggestion the Dagans dropped him at the New Gate, which was only a short distance from the Simonite monastery and church. Both had been built by the Crusaders in the eleventh century, destroyed by the Saracens in the twelfth, rebuilt under the Mamelukes, left to decay under the Ottomans, and restored to their present condition only in the nineteenth century. The monastery had small barred windows on the ground floor, a thick studded door beneath a Venetian arch, and an old-fashioned bell, which jangled within as Andrew tugged at the iron lever.

The door was opened by a sallow young monk and Andrew stepped into a cloister much gentler and prettier than the exterior of the monastery had suggested. It had the fat pillars and barrel vaulting of the twelfth century, and looked more like a monastery in Normandy or Burgundy than anything indigenous to the Middle East. The monk was an Italian, and spoke to Andrew first in his native language but then, on realizing that Andrew was one of that rare species, an English Simonite, changed with greater enthusiasm than skill into English as he led him toward the prior's office.

Andrew had been to the monastery before on several occasions, and it saddened him to remember that on almost all of them he had been in the company of Father Lambert. The news of the death of this eminent archaeologist had already reached Jerusalem, and the prior, a German Simonite called Father Manfred Stott, said at once how sad he had been to hear the news. "And he seemed so well when he was here," he went on. "A little affected by the heat toward the end, perhaps, but no one could have imagined that he would die just one day after his return."

It was clear from the way in which the prior expressed his sorrow that he had no inkling that Father Lambert's death was caused by either suicide or murder. Of course he knew that their general, Cardinal Memel, was coming to Jerusalem, and that Andrew's arrival was somehow linked to this, but it was part of the discipline of the order not to express unnecessary curiosity, so he simply informed Andrew that the cardinal was expected later that night, and then asked the Italian brother to show him to his room.

It was a pleasant cell, one in which Andrew had stayed before, with old-fashioned furniture, an enamel washstand and a jug of water. There were clean sheets, a clean towel and a view from the window over the roofs of the Christian quarter toward the two domes of the Church of the Holy Sepulcher. He unpacked his few belongings, then went along the wide corridor to take a shower in the huge, archaic bathroom. He was sticky after his journey and was relieved to change his trousers and jacket for the cotton habit that had been laid out for him on his bed. He put it on not just because it was cool, but because he dared not greet Cardinal Memel wearing anything but the robes of the order.

It was now five in the afternoon. At six there would be vespers, and at seven supper, so he had an hour free to go out into the streets of the Old City. Although the shops were shut because of the strike called by the leaders of the *intifada*, some Arabs had come out into the streets to take advantage of the cooler evening air. Andrew did not feel conspicuous in his gray habit, because here in the Christian Quarter it was common to see priests of every known denomination—Catholic, Orthodox, Maronite, Coptic— as well as monks and friars from different orders, and pilgrims from every country in the world.

This evidence of the universality of the Christian church had always exhilarated him when he had been to Jerusalem before. Now, however, as he passed through the gate into the paved forecourt of the Church of the Holy Sepulcher, he wondered what would happen when the news of Professor Dagan's find leaked out. Since the time of Constantine, pilgrims had come here to pray over the very tomb from which Jesus was said to have risen from the dead. Would the church be abandoned, or would it change its name to the Church of the Crucifixion, since Golgotha was also under its dome?

Andrew stepped between a group of American pilgrims and a party of German nuns to pass beneath the Romanesque arch into the gloomy church. He had never liked the hodgepodge of its architectural styles—the Latin pillars, the Byzantine icons—nor the shabbiness that came from the inability of the different denominations to agree about its repair and redecoration. Nor, in the claustrophobic little shrine within the church built over the tomb of Christ, with its suffocating smell of burning oil and stale wax, had he ever felt moved to pray. Now he did not even try, but simply watched the tourists and pilgrims file in to light the tapers handed to them by an Orthodox monk. He turned back toward the door, but before leaving the church climbed the narrow staircase to the ornate altar built over the spot where the cross had stood. Here again, where once he had knelt to pray, he merely studied the intricate silverwork that surrounded the painted faces of the Greek icons, looked up at the twinkling vulgarity of the candelabra and noted the naïve depiction of Christ on the cross.

It was not that Andrew doubted the fact of the Crucifixion itself, but if it was to turn out that there had been no Resurrection, it became nothing more than a public execution of a quite ordinary kind. He left the church, thinking dispassionately about Jesus, and the suffering he had endured. He felt he could love him and revere him whether or not he had risen from the dead; indeed, he could love him even *more* if, as now seemed possible, he had been merely human after all, because ever since his conversion he had felt daunted by those passages in the Gospels in which Christ claimed to be the sole means of human salvation. After all, neither Henry nor Anna believed in him, and it had been difficult for him to accept that both his brother and his closest friend might be damned.

He left the forecourt and walked south past the Mauristan, toward the Jewish quarter, remembering how he had put this problem to Father Lambert, and how he had given a somewhat evasive reply, saying that what was just to God might seem arbitrary to man, and referring dryly to the recurring theme in the Scriptures of God's apparently gratuitous exercise of choice: of Jacob rather than Esau, of Judah rather than Joseph—indeed, his choice of the Jews themselves. If it was now to be established that Jesus was not the Son of God, it seemed to offer the possibility that any man of good will might be saved. This not only appealed to Andrew's kindly instincts, but also to his sense of fair play. It made Jesus seem more human for having made such extravagant claims, and, because he was more human, more likeable—and certainly not to be blamed for what had been done in his name. If Christ was not

God, then he had never had the power either to deceive or to enlighten generations of gullible believers.

He had passed into the Jewish Quarter of the Old City and now came to the top of the steps that led to the Western Wall. Here he stopped and looked down on what remained of Herod's Temple. The view always astonished him, for, even though, as Jesus had predicted, not one stone of the Temple itself remained standing, the massive blocks of the retaining walls remained in place, and as always a row of Jews stood nodding and chanting as they prayed beside this relic of their Holy of Holies.

The sight of these Hasidim, with their frock coats, beards and ringlets, had always seemed bizarre to Andrew, sometimes even repulsive. Now, however, he felt a certain kinship with them. After all, why should it seem strange that they wore the costume of eighteenth-century Polish gentry when he himself was dressed in the habit of a medieval monk? Both bore witness in their eccentric attire to their faith in the same God. The Muslims, who had occupied the Temple Mount since Saladin had taken Jerusalem, like the Jews and Christians also believed in the existence of a single God. Perhaps this was all that mattered—to believe and to acknowledge that belief, whether by chanting at the Western Wall, prostrating oneself in the direction of Mecca or singing vespers in a church. Was there not a residue of righteousness in all religions? Did it matter whether or not one believed that God had given Moses the tablets of the Law, or that Jesus had risen from the dead, or that the Prophet Mohammed had ascended into heaven on the back of his horse, al-Buraq, from the rock beneath the golden dome that Andrew could see from where he stood? Didn't it accord not just with charity but also with common sense to recognize that all religions reflected elements of the same truth in their different ways, just as water, glass, chrome or silver reflect the light of the same sun?

That sun was setting behind him, its last rays giving a pink hue to the honey-colored ashlars of the Western Wall, reminding Andrew that he must return to sing vespers in the church of St. Simon Doria.

The nine Simonite monks in residence in Jerusalem were mixed in age, nationality and occupation, united only in their common calling and faith. Dressed in their gray habits, their faces half hidden by their cowls, it was hard to tell who was German, Italian, Irish or Arab. The reading during supper in the refectory was in Latin, still the lingua franca of the Catholic Church, and since the monk at the lectern was the same young Italian who had shown Andrew to his room, he read with a certain fluency from Eusebius's *History of the Church*.

Just as the prior, Father Manfred, was about to give thanks to God for what they had eaten, sounds of commotion came from the hall. Father Manfred hurried through grace and rapidly left the refectory. When Andrew and the other monks followed, they saw the tall figure of their general, Cardinal Memel. He was dressed in a black soutane with scarlet edging and a scarlet cummerbund as marks of his rank; a golden crucifix hung from a golden chain around his neck, as befitted a man who was the titular bishop of Ebolium. When Andrew caught sight of him, he was laying a friendly hand on Prior Manfred's shoulder as the prior knelt to kiss the episcopal ring. Then he stooped to help the German Simonite to his feet, and turned to present the young priest who had accompanied him from Rome.

The monks leaving the refectory hesitated for a moment, uncertain whether to greet their general or humbly make themselves scarce. Since few of them had ever seen Cardinal Memel at close quarters before, and since he was a gaunt, handsome, genial man who looked more like a film star than a cleric, they could not bring themselves to disperse and stood in a cluster around him; Cardinal Memel, alert despite his journey, and sensitive to the flurry of excitement, turned to welcome his fellow Simonites with the informality and friendliness of a modern prince of the Church.

Father Manfred, a shy and pious scholar, introduced those monks whose names he knew, but since several, like Andrew, had only recently arrived, he became confused because he could not remember their names. Therefore they introduced themselves—Father Xavier from La Plata, Brother Laurence from Cork, Father Ignatius from Cracow—filing past in a line like guests at a reception. Then Father Manfred, taking the cardinal's geniality more seriously than perhaps his visitor had intended, herded his flock into the monastery parlor and asked the Irish brother to open some bottles of Lebanese wine.

As they were walking from the hallway into the parlor, Andrew introduced himself. At first Cardinal Memel did not seem to distinguish him from the other monks, but the young priest accompanying him moved forward and whispered in his ear. The cardinal's expression became more serious, and he turned back to Andrew, saying, "Ah, yes. The young Englishman. Good. I'm glad you're here." Then his expression changed back to that of the fêted film star, and he swam into the group of chattering scholars, who with the innocence of the pious had grown tipsy from the excitement of the occasion even before tasting a drop of the order's Château Musar.

Later that evening, after Andrew had returned to his cell, he was summoned to the office of the prior. This was a large room on the ground floor with small barred windows giving onto the street and, opposite, larger ones that looked out over the cloister. These were shut, and although a big ceiling fan turned slowly above them, the room was unpleasantly hot. As Andrew entered, he saw in the dim light the cardinal seated on a sofa, and the prior, looking tired and miserable, on a wicker chair beside him. The young priest from Rome was standing behind them, propping himself up against the prior's desk.

Cardinal Memel stood as Andrew came in. "I'm sorry it's so stuffy," he said, as if reading Andrew's thoughts, "but we can't risk opening the windows. We mustn't be overheard."

"I understand."

The cardinal extended his hand, but before Andrew could stoop to kiss the ring, he felt his own hand grasped and then shaken. The cardinal took him by the shoulder and guided him toward a chair.

"You don't know my secretary, Father Pierre," he said, nodding toward the pale young Frenchman by the desk, "but you know Father Manfred, of course." He turned briefly to the prior. *"Sie kennen diesen Jungen schon?"*

"Natürlich, Eminenz."

Cardinal Memel pointed to a chair next to the sofa, and they all sat down in a circle, except for the secretary, who remained leaning against the desk.

"Father Manfred knows why I am here," the cardinal began in his deep, drawling voice, "and Father Pierre is also in our confidence, but it is of the utmost importance that no one else know. The Holy Father does not want the news of the find to leak out before we are ready to react. He has authorized me to make a preliminary assessment of the claims made by your friend, Professor . . ."

"Dagan," said Father Pierre.

"Dagan. That's right. Now as far as I know, the Church has

never pronounced upon the validity of the Slavonic additions to Josephus's *Jewish War*, let alone the Codex that turned up in Vilnius. However, the tendency among our scholars has been to accept their authenticity, and what reactions there have been to the Vilnius Codex have been affirmative. Of course this does not mean that we can discount the possibility of a fraud, or even a coincidence of some kind. Quite the contrary, we must bear that very much in mind. But we must not close our minds to the possibility that Almighty God now considers us ready for a new revelation that may alter our understanding of the faith."

Andrew nodded. The other priests were silent.

"Too often," the cardinal went on, "the Church has been caught on the rebound—by Galileo, by Copernicus, by Darwin. Too often, she has reacted to uncomfortable facts by burning those who brought them to her attention, or simply by anathematizing any awkward developments, as did Pius IX with his Syllabus of Errors."

"*Na, ja* . . ." murmured Prior Manfred, nodding his head in agreement.

"Therefore we must approach this discovery of Professor Dagan's with an open mind. Not so open, of course, that it should endanger our fundamental faith and provoke despair, but open with a total trust in Almighty God, who in his own good way and his own good time reveals to his children the truths of his creation."

Here the cardinal stopped, rather as if he had reached the end of a sermon, and stood up to suggest that they all should get a good night's sleep because they would need their wits about them the next day. Then he left the room, accompanied by the prior.

Andrew prepared to follow them, but the secretary, Father Pierre, motioned him to stay. Unlike the German prior, who had appeared devastated by what he had been told, the alert young Frenchman seemed calm. Almost as a courtesy, he asked Andrew whether he spoke French, but when it became apparent that it did not compare with Father Pierre's exquisite English, they reverted to that language to go over the arrangements for the following day.

"It is unfortunate," said Father Pierre, "that the cardinal is never willing to travel incognito. It means that there are many who will learn that he is in Jerusalem, and will wonder why. For example, the patriarch has not been informed, but he will certainly know by tomorrow morning, as will the Greeks, Armenians, Jesuits and Dominicans. We have therefore prepared a story that the cardinal is here for an informal conference of biblical scholars at the Ecumenical Institute at Tantur. Of course there is no such conference, and His Eminence rarely has time to meet his fellow exegetes these days, but it was the best pretext we could come up with at such short notice."

Andrew, who had not considered complications of this kind, merely nodded to signify his acquiescence to anything Father Pierre might propose.

"We have arranged to travel to the institute tomorrow morning dressed in our clerical habits, and there to change into something less formal before returning to West Jerusalem, where Professor Dagan is to meet us. He has been entirely cooperative in making these arrangements since he is aware of the sensitivity of the cardinal's visit."

"Of course."

"As the cardinal told us just now, the Holy Father is particularly anxious that the Church should not be seen to be taking this find seriously before it is validated."

"But how . . ." Andrew began.

"But," the young Frenchman interrupted, as if confident that he could express better what Andrew intended to say, "how can the Church validate or invalidate the find without investigating it, and how can it investigate it without appearing to take it seriously? That, my dear brother, is the kind of conundrum that is not uncommon in the Vatican."

"Does the cardinal himself intend to make the initial assessment?"

"Yes."

"But . . ."

"But you are wondering how a biblical scholar can decide upon an archaeological question?"

"Yes."

Father Pierre gave a Gallic shrug. "How indeed? He is not even much of a biblical scholar, and his theology is deplorable."

"Then why was he sent?"

"He sent himself, *mon cher*. Unfortunately, he was the first to know, and he told the Holy Father only yesterday, after all his arrangements had been made."

"But surely the Holy Father could have stopped him?"

"That might have been even more dangerous. At least if His Eminence feels himself to be responsible to the Holy Father, he may think twice before he opens his mouth to the press."

"Is he likely to do that?"

Father Pierre shrugged again. "He is an American. He feels that the people have a right to know, and there is nothing he likes better than a press conference."

"So what should we do?"

"Restrain him. Don't let him get carried away."

"But is he likely to . . . get carried away?"

The Frenchman closed the folder lying open on the desk, picked it up and started toward the door. "The cardinal has many virtues," he said in a lowered voice, "but humility is not preeminent among them. He is quite convinced that the Holy Spirit has already chosen him as the next pope, and he seems to think that the best way to ensure this destiny is to run for the post as one would for the presidency of the United States." He hesitated at the door. "Did you notice how he spoke German to Father Manfred?"

"Yes."

"He can hardly speak German at all, but he likes to practise for his blessings *Urbi et Orbi.*" Here Father Pierre mimicked a pope giving his blessing from the balcony of St. Peter's. "And he chose me as his secretary to teach him French," he added, as he ushered Andrew out of the room. "To be a candidate for the throne of St. Peter's these days, you must be a graduate not just of a seminary but also of Berlitz."

13

At seven the next morning a black Mercedes, having squeezed through the narrow streets of the Old City, drew up outside the Simonite monastery. Wearing his scarlet skullcap and black, red-trimmed cassock, Cardinal Memel got into the back seat with Father Pierre beside him. Andrew, also wearing his Simonite habit, but clutching a holdall containing jeans and a T-shirt, sat beside the driver. Under the curious eyes of the passing Arabs, the car edged away, drove down past the Casa Nova hospice, left the Old City through the Jaffa Gate, then crossed the Hinnom Valley and took the road to Bethlehem.

At the Ecumenical Institute everything was prepared. The cardinal was led off in one direction by an older man whom Andrew took to be the director, while a younger man in an open-necked shirt showed Andrew and Father Pierre to two bedrooms, where they changed from their habits into their more casual clothes. When Andrew met the French priest in the corridor, he looked more vulnerable without his habit, the *éminence grise* suddenly reduced to a precocious student. They followed their guide across the Institute garden to a second, smaller car, a white Peugeot, and waited beside it in silence until the cardinal appeared, dressed in white cotton trousers and a white short-sleeved shirt, as if ready for tennis. Then the young man who had accompanied Andrew and Father Pierre drove them back into Jerusalem to the Staedtler Institute of Archaeology.

There Jake, who must have been waiting, stepped forward to greet them. Andrew presented him to Cardinal Memel, who shook his hand vigorously and put his arm around his shoulder as if Jake were yet another young Simonite monk. Andrew saw Jake wince at this avuncular gesture, which he was obliged to endure until they reached the entrance to the Institute. Then he moved ahead to open the door, ushered them into the lobby, and led them up the stairs to Professor Dagan's office on the first floor.

The professor and Anna awaited them. Andrew stepped forward to introduce the cardinal and Father Pierre. He winked at Anna, who responded with a smile. Professor Dagan offered them coffee, but the cardinal said that he would prefer to move straight on. They returned to the cars, the cardinal and Father Pierre going with the professor in the white Peugeot, while Andrew and Anna went with Jake in his little Subaru.

"Is that guy really a cardinal?" Anna asked as they drove toward the Old City.

"He's the head of our order," said Andrew.

"His predecessors used to preside over the burning of Jews," said Jake dryly.

"You're thinking of the Dominicans," said Andrew.

"In 1486 the Simonites in Salamanca had a dispute with Rabbi Tagus. They tried to persuade him of the error of his ways. When he would not recant, they denounced him to the Inquisition and he was burned."

"I didn't know," said Andrew.

"You can never catch Jake out on a point of fact," said Anna.

Jake followed the Peugeot south around the Old City, skirting Mount Zion and going through the Dung Gate. Here they were stopped by the police, who recognized Michal Dagan and let them pass into the plaza, where they parked their cars. The two groups got out and followed the professor to the building adjacent to the Western Wall, near the entrance to the excavations. Here, Jake and his father took yarmulkes from their pockets and put them on; Jake took three paper skullcaps from a box by the door and handed them to the gentiles.

"We are entering sacred ground," said Dagan. "We must cover our heads."

"I should have brought my own," said Cardinal Memel, putting on the little cap.

They entered the excavations and made their way along a narrow passage toward the Western Wall.

"These foundations are from many different periods," said Dagan. "Some Hasmonean, some Herodian, much of it used by the Omayyads as foundations for the structures overlooking the Temple Mount."

They came out of the passage into a large, cavernous chamber formed by the span of an enormous arch, one end of which was embedded in the Western Wall. Dagan stopped. "That's Wilson's Arch," he said, "named after your fellow countryman"—he inclined his head toward Andrew—"who discovered it in 1868. The pillar is Herodian, but the arch itself was almost certainly demolished during the siege of Jerusalem by Titus, and was rebuilt by the Omayyads in the seventh or eighth century. Now, if you will follow me . . ."

He led them down a flight of steps toward the Western Wall, where half-a-dozen Hasidim were praying and a group of Israeli schoolchildren were being lectured by their teacher. "This is Warren's Shaft," he said, "dug by another Englishman, an army engineer named Charles Warren, which established that we are now standing at least four meters above the level of the Herodian pavement . . ."

Andrew had seen this before, as had Cardinal Memel, but he could not tell whether Dagan had failed to realize this, or whether he was merely playing at taking an American colleague on a guided tour, so he dutifully peered down the shaft, and then followed the group toward the iron gate at the entrance to the tunnel. Here Dagan stopped while Jake unlocked it. "As you can imagine," he said, "the whole question of excavating around the Temple Mount is very delicate, because we now have to pass under the Muslim quarter of the city. For that reason, this tunnel was not dug by the Department of Antiquities, but by the Department of Religious Affairs. Nevertheless, what has been uncovered is interesting, as you will see if you follow me."

Jake had pulled a number of switches that lit a series of lights along the tunnel. Then he stood back to let his father pass through, followed by Cardinal Memel, Father Pierre, Anna and Andrew, before closing the gate and following them.

The tunnel was long. The left side was made of concrete, so Andrew was unable to tell what soil or structures it had cut through, but the right side, being the Western Wall of the Temple Mount, showed all the exquisite craftsmanship of Herod's stonemasons. Every now and then, Dagan would stop to demonstrate, for example, how the unmortared joins between the blocks were so tight that it was impossible to insert a ten-agorot piece, or to point out the largest block in the whole edifice which, he estimated, would weigh four hundred tons.

As they proceeded, Andrew began to feel dizzy. He had visited excavations of this kind before—he had been deep into the pyramids in Egypt and the royal tombs in Mesopotamia—but as they continued walking through the musty air, he became oppressed by the fear that there might be a fall of rock that would bury them alive. The thought was absurd, because the tunnel had been in use for some time, but reason cannot always master the kind of irrational panic brought on by claustrophobia. Although they had been underground for only a quarter of an hour, he became convinced that this subterranean journey had lasted much longer, and to doubt that he would ever see daylight again. He felt faint. He wanted to cry out, but dared not for fear Jake and Anna would think him a fool. He kept his eyes fixed on the blue denim of Anna's jeans until Professor Dagan stopped once again.

"We have reached the point," he said, turning to face the cardinal, "where Herod's retaining wall leaves the side of the Tyropoeon Valley and cuts into the bedrock beneath the Antonia Fortress. To your right you will see how the rock face is dressed to look like the wall. Further along, we come to the point where the wall cuts through the cistern, and where the Hasmonean channel bringing water down from the north of the city had to be dammed."

Andrew peered over Cardinal Memel's shoulder and glanced cursorily at the narrow defile, but his eyes, like the cardinal's, were drawn to the black hole in the Western Wall where one of the massive stones had been removed.

Dagan, too, seemed to appreciate that he must abandon his act and get to the point. He turned toward the wall and showed them the points where the solid rock ceased and the manmade wall resumed. Then came a pillar of bedrock, which must have stood in the center of the cistern, with steps cut in the side to give access to the water. "What we suspected," said Dagan, "but wanted to verify, is that this cistern was connected to a series of others built beneath the Temple to meet the considerable demands which ritual purification made upon the water supply. Therefore it seemed plausible to go through the wall into the other half of the cistern, and from there to explore areas that have remained unknown, certainly since the destruction of Herod's Temple."

"What about the Muslims?" asked Cardinal Memel.

"We felt it could be done without disturbing them," said Dagan. "It was a matter of cutting around a single block and removing it from the wall."

They all turned to the wall and looked at the rectangular hole. As they did so, Jake flicked a switch behind them and a yellowish light became visible from the other side.

"We can go in," said Dagan. "When you go through, you will find a shelf of rock which is four or five meters above the bottom of the cistern. There is a ladder from there down to the floor. Please be careful where you walk. We have left everything exactly as it was found."

He walked to the wall, stooped, and went headfirst through the hole. The others waited to follow him in the same order as before. Standing in front of Andrew, Anna glanced back at him uncertainly. "Are you okay?" she asked.

He smiled to reassure her. "A little dizzy, but I'll be fine."

Anna went through the wall. Andrew followed and found himself standing on a narrow shelf of rock looking down into the other half of the cistern.

Like others he had seen before, it had probably been a cave that had been extended and rounded off by masons. The lights set up by the Israeli archaeologists were more than enough to illuminate the walls. Two pointed down at what looked like a pile of rubble, laid out on a plastic sheet on the floor of the cistern.

Since Jake was now coming through the hole in the wall behind him, Andrew climbed down the ladder, but as he reached the bottom and walked toward the plastic sheet, he stopped and started swaying from side to side. His dizziness had become acute, and he saw Anna as she turned toward him in a blur. He felt himself fall, then caught, held, and led back toward the wall.

"It's so stuffy," he mumbled.

"I know," said Anna, who was holding on to one of his arms. "You'd better sit down."

With Anna supporting him on one side and Jake on the other, he leaned back against the rock.

"I'm sorry," he said.

"Don't be silly," said Anna. "There's no air in here, and it's creepy. I'm not sure I want to see a skeleton, whether its Jesus Christ or John Brown."

Her words reminded Andrew why he was there: to use his

professional skill and judgment to form an opinion about something of overwhelming importance. The challenge restored him and he stepped forward.

"Rest a moment," said Jake, holding on to his shoulder.

"No. You see, I'm the archaeologist. The others cannot judge."

"There's plenty of time."

"I'm fine, really I am." His faintness gone, he walked unaided toward Dagan, Cardinal Memel and Father Pierre.

They stood looking down at a human skeleton which lay cradled in one half of an enormous earthenware jar. Andrew could see at once that the bones were exceptionally well preserved. Although the body lay in a fetal position at the bottom of the jar, he could tell immediately that it was that of a man around five-and-a-half feet tall, with short legs and a powerful torso. Some of the ribs on the left side had caved in, but those on the right remained in place. The jawbone had become detached from the skull, but the skull itself was in good condition. The teeth, in particular, were as sound as those of many a living man, and suggested death at a relatively early age. Most startling of all, however, were not the bones or the teeth but the huge rusty nail that still ran through both ankles.

"Is this how you found it?" asked Cardinal Memel.

"More or less," said Dagan. "The storage jar lay on its side, and was cracked. We did not expect to find anything of particular interest inside, and meant to remove it to the Institute in order to study its contents. Then we realized that it would be impossible to carry it up the ladder and through the hole in the wall without disturbing the contents, so we laid it on this plastic sheet and opened it just as you see it now."

"Nothing has been changed since then?"

"Nothing at all."

"That is most interesting," said Cardinal Memel, pointing to the nail transfixing the ankles.

"It seems that the legs were twisted before being nailed to the cross," said Dagan.

"There are other instances of crucifixions of this kind," said Jake.

"And did you realize at once that it might be Jesus?" asked Cardinal Memel.

"It is not for me to say whose skeleton it might be," Dagan answered.

"No, of course not. But it was inevitable, finding a body in a cistern . . ."

"It is not unusual to find a body," said Dagan, "because there are tombs cut into the rock all over and around Jerusalem, many of them close to cisterns. What was unusual was to find the body in a jar, not in an ossuary."

"Of course."

"If the family or friends of a dead man had taken the trouble to bury him deep beneath the Temple, you would assume they would have placed the body in a decorated ossuary, or even a sarcophagus. It also seemed curious that so much trouble had been taken to bury the body of a crucified criminal in this way."

"So you thought that it might be Jesus?"

"I had to be careful. I did not wish to jump to any conclusions."

"But it must have occurred to you . . ."

"Certainly when I examined the skeleton and found marks consistent with what was said to have been done to Christ . . ."

"The nail through the ankles?"

"Yes. And look at the skull."

Cardinal Memel took a pencil torch from one of his pockets and a magnifying glass from another, crouched and peered through the glass at the skull. "Yes. That's extraordinary." He looked up and turned to Andrew. "Here, Brother," he said excitedly. "Come look at this. You can actually see traces of the crown of thorns."

Andrew bent down and, sure enough, on the surface of the skull he could see a faint tracery of scratches.

"Because the cistern was airtight," said Professor Dagan, "the skeleton is better preserved than many others we have found. We have sent samples away for analysis and carbon-dating of both the bones and what remains of the skin. Preliminary reports suggest that there are chemical compounds within these fragments consistent with the theory that the lacerations could have been made by the curved spikes of what we now call *Sisyphus spina Christi*, which was indigenous to Palestine at the time."

"And the marks on the bones?" asked the Cardinal, turning his attention to the ribcage of the skeleton.

"The measurements taken are consistent with the known dimensions of the blade of a Roman spear."

"But all this could be a coincidence," said Father Pierre sceptically. "There were thousands of Jews crucified during this period. Many might have been given a coup de grâce with a spear."

"And crowned with thorns?" asked the cardinal.

The Frenchman shrugged. "Perhaps it was customary to torment prisoners in this way."

The cardinal turned to Andrew. "You're the archaeologist, Brother. What do you say?"

"We are trained never to jump to conclusions," said Andrew.

"But these are not conclusions," said Michal Dagan. "These are only preliminary findings, but we thought it proper to involve others at once."

"The Church appreciates your so doing," said Cardinal Memel, rather formally.

"I was thinking less of institutions," said Dagan dryly, "than of my fellow archaeologists, particularly Father Lambert."

"Of course, of course," said the cardinal, glancing at his secretary. "And he, quite clearly, was convinced."

"When did it occur to you," asked Father Pierre, "that it might be the body of Christ?"

"As a speculation? Almost at once."

"You remembered the Vilnius Codex?"

"Yes."

"And put two and two together?"

"Not at once. But when we found the marks on the bones . . ."

"You realized that it might be Christ?"

"I realized that I should call Father Lambert."

Cardinal Memel looked back at the skeleton. "Just think, gentlemen. If Father Lambert was right, then we are looking at the earthly remains of our Lord and Savior, Jesus Christ."

" 'I have gazed upon the face of Agamemnon,' " said Father Pierre scornfully.

"What's that?" asked the cardinal.

Father Pierre turned to Andrew. "Wasn't that what Schliemann said when he discovered the gold mask of a king at Mycenae?"

"Yes."

"And was it Agamemnon?"

"It is now thought that it was not."

"Father, Brother," said the cardinal reprovingly. "This is not the moment for chitchat. I suggest, if our Israeli hosts do not mind, that we kneel and say a prayer together." He grunted slightly as he knelt on the ground. Father Pierre gave Andrew a covert look as if to say, "What a clown," but in obedience to their superior both he and Andrew knelt beside the cardinal with bowed heads and clasped hands while the three Dagans withdrew discreetly to the ledge of rock.

"Almighty God and Father," prayed Cardinal Memel in his deep voice, "you have in your mercy drawn back the veils of mystery over the meaning of our existence and your creation, enabling us to rise out of our condition of sinful ignorance into a life of grace and truth. Help us now, we beg you, to understand the true meaning of what we see before our eyes, so that we may go forth from this cavern beneath the foundations of your holy Temple, and carry its message to the waiting world."

Walking back down the long tunnel to the plaza in front of the Western Wall, Andrew's thoughts and feelings about what he had just seen were constrained by the role he had adopted in the cistern, that of an archaeologist whose judgment could affect the future history of the world. He even wore a thoughtful and slightly self-important expression, as if pondering a question of science, not reconsidering a matter of faith.

When at last he took off his paper skullcap and stepped out into the hot, bright sunshine, he did not drop this role for that of an anguished believer who had just had the rug pulled out from under his feet. Instead, he felt a sudden, irrepressible burst of high spirits, which made him want to run across the plaza and jump for joy. He told himself it was only relief at escaping from the confines of the tunnel that had changed his mood in this way, and he was restrained from obeying the impulse to run, skip or even smile by the presence of the cardinal and Professor Dagan. He satisfied himself by catching Anna's eye and giving the kind of complicit wink that one mischievous child directs at another, which elicited one of her ironic smiles. It was only when he reached the car that he understood that the relief he felt was not just at escaping from the tunnel, but also at returning unaffected from what he had seen.

He knew, of course, that it would be irresponsible and unprofessional to reach any fixed conclusion without further painstaking research. Even then it was unlikely that anyone would ever be certain one way or the other. Father Lambert had apparently accepted that the balance of probability came down in favor of the hypothesis that this was the skeleton of Jesus Christ. What made Andrew so happy was that, unlike Father Lambert, he had discovered the truth before it was too late.

He also knew that this was an entirely egotistical reaction, and for a moment felt the usual twinge of bad conscience, but this twinge was overridden by the liberating realization that if Christ had not risen from the dead, then all the struggle to be unselfish was futile. So what was the point of continuously chastising himself for being what he was, someone young, healthy, intelligent and, at that particular moment, in enormously high spirits?

They drove back to the Staedtler Institute in the same cars as before, Andrew sitting in the back, Anna next to Jake in the front. She turned to Andrew. "What did you think?"

"It could be Jesus," he said.

"Do you really think so?"

"In itself the discovery of a skeleton with those marks, and hidden like that, would lead one to wonder. But add to that the quite separate discovery of the fragment of Josephus. Clearly Father Lambert thought that this proved it was genuine."

"Doesn't that upset you?"

Andrew looked perplexed. "It should, shouldn't it? But somehow it doesn't."

"The French priest seemed sceptical," said Jake.

"I think he was just playing devil's advocate," said Andrew. "Or perhaps one should say the advocate of the risen Christ."

Jake did not laugh. "Will he influence the cardinal?"

"I doubt it. He was only chosen as his secretary to teach him French."

When they reached the Staedtler Institute, the cardinal was already taking leave of Professor Dagan. "This has been a most memorable occasion, Professor," he said, shaking Dagan's hand vigorously. "One way or the other, it has been a most memorable occasion."

"For me, too," said Dagan.

"Now I know you won't expect me to pronounce on your find before I have had time to think about what I have seen, and to discuss it with some of my colleagues. I would be grateful if you would continue to regard our visit as confidential until we are ready to make the Church's position clear."

"Certainly," said Michal Dagan. "As I have told you, the government, and I myself, are all too aware of the implications of this find, and are most anxious to cooperate with the Christian churches."

With a few more courtesies of this kind, the clerics took leave of the Israelis. Suddenly realizing that he was about to part from

Anna, Andrew drew her aside and said, "Can we meet later on? Where will you be?"

"Call me at home. I'll be there this afternoon."

She smiled, then followed Jake and her father. When she reached the door of the Institute she turned and waved to Andrew as he was driven off in the white Peugeot with Cardinal Memel and Father Pierre.

14

The three Simonites could say little in the car because of the driver, but upon reaching the Ecumenical Institute at Tantur, Cardinal Memel instructed them to change back into their clerical clothes and then meet him in the garden. When they reassembled, the cardinal was accompanied by Prior Manfred, and by the thin, gray-haired man wearing a beige jacket and open-necked shirt who, when they had arrived that morning, Andrew had taken to be the director of the Institute. However, the cardinal now introduced him as "Father van der Velde, whom we have taken into our confidence in this matter," and Andrew realized at once that this was the distinguished Dutch Dominican from the Ecole Biblique.

Van der Velde led the four Simonites to a room and showed them to seats around a polished table. He then brought in a jug of fruit juice and five glasses on a tray, filling the first for Cardinal Memel, who now that he was wearing his red-trimmed cassock and scarlet cummerbund again took on some of the dignity of a prince of the church, then the other glasses, before sitting down with them to listen to the cardinal.

"I have told Prior Manfred and Father van der Velde what we have seen this morning," said Cardinal Memel to the two younger men, "but I think that having heard from me, they should also hear from you—particularly from you, Brother Andrew, because of your archaeological expertise."

Andrew blushed, a little awed by this formal confrontation with such eminent priests. Father van der Velde, who had seemed so modest while pouring out the fruit juice, was well known as one of the most eminent and influential theologians in the Roman Catholic Church, a Dominican who had served as a theological adviser during the Second Vatican Council, and who had gone on to work so hard for the reunification of the different Christian churches that he had become known as "the apostle of ecumenicism." He had occasionally been rebuked by theologians such as Cardinal Ratzinger, and whenever his name had come up in conversation with Father Lambert, Andrew had noticed that tight look which came onto his professor's face when he had difficulty in suppressing uncharitable thoughts.

Now, under the scrutiny of this penetrating theologian, as well as that of the general of his order, Andrew became confused. He dared not give free expression to the wild and heterodox thoughts that were running through his mind, yet he knew that as the pupil of Father Lambert he was expected to have something to say. "You will appreciate," he began, "that it is difficult to form any judgment of my own on the archaeological data because I have not had the opportunity—"

"We understand that," the cardinal interrupted. "But what were your impressions?"

"My impressions? Well, clearly this was the skeleton of a crucified man with marks on the bones consistent with the descriptions in the Gospels of what Our Lord suffered. It is in a cistern that matches the location of the cistern in which Pilate, according to the Vilnius Codex of Josephus's *Jewish War*, buried the body of Jesus of Nazareth. Therefore at first sight, it seems, or rather it seemed to Father Lambert, who was a far greater archaeologist than I am—it seemed to him that this was indeed the mortal remains of Our Lord."

Father Pierre opened his mouth to protest, but Cardinal Memel held up his hand to silence him. "How can you be so sure," he asked Andrew, "that the whole thing is not a hoax?"

Andrew, who had hardly considered this possibility, felt like a student who had forgotten an essential point in his presentation. "I cannot be sure. I cannot even speculate one way or the other until I have made a more detailed study of the find, but I have known Professor Dagan for some years, because he was not just a colleague but also a close friend of Father Lambert's and it is inconceivable to me that he would have anything to do with a hoax."

"Clearly Father Lambert thought the same."

"Yes. And then there is the Vilnius Codex. That too would have to be a fraud."

"But why?" asked Father Pierre.

"Just a moment," said Cardinal Memel, holding up a hand to restrain his secretary. "Before we move on to you, Father, I want to be sure that Brother Andrew has had his say."

"There is nothing I can think of at this moment to add to what I have said," said Andrew, as he might have at the end of his confession.

"Very well. Father Pierre. *On vous écoute.*"

"I think it would be absurd," said the young Frenchman, arching his eyebrows with Gallic contempt for the illogical, "to accept one hypothesis or the other at this stage."

The cardinal frowned at the word "absurd." "No one suggests," he said, "that we either accept or reject any hypothesis. However, we do have to decide whether or not Professor Dagan's discovery merits an investigation by the Church. If we decide that it does, then we are, to some extent, acknowledging the possibility that he may have discovered the mortal remains of Our Lord Jesus Christ. If we do not, however, we are open to the charge, which has been made over and over again in the Church's history, that we are afraid to put the tenets of our faith under any kind of scientific scrutiny."

"A comparable case was the Turin Shroud," said Father van der Velde in a quiet, high-pitched voice.

"Exactly," said Cardinal Memel. "And the Holy Father himself authorized the carbon-dating of that fragment of cloth."

"Certainly," said Father Pierre, "if prima facie evidence emerges that this skeleton is that of a crucified man from the period of Pontius Pilate, there will be speculation that it is the body of Christ."

"And the Church will be asked to comment."

"Yes. But as well as investigating the archaeological data, if that must be done, we should also investigate the possibility of a fraud."

"Of course," said Cardinal Memel. "But at this moment do you feel sufficiently confident that it is a fraud to recommend that we denounce it as such?"

Father Pierre hesitated. "I mistrust the Jews," he said.

"What motive would they have for a hoax of this kind?"

The priest gave another Gallic shrug. "They have always been the enemies of Christianity."

"I think that is untrue," said Father van der Velde.

"Yes. I too," said Prior Manfred.

"Certainly," the Dutchman went on, "there have been attacks on Christian churches here by some fanatics, but the Israeli government has always shown great sensitivity about our feelings for the holy places."

"Naturally," said Father Pierre. "Pilgrimages are a source of foreign currency. But even here they try to denigrate our faith by turning the Holy Land into a Disneyland."

"How do you mean?" asked Cardinal Memel.

"They take pilgrims to an old Turkish caravanserai and call it the Inn of the Good Samaritan. Think how many thousands more would come to see the body of Christ."

"I cannot believe," said Andrew, "that Professor Dagan would be party to a hoax for the promotion of tourism."

"Nor does your hypothesis deal with the strong link between the discovery of the cistern and the Codex in Soviet Lithuania," said Cardinal Memel, "unless, of course, you are suggesting some collusion between the Israelis and Russians."

"That seems very unlikely," said Father van der Velde. "What interest would the Russians have in a fraud of this kind?"

"The discrediting of Christianity," said Father Pierre.

"But as I understand it," said Father van der Velde, "the Soviets under Gorbachev are seeking to rehabilitate Christianity, not discredit it."

"That is also my understanding of the international situation," said Cardinal Memel.

"But surely," said Prior Manfred, who until this point had remained silent, "surely we are approaching this question from the wrong direction."

"How do you mean?" asked Cardinal Memel.

The face of the pious German was creased and twisted, the evidence of much anguish. "What we are asking, are we not, is whether this is a fact or is not a fact—whether these bones are the bones of Jesus of Nazareth. But surely we should be listening in our hearts for the voice of God to tell us."

"Certainly," said Cardinal Memel.

"I feel sure," Prior Manfred went on, "that this discovery is sent to test us, but in what way, *dass weiss ich nicht.*"

"Blessed are those who *have* seen and yet still believe, perhaps?" asked Father Pierre.

"There is a certain levity in your attitude, Father," said Cardinal Memel to his secretary, "which seems to me inappropriate under the circumstances."

"Yet," Prior Manfred went on, his agitation forcing the words out like puffs of vapor from a steam engine, "yet he is right to refer to doubting Thomas because if these are the bones of Christ, perhaps they have been uncovered to test us further, to see if our faith in Christ can survive despite the evidence that there was no bodily resurrection."

"Are you suggesting," asked Cardinal Memel, "that it does not really matter whether these are the bones of Our Lord or not?"

"*Ja . . . nein . . . das ist . . .* that is to say, when it *is* established, if it can be, that they are, does it mean that all our faith is in vain?"

"Those are the words of St. Paul," said Andrew.

"Yes, but St. Paul is not Jesus," said Prior Manfred. "There are many things he said that the Church now rejects—about the role of women, for example. And there are many theologians and exegetes who have for some time harbored doubts about the bodily resurrection of Christ."

"Certainly," said Cardinal Memel.

"These doubts have not destroyed their faith," said the German Simonite, "so why should this destroy ours?"

There was an almost crazed look in the prior's eyes as he spoke, and it was evident to Andrew that for all the reassurance his arguments conveyed, he was closer to a crisis than any of the others. It was apparently evident to the cardinal, too, because he turned from Prior Manfred to Father van der Velde. "You, Father," he said, "are more up to date than any of us, I think, on the latest developments in Biblical exegesis."

The Dutch Dominican sat back in his chair and reached into the pocket of his jacket. "I am very much of the opinion of Father Manfred," he said, taking out a packet of Gauloises and looking down at it as if wondering whether to have a cigarette. "We may look at the question of whether Jesus rose from the dead or not in a literal sense—and whether, in consequence, the skeleton discovered by Professor Dagan could be his—without doubting any article of the Nicene Creed."

"Go on," said Cardinal Memel.

"As most of you know, for some time many theologians and exegetes, such as Father Schillebeeckx in Holland or Father John

Coffey in Sydney, have had serious reservations about accepting that the Christ of the Resurrection was the physically reanimated corpse which was placed in the tomb. The evidence of the Gospels themselves hardly sustains such a hypothesis, for though it is clearly stated that the body was gone—and we need not doubt that—it is also a fact that those who saw the risen Lord did not at first recognize him as Jesus."

"Mary Magdalene thought he was a gardener," said Cardinal Memel.

"And the two disciples on the road to Emmaus," said Andrew, "walked and talked with him without realizing who he was."

"Exactly," said Father van der Velde in the tone of an approving tutor. "If you read the Gospels simply as narratives, they all founder when it comes to the risen Lord. On the one hand, they are eager to show that he is flesh and blood, eating with the Apostles on the shores of the Sea of Galilee. On other occasions, however— in the upper chamber in Jerusalem, for example—he appears to them out of thin air."

"Yet," said Prior Manfred, "it was there that Christ showed Thomas his wounds and told him to touch them, and it was also there that he blessed those who believe without seeing."

"Yes," said Father van der Velde, "but believe what? That he rose from the dead, certainly, but must it be in a literal sense? Were those wounds bleeding? Were they bandaged? And where did Christ go when he disappeared once again into the ether? And was it the same Christ who appeared to St. Paul on the road to Damascus *after* the Ascension?"

"St. Paul certainly thought so," said Prior Manfred.

"Are you suggesting, then," asked Cardinal Memel, "that Our Lord did *not* rise from the dead?"

"The question we must consider, Your Eminence, is not 'Did Christ rise from the dead?,' because it is an article of our faith that he did, but 'What do we mean when we say that Christ rose from the dead?,' or 'In what way did Christ rise from the dead?' In other words, is it possible that Christ rose from the dead in a way that left his body itself on earth?"

"For God, anything is possible," said Cardinal Memel.

"So the answer must be yes, because before the Crucifixion Jesus did not disappear into thin air, whereas the risen Jesus did, and so, we must suppose, was physically real only in a spiritual sense and not in an actual, scientific sense that would exclude the existence of his mortal remains." Here Father van der Velde paused and looked down at his packet of Gauloises, as if considering again whether it would be appropriate to smoke.

"I follow your theology and your exegesis," said Cardinal Memel, "but how does this hypothesis explain the empty tomb? Was that a hoax by the Apostles to help us believe in the Lord's spiritual resurrection?"

"That is most unlikely," said Father Pierre, "because the Pharisees believed that those saved would rise again with a new body."

"That's quite true," said Father van der Velde. "The disciples could plausibly have claimed a resurrection even if the tomb had not been empty. Moreover, the passages in the Gospels that describe the finding of the empty tomb, though contradictory in places, are nevertheless as vivid and convincing as the descriptions of Christ's Crucifixion. Yet if one accepts that Peter, John and Mary Magdalene did find the tomb empty, but that Christ did not rise from the dead in a literal sense, then who removed the body and how was it done?"

"It must have been the disciples," said Andrew. "They were the only ones with anything to gain."

"But the chief priests were aware of that," said Father van der Velde. "They knew that Christ had in some sense predicted his own resurrection, and that his disciples might therefore steal the body and claim that he had risen from the dead. That was why they asked Pilate to place a guard over the tomb, and, according to both the Evangelists and Josephus, he did so."

"Josephus states, I seem to remember," said Cardinal Memel, "that the Jews also put a guard of their own at the tomb."

"I know, but that is unlikely. Remember, it was the Sabbath, and no Jew could bear arms on the Sabbath."

"So they had to get Roman soldiers to guard the tomb."

"Precisely. Now, even before the discovery of the Vilnius Codex, which suggests that it was Pilate who ordered the removal of the body from the tomb, it had become clear to many exegetes that it was probably removed upon his orders. We discovered this by approaching the question from another direction—looking back, as it were, upon the Gospels with the benefit of our knowledge of the Acts of the Apostles, which come after them in the canon but were almost certainly written earlier. To begin at the end, we have St. Paul sent to Rome for trial on charges brought against him by the chief priests. What is interesting if you read between the lines of Luke's narrative is the cordial relationship between Paul and the Roman authorities. For example, when Paul is threatened with assassination by the Jewish leaders, the Roman tribune in Jerusalem provides a cohort of Roman soldiers to escort him to the safety of Caesarea."

"But wasn't that because Paul was a Roman citizen?" asked Cardinal Memel.

"Or was it Roman policy to protect the fledgling Christian Church?"

"And what about Nero?" asked Father Pierre.

"But that's just the point. We are so used to thinking of our martyrs in Roman arenas, and the persecution of Christians under Nero and the later Roman emperors, that it seems inconceivable that in those early years in Palestine it was Roman policy to *encourage* the spread of Christian teaching."

"But it was the Romans who crucified Christ," said Father Pierre.

"Yes, for though power was to some extent shared at that time between the Roman procurators and the leaders of the Jews, the one power which was reserved to the Roman procurator alone was that of sentencing a man to death. This was why the Jews were obliged to ask Pilate to authorize the crucifixion of Jesus."

"Why did he agree?" asked Father Pierre.

"Because he was afraid of a riot if he refused," said Cardinal Memel.

"That is what the Evangelists imply," said Father van der Velde, "but is it consistent with the fact that Festus would not hand over the lesser figure of Paul? Was it not rather, as Josephus states, because Pilate was bribed by the Sadducees?"

"That is more likely," said Prior Manfred, "from what we know about the behavior of Roman procurators at the time."

"Then why," asked Father van der Velde, "did the Evangelists not say so? Why, indeed, did they portray Pilate as a reasonably decent man? Was it not because they themselves were being protected by the Romans and did not want to offend them?

"Look at the martyrdom of James, the brother of the Lord," Father van der Velde went on, "which is described by Hegesippus and also by Josephus in his *Antiquities*. He was the leader of the Christian Church in Jerusalem, and was widely respected by both Christians and Jews. Ananus, the chief priest, wanted to get rid of him but dared not do so while there was a Roman procurator in Palestine. It was not until the interregnum between Festus and Albinus that he took advantage of the absence of a Roman procurator to condemn James, a misuse of his power for which he lost his position as chief priest. Look, too, at Peter who, soon after Pentecost, was arrested and imprisoned by the chief priests, and was then miraculously released by an angel. As we all know, an angel was the conventional device used by the Evangelists to describe divine intervention in the affairs of men, but is it not possible that it was the Roman authorities who secured his release? Is it not even possible that the sudden change in the behavior of the Apostles at Pentecost, when they no longer cowered afraid in an upper room, but came to speak openly of Christ in the marketplace, occurred not just because of the descent of the Holy Spirit but because of assurances by the Roman authorities that Christian preachers would be protected? Is it not even conceivable that the message of the Apostles, heard by many men of different nationalities, each in his own tongue, was not the result of a miracle, but because the Romans themselves provided interpreters to spread the message of Our Lord Jesus Christ?"

"But why?" asked Cardinal Memel. "What interest could the Romans have had in promoting the Christian Church?"

Father van der Velde leaned forward with an animated expression on his learned face. "Consider the Roman predicament. Consider the task assigned to Pilate, and then the problems he faced. Palestine was essential to the Roman Empire because it controlled the eastern seaboard of the Mediterranean—'our sea,' as they called it. Should the ports of Sidon, Tyre, Caesarea and Jaffa fall into the hands of the Parthians, the Romans' unconquered enemies in Mesopotamia, they could threaten the sea routes from Egypt to Italy."

"But what has this to do with a new religion?" asked the cardinal impatiently.

"It had everything to do with a new religion," said the Dutch Dominican, "because the stability of Palestine had so much to do with the old one. The Jews considered themselves the chosen people. It irked them to submit to the Romans, to pay taxes to Caesar—to be ruled, in effect, by men they despised as pagans. They were by nature a volatile, almost ungovernable people. The Romans lived in constant fear of a rising in Israel that would give an opening to the Parthians. And the Jews themselves, at the time of Our Lord, were in a state of incipient revolt, not just as a reaction to the Roman occupation, but in anticipation of the advent of their Messiah, the all-conquering king promised by the prophets, who would lead them to power and glory."

"So," said Cardinal Memel, "along comes a leader who says that his kingdom is not of this world."

"Precisely. Jesus of Nazareth, with his meekness, his humility, his injunction to love one's enemy, to return evil with good, to turn the other cheek, and, above all, to render unto Caesar the things that are Caesar's, was the ideal man from the Romans' point of view to divert Jewish rebelliousness into a harmless religion. If the Jews could be persuaded that their Messiah was leading them to paradise in another world, and that it really did not matter who ruled them in this one, Pilate's task would be made much easier. Moreover, since Jesus had made cryptic references to rising again from the dead, and would do nothing to save himself from crucifixion, Pilate must have felt that he could kill several birds with one stone. He appeased the Sadducee establishment, represented by the chief priests, by taking their bribe and crucifying their troublemaker. Then he spirits away the body, under cover of the Sabbath, and protects Christ's disciples when they step out into the street proclaiming that Jesus has risen from the dead."

"Did this theory of yours," asked Cardinal Memel, "predate or postdate the discovery of the Vilnius Codex?"

"Please," said Father van der Velde, "this is not *my* theory, but a conclusion reached by several theologians and exegetes, and it evolved some time before the discovery of the Vilnius Codex. A certain caution had to be maintained, as I am sure you will understand, in expressing such thoughts in public. Many of us held posts in Catholic universities and would have undoubtedly lost our jobs if we had promulgated them."

"I cannot imagine them going down well with Cardinal Ratzinger," said Cardinal Memel with a laugh.

"Particularly as they are not susceptible to any kind of proof. Even with the discovery of the Vilnius Codex, which seemed to confirm much of the theory, we could not prove that it was correct. Even now, with Professor Dagan's find beneath the Temple, nothing can be proved, but evidence is accumulating that suggests Christ did not rise from the dead in a literal sense."

The cardinal sat back in the practiced manner of a chairman who wishes to conclude a meeting. "Father van der Velde, fellow monks of St. Simon Doria, I want to thank you for what you have done today. We should each now go and ponder on these things in our hearts, but maintain the strictest secrecy as before. I myself shall make my report to the Holy Father, and it will be for him to decide how to handle Professor Dagan's find. I can tell you now, however, that my advice to him will be that it must be taken seriously, and that far from representing a threat to our faith, it may be a vitally important sign of the times—the culmination of the new spirit in the Church which came with Vatican II, and the portent of a new maturity in our relationship with our Creator. Remember the words of the Apostle Paul: 'When I was a child, I spake as a child, I understood as a child, I thought as a child: but when I became a man, I put away childish things.' It may be that now the Deity, who is the source of all life and all good and all understanding, considers us ready to discard the props of the miraculous that have hitherto sustained our faith, and to walk freely toward a full and rational understanding of the bond between God and man."

15

After the departure of the three Simonites from the Staedtler Institute, Anna followed her father and brother up to her father's office, but sensed at once that they wished her to leave. Indeed, Professor Dagan said pointedly, "I think it would make your mother happy if you went home for lunch."

She left and caught a bus to Rehavya. For all the comforting smiles she had directed toward Andrew, her mood was black. Her father's find, which should have excited her—not just as his daughter, but as an archaeologist in her own right—had done nothing to relegate the private preoccupations that tormented her whenever she returned to her family in Israel. She had come to witness her father's triumph, but as she had looked down at the skeleton marked by a spear and a crown of thorns, she had been overwhelmed not by excitement or exaltation but by acute irritation with her brother Jake.

There was something about his manner as he escorted them underground that exasperated her: an aloofness, a reticence, a conceit, as well as that same sneer which he had so often directed toward her when, as a child, he had been told secrets that had been kept from her. To be sent home to have lunch with her mother only exacerbated her irritation, and she was exasperated with herself for being entrapped by the emotional reflexes of her childish self. She had told herself in the plane the day before that she was now an adult with adult feelings, yet no sooner did she set foot in Israel than she was drawn back into the passions provoked by her immediate family.

The contrived way in which her father had embraced her at the airport, and a similar reserve in her mother's kiss when she had arrived at the flat in Rehavya, had made Anna angry, and the polite questions over supper about her life in London had only reminded her of how little either of her parents seemed to care about what she was doing. That night she had cried, muffling her sobs in the pillow. She could have coped with the coldness of her parents if Henry had been waiting for her in London; alternatively she could have handled his jilting more easily if she had found affection at home. However, the double rejection—one explicit, one implicit—was more than she could bear. She had been temporarily distracted the next morning by the visit to the excavations beneath the Temple Mount, but now that she was returning home, she again felt all the wretchedness and resentment of the night before and prepared to face her mother in an angry frame of mind.

Rachel Dagan seemed surprised to see her daughter. She was watering the plants on the balcony, and looked down at the watering can as if wondering whether she could go on with what she was doing or should abandon it to talk.

"Can I get a drink?" asked Anna.

"Help yourself," her mother replied. "There's lemonade in the icebox."

Anna brought the glass to the balcony, which was just wide enough for two battered canvas chairs and an old chaise longue, sat down and watched her mother.

Rachel Dagan was as small as her daughter, but while Anna had her father's sharp but delicate features, Rachel's were rounded and bland. Her spirit was also quite different, so that while Anna's face was lean from the many changes of expression that reflected her changing moods, Rachel's was plump and smooth, not just because she had grown heavier over the years but because her character was placid, her mood always calm. As if to match this psychological trait, her voice was soft and her movements gentle. Anna had never known her to be angry; at worst, if crossed or frustrated, her gray-green eyes would widen and her reticence give way to silence. Even then she remained patient, the calming, soothing influence in a highly strung, idiosyncratic family.

It was because Anna was temperamentally so different that she had found it impossible when growing up to model herself on her mother. The primary influence had always been her father, who, though shy and introspective to the outside world, played the part of a pasha in his own home, sometimes sulking, sometimes raging if his wishes were thwarted.

Anna had often discussed her parents with her aunt in London, and it was partly because she sensed that Miriam had feelings for her brother Michal similar to those felt by Anna for Jake, that she got on so well with her. "You must always remember," Miriam once said, "that your father had no parents after the age of fourteen. He was always looking for a mother, and he found her in Rachel."

"So she was too busy mothering him to mother us?" Anna had asked.

"Perhaps. Who knows? It sometimes happens."

Now, on the balcony, as Anna watched her mother, she felt hostile toward the woman whose gentleness and calm seemed like a varnish protecting her from any involvement in the lives of her children. The silence, clearly, was to save her from comment; the patience was to save her from action. Her obligations were completely focused on the delicate handling of her husband's fragile ego, or so it seemed to Anna.

As if sensing some of her daughter's angry thoughts, Rachel prolonged the watering of her plants for as long as she could, but when it was clear that the cactuses and geraniums were soaked through, she put down the watering can, looked at her watch and asked, "Are you hungry? Would you like some lunch?"

"Why don't you sit down? We could talk."

"Yes. If you like." She sat upright on one of the canvas chairs. "What would you like to talk about?"

"Don't you want to know about the visit to the dig?"

Rachel looked away. "I think three archaeologists are enough for one family."

"But you must feel *something* about Dad's find."

"Of course I do."

"Pleased?"

"For him, yes, but I also feel . . . afraid."

"Why?"

"Because it will make many people angry."

"Revolutionary discoveries always do."

"I know. Of course your father was prepared for anger and controversy, but not for the death of Father Lambert. That upset him. He wanted to bury the skeleton and pretend that it had never been found."

"So why didn't he?"

"Jake wouldn't allow it."

"What the hell has it got to do with Jake?"

"He was working with him. It was Jake who persuaded him to go into the cistern."

"I don't understand why he left the IDF," said Anna.

"He still is in the IDF," said Rachel. "They gave him leave to help your father."

"If Dad had needed help, he could have called on me."

"You would have had to serve in the army."

"He could have fixed that."

"He thought you were better off in London."

"Out of the way."

Rachel looked at her daughter nervously. "We only want what is best for you."

"You know," said Anna, sitting up and turning away to hide her tears, "you always say that, but now, looking back over my life at the age of twenty-two, I feel that you've always wanted to get rid of me."

Her mother did not deny this. "It was very difficult," she said, "because you were in school when we were in America, and when we came back, we thought it best to leave you there."

"But not Jake?"

"Jake was always an Israeli."

"Like Dad and you?"

"Yes."

"But not me?"

"You never learned Hebrew."

"It seems to me now," said Anna, her voice trembling with a mixture of misery and anger, "that you never really *wanted* me to become an Israeli."

"That isn't true."

"Or that you didn't care whether I did or didn't, whereas with Jake . . ."

"Your father always wanted a son."

"And you?"

"I wanted to make your father happy."

"But not a daughter."

"God gave you to us . . ."

"I was an *accident*?"

"Nothing from God can be called an accident."

"But I was unexpected?"

"I was already forty . . ."

"Then why the hell didn't you abort me?"

"Anna, dear," her mother said gently.

"Can't you understand what it was like for me, growing up with this sense that I was less loved and less wanted than Jake was?"

"We did want you, Anna. We did love you. But you must realize that we were . . . inhibited."

"What?"

"By our own inheritance. Our own childhood."

"Why should that make you love me less than Jake?"

Rachel sighed—a sigh that sounded terrible to Anna, because it signified that her mother could not deny that they had indeed loved Jake more than they had her. "You must try and understand," Rachel went on, in her calm, almost monotonous voice, "what your father suffered as a child."

"I know," said Anna impatiently. "I know all that. I've heard it a thousand times."

"It was not just that he and Miriam lost their parents in the camps. That was bad, but it happened to others. Worse, however, were the years before. You see, Michal's father was a rich and successful man, one of the best lawyers in Hamburg. He didn't think of himself as a Jew, but simply as a cultivated, urbane, liberal-minded member of the German middle class. They didn't go to the synagogue, and your father and your aunt didn't even attend a Jewish school.

"Then came Hitler and the first Nuremberg laws, which said that Aryans could not be employed by Jews. The servants had to leave, even the old cook who had worked for them for over twenty years. His secretary, too, had to go, and after that his Aryan clients. He could only act for Jews. His practice shrank, and with it his income. They had to sell their large house outside the city and move into a flat in the center of town. Then the insults started. Once your grandfather was taking your father for a walk in the park when a group of storm troopers stopped him, spat at him, shouted *Juden 'raus*, and kicked him out of the park—literally kicked him in front of his son."

"Why didn't he leave?"

"To go where?"

"The States."

"To do what? He was old, he was becoming deaf, he spoke only German and knew only German law. And it wasn't easy to find a sponsor."

"What about Uncle Eleazar?"

"He offered to take the children, but he wouldn't sponsor your grandparents because he might have had to support them for the rest of their lives. And, besides, your grandfather was an optimist. Even when he had to sew a Star of David on his suit, he thought that the bad times would pass, that Hitler would mellow, that all would be well."

"But they sent Dad and Miriam to America . . ."

"Yes. They saw the war coming, and sent them to Chicago."

"To their Uncle Eleazar?"

"Yes. He wasn't really their uncle, only a cousin, a vulgar man who lived in a nasty apartment with his Irish housekeeper. The two children thought that it was going to be just for a holiday, but they never went back. For a time there were letters, then postcards, then news from friends and the Red Cross, then nothing."

"They were taken away?"

"Yes. When they came for your grandfather the first time, a doctor friend gave him an injection that made it look as if he'd had a heart attack. But they came again and took your grandfather and grandmother, your great-uncle and your aunts—all of them— to Riga, and they were never heard of again."

"I know, Ma," said Anna, her voice softer and less aggressive than it had been before, "and it's all terrible, but we can't go on agonizing about it forever."

"I don't want you to agonize," said Rachel Dagan. "I'm only asking you to try to understand the effect of it all on a boy who first sees his parents humiliated and then learns that they have been gassed and burned."

"It must have been bad."

"It was. He has never got over it. Always, within him, is his anger, his desire to do something to save them, or to take revenge on those who murdered them."

"But how could he?"

"How, indeed? He fought in the last year of the war, but against the Japanese, not the Germans. Then, afterward, when we all hoped that justice would be done, we were told to forget about the Nazis because the Communists were the enemy now. But your father could not forget, so he came to Israel—not just because there were great opportunities here for an archaeologist, but because he felt that here he could be proud to be a Jew."

"I don't know why he can't just forget about being a Jew."

"As your grandfather forgot?"

"That can't happen again."

"Don't be so sure."

"It's more dangerous for Jews in Israel than it is in Europe or the States. You don't dare go to the Old City, or even for a walk in the park."

"That's only because of the *intifada*."

"Which has made Jews into torturers and killers."

"That may be true of some," said her mother, "but at least we are masters of our own fate here. That is what your father wanted—not just to be in control of his individual destiny, but to have a son who would be untainted by the shame he felt at his own father's humiliation. It's not true that Michal loves Jake more than he loves you, but Jake is everything that he wanted and needed in a son. He is clever, he is brave, he is proud. Even his worst qualities—his contempt for the Arabs and the Bedouins—delight your father, for he sees in him a phoenix who has risen out of the ashes of Auschwitz."

Anna sat back, the tears gone from her eyes but not the look of resentment. "But do *you* believe all that crap?" she finally asked her mother.

"What . . . crap?" her mother asked.

"The phoenix rising from the ashes?"

Rachel turned away as if to hide her reaction to Anna's question. "You should understand," she said to Anna, "that men are different from women . . ."

"Humph."

"And while women are often content with a home, men . . . their pride, even their self-respect, depends on the fortunes of their tribe or their nation."

"You mean that Dad felt like a wimp because his father was kicked around by the Nazis, but Jake feels like a man because the boot is now on his foot and he can kick the Arabs around?"

"It isn't as simple as that. Jake—and your father through Jake— can respect themselves now as part of an ancient nation. They are no longer *schnorrern* in Poland or dentists in New Jersey, but masters in the land given them by God."

"That's fantasy, Ma, and you know it. I doubt that either Dad or Jake even believe in God except as an excuse for screwing the Arabs. Even if they do, it's plain that if God ever *did* give Israel to the Jews, he changed his mind and took it away from them a couple of thousand years ago. I mean, Dad can dig up the whole damned country, and all he's ever going to uncover that's authentically and undeniably Jewish are a few piles of stones from the time of Solomon. The Hasmonean remains are really Greek, the Herodian remains are really Roman, and everything else is either Christian or Muslim."

"That's not true, Anna."

"Look around you, Ma. What do you see when you look at Jerusalem? Turkish walls, Christian churches and on top of it all the golden dome of a mosque that has been sitting on the site of the Temple for at least thirteen hundred years."

"But there are Jewish monuments . . ."

"Sure. The Hilton, the Sheraton and the Laromme."

"You're too harsh, Anna."

"If I am, it's because I feel cheated."

"No. You have not been cheated."

Tears returned to Anna's eyes. "I have, Ma, because you let me out of this crazy country to see it all from the outside, and then you didn't really want me back because I wouldn't swallow the mad myth that makes Dad and Jake feel like real men."

"We need a myth," her mother said gently.

"Perhaps we do," said Anna, tears running down her cheeks, "but you never thought about a myth for me. You left me to salute the Stars and Stripes, then sent me to sing 'God Save the Queen,' so I'm left without a myth or a country or a family . . ."

"We didn't mean it that way," said Rachel Dagan.

"You may not have meant it," said Anna, "but it happened, and you let it happen because you cared more about them than you did about me."

"Not them, Anna," her mother said in a voice so low that it was almost a whisper, "but him perhaps . . ."

"Then him, yes. You were such a perfect mother to Dad that you had nothing left for me."

"He was the first, Anna."

"Then why did you have me?"

"You came . . ."

"Well, I wish to God that you'd aborted me and fed me to the dogs . . ." With that she fled and shut herself in her room to sob once again into the pillow.

Anna did not wake until around five, when she heard her mother tapping on the door. "Anna. The telephone. It is Andrew."

Anna went out into the living room. Her mother was in the kitchen, and the receiver lay on its side next to the telephone.

"Hi," she said, trying not to sound sleepy.

"Anna?" He seemed agitated.

"Yes."

"Are you busy?"

"No."

"Could we meet?"

"Sure."

"Can you get to the Jaffa Gate?"

"Yes."

"I'll wait for you there."

Anna was glad to escape from her parents' flat. If she could have, she would have left Israel that evening and returned to London. However, meeting Andrew amounted to much the same thing; now he seemed to be her only friend.

He was sitting on the steps beneath the citadel, wearing the same jeans and shirt he had put on that morning. Since Anna had expected him to be back in a Simonite habit, or at least the kind of dark, quasiclerical costume he wore when in London, these clothes struck her as odd but agreeable; he was decidedly better-looking when not dressed as a priest.

When he stood to greet her, she sensed at once that he was in an unusual mood. His manner was almost frenetic, like someone who has missed a night's sleep but has kept awake by drinking frequent cups of strong coffee. He said at once, "I am glad you could come," as if she was doing him a great favor in meeting him in this way. "Where shall we go? Would you like a drink? Or shall we go for a walk? Where can we go? There's a nasty little café over there. The rest seem to be shut because of the strike."

"They'll be open in the Jewish Quarter."

"That's true. Let's go there." They started walking toward the Armenian Patriarchate. "And if nothing's open, we can take a cab to my hotel."

"Your hotel?"

"Yes. I've taken a room at the American Colony, just for a night. I could probably stay longer but I don't know what it costs."

"I thought you were staying at the monastery?"

"I was, but suddenly . . . Well, that's what I wanted to tell you. I've decided to leave, for the time being . . . probably forever. The order, that is . . . And having made up my mind to do that, it suddenly seemed quite wrong to go on living as a Simonite, even for a minute longer. So I rushed out into the street with my bag, but then I thought it was discourteous simply to leave like that, so I went back and told the prior—he's a nice old German—and he was very sympathetic. I think he was upset about what we all saw this morning, and he rang the American Colony."

"But why? Is it because of Dad's find?"

"Yes, well, not just the find as such but more what we made of it afterward, especially Father van der Velde and Cardinal Memel."

"Do they know you've left the order?"

"No. They went straight from Tantur to the airport."

"What did they think of the find?"

"Different things. Father Pierre—that's the cardinal's secretary—thinks the whole thing is a fraud, but the other two seemed to accept that even if this particular skeleton is not that of Christ, it is almost certainly somewhere else, because he almost certainly did not rise from the dead in the literal sense that we had always supposed."

"And is that what you believe?"

"Yes, I think I do, not just because Cardinal Memel and Father van der Velde believe it, or even because Father Lambert seems to have come away convinced that the skeleton was that of Christ, but really because it suddenly seems to me wrong to insist upon something so inherently improbable when doing so separates us from others who believe in God."

"But surely the whole point of Christianity is that Christ was the Son of God?"

"Yes. And the whole point of the Muslim religion is that Mohammed was God's prophet, and for the Jews it was Moses, and for centuries now we have been slaughtering one another. People are being killed right now here in Israel because the Muslims insist that Mohammed rose up to Heaven from the rock under the Dome, and we insist that Jesus rose from the dead from under that kiosk in the Church of the Holy Sepulcher, and you insist that God gave you Palestine."

"I don't insist on anything."

"No, of course not you, but your father and Jake."

"Sure."

"What struck me yesterday, even before I saw the skeleton, was that if there *is* a God, and this God wants us to love one another, then we should build on what we have in common, and not insist on the beliefs that divide us."

"But what do we have in common?"

"Our faith in God, whether we call him God, Yahweh or Allah."

"And if you don't have that faith?"

"Then build on our common humanity."

They had reached the Jewish Quarter and stopped at a café, where they sat down and asked for two Cokes. Anna watched Andrew uneasily across the small table, wondering paradoxically whether his speaking such sense was a sign that he had gone out of his mind.

"All this . . ." she began cautiously.

"All what?" he asked.

"All this belief in the same God and a common humanity—isn't it kind of the reverse of what you believed before?"

Andrew gave a self-deprecating smile. "Like St. Paul? A vision on the road to Damascus? Yes, I suppose it is. But it makes me feel . . . I don't know . . . so excited and happy and free, like getting out of prison or leaving school."

"I can imagine."

"My only sorrow is the thought that Father Lambert must have come to just the same conclusion, but because he was so much older felt that he had wasted his life."

"I know."

"He must have realized, as I do, that once you accept Jesus as simply one among many good men—one of the best, certainly, but not the unique source of truth—then you can take from his teaching what leads to the common good, and discount some of the harsher ideas, which really, when one thinks about it, serve no purpose at all."

"Such as?"

Andrew blushed. "Well, celibacy, for example. It only entered anyone's head because Jesus blessed those 'who made themselves eunuchs for the sake of the Kingdom of God,' and St. Paul built on that, teaching that it was good to be married but better to be celibate. Then along came St. Augustine, who, to judge from his *Confessions*, was obsessed with sex and couldn't distinguish love from lust."

"And you?" Anna asked, looking at him with a trace of her old mockery. "Can you distinguish love from lust?"

He blushed again. "I think so, yes. Anyway, perhaps lust isn't as bad as it's been made out to be."

"So it's off to the fleshpots of Egypt?"

Andrew laughed and said, with hollow bravado, "No. I'm not suddenly desperate to lose my virginity."

"Father Lambert was."

"Because he was in love."

"So if you were in love . . ."

He looked away, as if to avoid her eyes. "When you are committed to celibacy, you have to discipline yourself to prevent your thoughts from wandering in certain directions, and you have to cultivate a certain mistrust of your body, not because it's bad in itself, but because its appetites and passions can lead one astray."

"But now you think they're a good thing?"

"Yes, now I do." He looked up at her earnestly. "It must be difficult for you to understand, but my concept of celibacy was tied to my belief in the Resurrection. It was as if the sexual act somehow initiated the decay of the flesh, as a fig must split open to release its seed. The Resurrection of Jesus, like the Assumption of Mary, was linked in my mind to their virginity. Suddenly this afternoon, when I realized that Jesus and Mary had bodies like yours or mine, which flourished when they were living but eventually putrefied like the corpse in the cistern, then virginity seemed absurd—in fact not just absurd, but wrong, sterile, a denial of life. That's what suddenly made the monastery seem intolerable, the thought that behind those doors were fifteen or twenty wretched men struggling to suppress their God-given desires."

"And you think Father Lambert reached the same conclusion?"

"I felt as if his spirit were hovering over me, guiding my thoughts in that direction."

"But he had Mrs. Dunn. He knew the difference between love and lust."

"So do I."

"I'm not sure I do."

"Perhaps you've never been in love."

Anna thought of Henry and frowned. "It's all more complicated than you imagine."

"I daresay." He smiled.

"You can love someone who doesn't love you."

"I'm sure."

"Or fancy someone you don't love."

"Or love someone without realizing it."

"Of course. Or not know what you feel at all."

"Yes." He hesitated, his voice calmer than it had been before, as if he had reined in his thoughts and brought them under control. "But you see, I have an advantage over you."

"What's that?"

"Well, you went into the game before you knew how to play it, but I've had a long time to learn the rules while watching from the sidelines."

"As a substitute?" She looked up at him with one of her little sneers, but met only an expression of tenderness.

"A substitute. Yes, I could hardly expect to be anything more."

Anna opened her mouth to make some ironic rejoinder but was suddenly struck by the thought that if Andrew was so sure that he could distinguish between lust and love, it was because he felt he loved someone already, and if he loved someone already, it might be her. This realization filled her with panic, not merely because it is always awkward to be faced suddenly with love or desire from an unexpected source, but also because a week earlier she had been sleeping with his brother, something Andrew did not know.

Compounding her confusion, the idea that Andrew might love her did not appall her as she might have expected. Indeed, it had no sooner entered her head than the kind of vague admiration she had felt when she had seen him waiting at the Jaffa Gate returned as a brief spasm of sexual desire. She shifted in her seat, as if someone might notice, and said, because she had to say something, "Do you think I could have another Coke?"

"Of course." He smiled and turned to call the man who had served them.

When he faced her again, Anna noticed that he had the kind of sardonic smile on his face which was more usually found on hers, as if he was more in control of what was going on between them than she was, and was amused to see her floundering in her confused and contradictory emotions. Was he so assured because he had declared himself? *Had* he declared himself? And did he also understand that after a couple of years of comradely friendship she too now considered him in a different way? Yet, she told herself in the cynical tone she always adopted in her inner monologues, if he did think he loved her, it must be because she was the only girl he knew. Once he had abandoned his commitment to celibacy, it was inevitable that he would think of her in such terms. Suddenly, with an anguish that belied the cynical tone of her thoughts, she became afraid that the friendship he had felt for her had always been only the sublimated love of a celibate monk. Now that it had surfaced as sexual desire, it would wane with its satisfaction, as in her experience sexual desire always did. She would have gained one more lover but lost her only friend.

When their drinks came, they sipped but did not speak, and the very fact that their earlier chatter had stopped so abruptly told Anna that Andrew, though he had said nothing, and had heard nothing from her, was aware that they had established a bond of a quite different kind. Yet if, as she now supposed, they were destined to become lovers, it was in a way that she had never known before, nor even imagined. He had said nothing; he had done nothing; no pass had been made, no innuendo slipped into a casual conversation; there had been simply a humble acknowledgment that he could only serve as a substitute for someone better.

He was silent now, as if also aware that anything either of them might say would be beside the point. He seemed shy, certainly, but not awkward or uneasy. His manner was that of a bridegroom who after a long engagement has finally reached the day of his wedding. She, too, looked back on their friendship as on the courtship of an arranged marriage, with providence the matchmaker and love an unexpected surprise.

When they had finished their Cokes, they went out into the warm streets and walked toward the Temple Mount to watch its honey-colored ramparts turn pink from the light of the setting sun. There they held hands, as did a number of other courting couples. Then, as it started to grow dark, both discovered they were hungry, and returned to the Jewish Quarter to eat pancakes and drink beer at a table in the open air. Again they hardly talked; there was nothing new to say. Only when they had eaten did Andrew ask, "Will your parents wonder where you are?"

"They will if I don't go home."

"And will you go home?"

"Do you want me to?"

"No." He shook his head almost sadly.

"Is there room at the inn?"

He smiled. "I think so."

"Good. Then I'll call them from there."

16

On the day Andrew and Anna had left for Israel, Henry awoke as usual at seven o'clock in the morning and went barefoot to the bathroom. As he rinsed his face after shaving, he saw a scarlet stain in the soapy water and was at once seized by panic. He spat into the basin; there was also blood in his saliva. He felt himself turn pale, imagining that these were signs of internal bleeding, that his lungs had ruptured, and that in half an hour he would be dead. But a few seconds later he saw that the blood came from his nose, and could be staunched with a tissue. Still with the taste of blood in his mouth, he shuffled through to the kitchen to make some coffee, feeling relieved to be still living and foolish that he had thought himself so close to death.

This was not the first such scare. Three months earlier he had panicked because his weight had begun to go down. He had imagined some malignant growth devouring all the nourishment that would normally have fed his body. Then he remembered that he had given up alcohol for a spell, and that since he was used to drinking several glasses of whisky every evening, he had reduced his consumption of calories by about a thousand each day.

Now, as he sat down to a breakfast of freshly squeezed orange juice, freshly ground coffee, whole-wheat toast and thick-cut marmalade, with a copy of the *Financial Times* on the table in front of him, Henry tried to return to the solitary contentment he usually felt at this moment of the day. However, while it did not persist, the fear he had felt left a residue of anxiety of an imprecise kind. It was not that he feared death, which he supposed was simply oblivion; rather, he was annoyed in advance by the business of dying, just as he was exasperated when any of his machines broke down. He expected his body and brain to function as efficiently as the engine of his BMW. He was tormented by petty malfunctions like nosebleeds or toothaches far beyond the parameters of the pain itself.

He was equally fastidious about his clothes. When he had finished his breakfast he went to his dressing room, where nine suits awaited him on heavy mahogany hangers. Before deciding which to wear, he thought of the day's appointments. Having chosen an appropriate suit, with shirt and tie to match, he dressed in front of a full-length mirror, inspecting each garment as he put it on for a sign of wear, ready to throw it aside for the husband of his Spanish cleaning woman.

He used to be as demanding about the furnishings of his flat as about his choice of clothes. A mark left by a glass on the leather top of his upholstered fender, or by a greasy hand on the arm of his sofa, would have led him to call in the cleaners and, if the stain could not be removed, have the upholstery replaced. If he now tolerated the occasional signs of grime or wear, it was not because it did not pain him, or would cost too much to fix, but because he could not be bothered to telephone the shops which had provided the furniture or the girl who had decorated his flat.

As a result, although he seemed to others to be a man in control of his own fate, Henry felt himself the victim of a creeping decrepitude brought about by the weakening of his will. Far from the heroic destiny he had once envisaged, he now foresaw nothing but a grumbling war of attrition against dirt, dilapidation and disease, ending in a final defeat by cancer, a heart attack, emphysema or a stroke.

Only the demands made upon him by his work distracted him from this pessimism. Having dressed, he now drove from Belgravia to Soho, left his car in a garage, and walked from it to his office. It occupied one floor of an old brick building, with an architectural practice above and a film-cutting studio below. At ten, he held a meeting of his editors and researchers to discuss a proposed newsletter on barter in international trade, which, he believed, would increase over the next decade. Many countries in Africa and Eastern Europe were virtually bankrupt, their currencies worthless, their credit exhausted. Even the Russians needed most of the hard currency earned from the export of oil to import food for their hungry population. Those Western businesses who wished to trade with the Soviets in the future might have to return to the kind of barter that had existed at the time of Ivan the Terrible, when English merchants had exchanged pitch and iron for Russian furs and timber.

With this newsletter in mind, Henry had arranged to have lunch with Edward Meredith, a friend from his days on *The Economist*, who was now the Moscow correspondent for a London daily. They usually met when Meredith was in London, and on this occasion, eager to pick his brains, Henry had asked him to lunch in a restaurant in Charlotte Street.

On his way there Henry was crossing the east side of Soho Square when a woman came out of St. Patrick's Church whom he recognized but could not place. It was too late to avoid her, so he smiled and prepared to walk on, but she stopped and greeted him.

"I thought you might not remember who I was," she said with a coy smile.

"Of course I do."

"I was reminded of you because I met your brother the other day."

"Andrew?"

"Yes. I had heard about him from the Simonites, but I never realized that he was your brother."

Henry now remembered that this was Veronica Dunn, the woman seduced by Father Lambert. "We're very different," he said.

"I rang him this morning, but they said he was away."

"He went to Israel."

She nodded, a grave expression on her face. "Did he go because of . . . Father Lambert?"

"Yes."

"To find out what might have happened to him there?"

"He knew already."

"He didn't tell me."

"He was very agitated."

"Why? What was it?"

"It appears that Professor Dagan has discovered the skeleton of Christ."

"Ah." She made a sound, half an exclamation, half a cry, and a look passed over her face of mixed pain and relief, as if Henry had just removed the point of an arrow from her flesh. She listened gravely as he told her about the Vilnius Codex and the discovery of the jar in the cistern.

"And Father Lambert believed that it was Jesus?"

"So it would seem."

"The poor man."

"It seems to explain why he killed himself."

"Yes." She nodded with the same grave look on her face, then frowned as some new anxiety came to mind. "And your brother?" she asked. "How did he take it?"

"He was shocked, I think, but also glad to know the truth."

"What truth?"

"That Christ did not rise from the dead."

"Is that established with certainty?"

"Why surely, if Father Lambert accepted it . . ."

"Can we be sure that he did?"

Henry frowned. "I would have thought so, from the very fact that he took his own life."

Mrs. Dunn closed her eyes for a moment, and Henry, afraid that she might be about to faint, led her across the street to a bench in the garden of Soho Square.

"There might have been other reasons why he took his own life," she said as they sat down.

While sympathetic to her physical frailty, Henry was irritated by this refusal to face the facts. "Surely you can't deny," he said, "that his suicide now seems certain to have been an act of despair?"

"Yes," she said. "I am sure . . . I have reasons of my own for believing that on that afternoon he was in a state of great confusion . . . perhaps despair. He doubted, yes, he doubted, but . . . You are not a Catholic, are you?"

"No."

"I thought not."

"Why?"

"Because you cannot understand doubt unless you have known faith."

"They are both attitudes of mind."

"No."

"What are they, then?"

"Faith is to find God. Doubt is to lose him, or rather to lose sight of him."

"And hadn't Father Lambert lost sight of God, or at least God as he had previously conceived of him?"

"We all lose sight of God from time to time. He withdraws."

"Why?"

"Perhaps to teach us that he is a person, not an attitude of mind."

Henry frowned, annoyed that this woman was trying to evade the ramifications of her lover's suicide. "I daresay," he said, "that Father Lambert must have had doubts before . . ."

"Grave doubts."

"Any sane man would."

"Any man at all."

"All the same, the doubt he entertained that afternoon, knowing, as he did, that Dagan had found the body of Christ . . ."

"He cannot have known it."

"Why not?"

"Because he had not had time to study the findings."

"That's true, but prima facie . . ."

"Prima facie it was enough to make him vulnerable to doubt, but we know he cannot have reached a reasoned conclusion because he behaved so irrationally . . ."

"In killing himself?"

"And in other ways."

"What other ways?"

"I think you know."

"Andrew did mention that . . ."

"I don't blame him. He's young."

"But that was not the act of a man who still believed in the Resurrection."

"It was the act of a man wrestling with Satan."

"Satan?" Henry gave a grunt of derision.

"If you don't believe in God, then I daresay you don't believe in Satan."

"I didn't know that anyone did these days."

"That only goes to show his cunning."

"Why?"

"Because, prima facie . . ."—she repeated Henry's Latin tag with an ironic smile—"there is so much evil and suffering in the world that it should be easier to conceive of an evil creator than of a good one."

"Does one need to conceive of a creator at all, post-Darwin?"

"He explains how one species evolves into another, but he doesn't explain how the first species came out of nothing."

"And a god, I realize, provides an easy answer," said Henry scathingly, "particularly if he is all-powerful and totally mysterious."

"But he is not totally mysterious. He makes himself known."

"To whom?"

"To anyone who prays and listens."

Henry scowled. He disliked what he considered Mrs. Dunn's archness and complacency. "How lucky you are to have all the answers," he said.

"But I don't."

"Well, you seem better equipped than Father Lambert to cope with the news of Dagan's find."

Suddenly she looked perplexed. "He went through periods of great depression."

"About his vocation?"

"No, no. He never doubted that."

"About what, then?"

"About the state of the Church."

"Surely it's in better shape now than it has ever been."

"In most ways, yes. But even when the popes were utterly corrupt, they maintained the claims of the Catholic Church to be the only institution founded by God."

"And they don't now?"

"A year or two ago—you may remember it—our present pope held a meeting in Assisi of the heads of several different religions, not just bishops from other Christian denominations, but a Muslim, a Hindu, a Shintoist, even a Red Indian chief or medicine man."

"I remember. They were all photographed together."

"Exactly. And that photograph seemed to proclaim that the pope now accepted that the Catholic faith was just one among others. He may not have intended this, but that was its effect, and to Father Lambert it was very disheartening."

"It seems to me to be stating the obvious."

"Of course, but what is obvious to those who doubt is not obvious to those who believe."

"So faith can not only move mountains, but can see through them, too."

"It is quite as valid a way of knowing what is true as deductions based upon archaeological data."

"So it can rise above awkward facts, like a skeleton found just where Josephus said it was buried, with marks consistent with what the Evangelists say was done to Christ?"

She smiled. "I really think that it is faith of a different kind which makes you so sure that those bones are those of Jesus."

"Why?"

"Because after so many years it is quite impossible to know something like that."

"They found the body of Tutankhamen after many more years than that."

"Certainly, but in that case there were inscriptions . . ."

"And here there is the description in Josephus's history."

"Discovered when?"

"A couple of years ago."

"Isn't that in itself an unlikely coincidence—two finds that fit so neatly together within such a short space of time?"

"Are you suggesting that the find is a hoax?"

"Yes."

"Will you bet on it?"

"If you like."

"Whose judgment will you accept? An archaeologist's? Or must it be the pope's?" Henry asked.

"I'll accept yours."

"*My* judgment?"

"Yes. If you look into it."

"But I'm not an archaeologist."

"If it is a fraud, then it isn't really an archaeological question."

"No. It would be personal, or political."

"There may be some link, if my hypothesis is true, between Vilnius and Jerusalem," Mrs. Dunn said.

"Possibly."

"Some complicity between two people."

"Yes."

She stood up. "I must go."

"And what are the stakes?" asked Henry, glancing at his watch, then also getting to his feet. "Ten pounds? A hundred pounds?"

"It is worth more than that, surely."

"A thousand?"

"I think bets of this kind are usually in a different currency." When Henry looked puzzled, she went on. "Souls."

"Ah. You mean I'm wagering my soul?"

"And I mine."

"Very well."

"Ring me when you know." She held out her hand and he shook it, whether to say good-by or seal their bet he did not know, before walking toward Oxford Street.

Henry was now late for lunch and found Edward Meredith waiting at his table. After his encounter with Veronica Dunn, he was particularly pleased to join his sceptical friend. Meredith had changed a little since he had last seen him—his hairline an inch further back on the brow, his eyes a little more bloodshot and bleary, his face heavier around the jowls—but his personality was the same, and they at once re-established the familiar manner of their early days in journalism. After conventional enquiries about the well-being of his wife and children, Henry plunged straight into the question of the Soviet economy.

"It's a fascinating time to be there," said Meredith, "because the country is doubly bankrupt, both economically and ideologically. You're right about barter; they're reduced to that, not just in their trade with hard-currency nations, but also with other socialist countries which don't want their worthless rubles. Even in trade between the Soviet republics themselves, they may be reduced to barter. I wrote a piece about a paper mill in Lithuania that suddenly stopped receiving pulp from Siberia. The director telephoned the sawmill and was told that they would only continue to provide the pulp in exchange for sausage, cabbage, beer, potatoes and beans. It's an extraordinary situation. Anything could happen . . ."

They ordered their lunch—not sausage, cabbage, beer, potatoes and beans, but *feuilleté d'escargots*, rack of lamb, *fraises des bois*, a half bottle of Chablis and a full one of Clos de la Roche.

"I gather from what you write in your paper," said Henry, "that the Lithuanians are determined to secede."

"So are the other two Baltic republics, and possibly Armenia and Azerbaijan as well."

"Will Gorbachev let them?"

"It's difficult to see how he can stop them except by using brute force, which would lose him the support of the West."

"Are those republics viable as independent nations?"

Meredith shrugged. "With a little help from their friends. Particularly Lithuania."

"Why?"

"Because its industries are advanced by Soviet standards, and its agriculture retains some of its efficiency from the time when the land was privately owned. But above all because of the Catholicism of the Lithuanians, which has kept them socially and culturally distinct."

"Is the Church still that strong?"

"As in Poland, it's the principal ideological opposition, and until recently it was ruthlessly persecuted."

"And now?"

"Now there's a thaw. The archbishop has been released from house arrest and given back his cathedral."

"A change of heart?"

Meredith looked doubtful. "More a change of tactics."

"Could the Communists still see it as in their interest to discredit the Catholic Church?"

"Yes, I would think so. Why do you ask?"

Henry hesitated, then said, "My brother . . ."

"The monk?"

"Yes. He's stumbled on a story that might interest you."

"About Lithuania?"

"Indirectly. But if I tell you, it will have to be off the record."

"Very well."

Henry leaned forward, and in a quiet voice told Meredith the story of Dagan's find.

"And they really think it could be the skeleton of Christ?" Meredith asked him when he had finished.

Henry shrugged. "I don't know. If he didn't rise from the dead, he has to be buried somewhere."

"Of course. But this body would never have been identified if it weren't for the Vilnius Codex."

"So if the Codex is a fake, then the find must be a hoax."

"Even if the Codex is genuine," said Meredith, "the find could be a hoax because this man Dagan might have put a skeleton into the jar and the jar into the cistern."

"It would be difficult, wouldn't it, to make it convincing?"

"Not really. It certainly wouldn't be difficult to find the skeleton of a crucified man, since thousands were executed at that time in that way, and then to add the marks of the thorns and spear. It wouldn't be hard to fake the Codex either . . . if, that is, the forgers had access to the laboratories of the KGB."

"Would it be possible for a private individual to fake the Codex?"

"In Russia? Unlikely."

"Could the Israelis have smuggled it into the country?"

Meredith hesitated. He was said to have links with various intelligence services, and now seemed to be considering not just what he knew but how much he could say. "They might have smuggled it in," he said, "but there would have to be half-a-dozen people to connive at a fraud of that kind, and people placed in the right positions: the monks in the monastery, the officials in the library, and of course the young woman who discovered it."

"Miss Vesoulis."

"Yes. She'd have to be part of the hoax, and I would have thought it would be beyond the capacity of Mossad to position people in that way. In Israel certainly, in the West probably, but in the Soviet Union no."

"But it would be possible for the KGB?"

"Of course. You see, what Mossad and the KGB have in common is that they enroll almost every citizen as a potential auxiliary, so you can never say precisely that anyone is or is not an agent. Through zeal in Israel, and through fear or opportunism in Russia, anyone can be a kind of stringer, asked to report on a colleague or to perform a small part in a much larger intrigue."

"So it's not impossible that the Codex is forged?"

"Not impossible, no."

"Improbable?"

Again Meredith hesitated. "One would have to come up with a motive, not just for forging the Codex but also for collaborating with the Israelis."

"Who are surely the Soviets' enemies rather than their friends?"

"In theory, certainly."

"What might be the motive?" asked Henry.

"Well, if one discounts the theory that it's an elaborate and expensive practical joke, then one must assume an intention to discredit the Christian religion."

"Yes," Henry agreed, "and one can concede that both the Soviets and the Israelis are to some extent antagonistic toward Christianity."

"They have that in common."

"But it would surely be inconsistent for Gorbachev, on the one hand, to stop persecuting the Christian churches and to try to enlist their support for his policy of perestroika, and on the other to play a dirty trick of this kind to discredit them."

"I don't think that necessarily follows. Gorbachev may well feel that though it's a mistake to make unnecessary enemies among believers, Christian beliefs are nonetheless absurd and reactionary superstitions."

"So he could be behind a fraud of this kind?"

"I doubt that he would be behind it, but he might have allowed it to placate those opposed to his policy of religious toleration."

"Could it have been done without his knowing about it?"

"Certainly, and here the fact that the Codex was discovered in Lithuania may be relevant."

"Why?"

"Because Lithuania is the only one of the Soviet republics with a Catholic population. There, as in Poland, the Church is the only institution that can effectively oppose the regime."

"But all that is in the past, surely? The persecution has stopped."

"Only direct persecution. Atheism is still the ideology of the state. For quite practical reasons, Gorbachev may want to enlist the support of the Christian churches for his particular faction in the Party, but he must still counter an institution which implicitly denies his right to rule."

"I don't follow," said Henry.

"It's misleading," said Meredith, "to see the Communist Party simply as a political party. In the eyes of its members it is more than that; it is, in fact, more like a church."

"In what way?"

"In the West the legitimacy of a government depends upon democratic choice. In Russia it comes from its historical mission to lead mankind toward the socialist millennium."

"But surely they don't believe that today?"

"You'd be astonished how many still do, not least because it justifies their right to rule."

"So your hypothesis would be that some old apparatchik in the Lithuanian KGB dreamed up a scheme to discredit the Christian religion?"

"Yes. Or if not to discredit it, to remove its otherworldly expectations, so that Christians, like Communists, can set their sights on a paradise here and now."

"But how could they think that a hoax of such a kind could work?"

"Why shouldn't it work?"

"Because in the end they would be exposed."

"Perhaps. Perhaps not. But by then the damage would be done. Remember the Zinoviev letter, or the Protocols of Zion."

"But doesn't your hypothesis presuppose collusion with the Israelis?"

"Yes."

"So some link would have to be established between the Soviets and Professor Dagan."

"Yes, and of course that makes it less plausible if, as you say, Dagan is a man unlikely to commit fraud."

"I don't know him myself, but my brother is sure he would be incapable of it."

"And do you trust your brother's judgment?"

Henry frowned, then said, "Not really, no."

"The way to proceed," said Meredith, taking an address book from his pocket, "if you really want to get to the bottom of this, is to find out what you can about the people who were involved in the discovery of the Codex. Ask the Lithuanians here in London about this Miss Vesoulis. Phone this man." He wrote a name and a number on a piece of paper. "He may know of her, or he can find out. Lithuania is a small country, and almost everyone knows everyone else."

17

When Henry got back to his office, he returned to work on the question of barter but found that his mind was unable to concentrate on the papers spread out on his desk. Normally he could interest himself in matters that others found intrinsically dull, but now some irritating inner voice kept whispering that matters like the convertibility of the ruble were trivial compared to the authenticity of Dagan's find.

At four he gave up and sent for one of his researchers, a girl named Sandy Wells, who though plain and unimaginative, could speak German and Russian and unearth information in a remarkably short space of time. He told her to stop working on contracts within Comecon and instead go to the British Museum to find out what she could about the Vilnius Codex and the Slavonic additions to Josephus's *Jewish War*. She looked surprised, but since Henry paid her salary she did what she was told. Then Henry rang the number that Meredith had given him and asked to speak to a man named Algirdas Sostakas. The voice that answered sounded cautious until Henry mentioned Meredith's name, and they agreed to meet at six at a pub in Notting Hill.

When Henry got there, the bar was not crowded, and he spotted Sostakas easily because of his blond mustache and Baltic physiognomy. He was about forty-five, perhaps the child of a refugee from the Second World War, but he still spoke English with the accent of someone who had learned it as a second language.

He ordered beer, Henry whisky, and once they had their drinks they went to sit at a small table.

"It's very good of you to see me," Henry began.

"Mr. Meredith tells me that you are a very old friend."

"You spoke to him?"

Sostakas shrugged his shoulders as if to say, "What did you expect? I had to make sure."

"Did he tell you what I wanted to know?"

"He said you would explain."

"It concerns a Codex, a fragment of an ancient manuscript, in the State Library in Vilnius. It disappeared during World War One, but was discovered four or five years ago in an Orthodox monastery."

"You want to know if it is a fake?"

"Yes."

"You are buying it?"

"No, but its authenticity has certain political implications."

"There are many fake icons, fake manuscripts, fake relics. They earn currency that way. Dollars, deutsche marks."

"I realize that. But this Codex would have to be faked for a specific political purpose."

"By Chekists?"

"Yes. If by that you mean the KGB."

"We know, more or less, who the Chekists are."

"But the conspiracy, if there is one, would implicate Orthodox monks as well."

"Many of them are Chekists, especially in Lithuania."

"And also officials at the State Library, in particular a Natalija Vesoulis."

Sostakas took out a grubby scrap of paper and scribbled down the name with a ball-point pen.

"We are also curious to know," said Henry, "if any of the people involved in the rediscovery of the Codex have any links with Israel."

He nodded. "Many Chekists in Lithuania are Jews."

"Why?"

"You know our history?"

"Not well."

"In Lithuania there were always many Jews. In the cities especially, in Vilnius and Kaunus. They were always on the side of the Russians. They didn't want an independent Lithuania. For this reason, and because they were in the cities, many of the Bolsheviks were Jews. They helped the Soviets when they invaded our country, arresting, deporting, torturing and liquidating. In some areas, most of the militia were Jews. They closed our churches and imprisoned our priests."

"And later," said Henry tartly, "they paid the price."

"Of course," said Sostakas. "When the Germans came, we killed them."

"All of them?"

"Most of them." He did not seem discomfited. "Some escaped to Russia and came back at the end of the war."

"As KGB?"

"Of course."

"And today?"

"Also today."

"Is it possible that any of them would have links with Israel?"

Sostakas frowned. "I don't know, but I can enquire."

"How long will it take?"

"A telephone call."

"Is that safe?"

"We have ways of putting things. 'How is my cousin Natalija Vesoulis? Is she still working at the State Library? We should like so much to know what she is up to these days.' If it sounds innocent, it does not trigger the tape recorders of the Chekists."

"You must let me know if you incur any expenses."

"Please." He held up his hand as if Henry was pressing a banknote into it. "It is a pleasure to do a favor for a friend of my friend Meredith."

From Notting Hill, Henry drove to his flat in Eaton Square. There he played back the messages on his answering machine, poured himself a drink and lay back on the sofa. He was expected to dinner by some friends, but he knew that he could not face going and waited for the strength to phone to say he was ill. He told himself that he was tired, and certainly his limbs felt weary, but the reason he balked at the thought of a social occasion was his consuming curiosity about Dagan's find.

When Anna had first told him that her father had discovered the skeleton of Christ, he had been neither much surprised nor interested. Now, he realized, the truth or falsity of her claim could not only affect the psychological state of those who had faith, like Andrew or Veronica Dunn, but it could also have considerable political ramifications all over the world, particularly in Eastern Europe, Africa and Latin America. Isolated for so long among like-minded agnostics whose values were all of a secular kind, it came as a shock to Henry to realize how many people throughout the world still believed in the Resurrection of Christ. Seldom since adolescence had he himself stopped to consider questions of this kind. There had been moments, mostly on holiday, when, staring at the stars, he had been awed by the mystery of infinity, and had wondered about the origin of the universe, but almost at once on returning to London he had become distracted by the practical concerns of his daily life.

Now, however, he had the uneasy feeling that there might, after all, be more to life than he had supposed, that perhaps the imperatives of instinct did not lead to fulfillment, and that perhaps the faculty of reason, unique though it was to the human species, was insufficient to explain the mystery that was the kernel of the human condition.

He sat up, put down his glass, and made the telephone call to the friends who were expecting him for dinner. The wife answered. He lied about a sudden sickness. She spoke the appropriate words of sympathy, but he could tell that she did not believe him.

He went out onto the small balcony at the back of his flat, a space between the sloping roof and the parapet. He watered the plants he kept there—a camellia, some herbs and a bay tree—and breathed in the scented air of the London summer. But this taste of nature did nothing to calm his mind, and while he picked the chives and parsley for an omelet for supper, he continued to think about the skeleton, and grew increasingly agitated by the thought that if reason could not explain the human condition, it was unreasonable to be so certain that there was no God. Nor could it be impossible, if there was a God, that he had been born a Jew, had died on a cross, and after dying had risen from the dead.

If such a story was not *certainly* false, then it must be *possibly* true. Thus, incontrovertible evidence, even that which pushed the balance of probability one way or the other, would be of critical importance, not merely to those political institutions in different parts of the world that were influenced by people's religious convictions, but also to the individual speculations of a man such as himself about the value of his actions or the meaning of his life.

Henry cooked his omelet and ate it in the kitchen, his mood swinging between excitement and gloom. He still felt a repugnance for religion, and thought it absurd to suggest that a God powerful enough to bring the whole universe into existence should choose to become a sweating, defecating, suffering man. Yet he had to acknowledge that if there was a God, then what appeared absurd to us might seem sensible to him. He would be privy to knowledge beyond the range of human understanding that made it necessary for God to become man in order to enable man to become a god.

Yet if he himself was potentially a god, a creature whose existence would continue beyond death but one whose condition in that unknowable dimension would be determined by his attitude to the crucified Jew, clearly his life up to this point would have earned him not bliss but torment. So too would the lives of almost everyone he knew. It followed that if there was a God with power over the destiny of human beings, the first prayer to be addressed to him should be a plea to be spared this awesome choice, to be reassured that Professor Dagan was right, and that the skeleton was indeed that of Jesus of Nazareth.

As if in answer to such a prayer, the telephone rang and Henry heard the flat, matter-of-fact voice of his researcher, Sandy Wells. "I thought you'd like to know what I've uncovered so far," she said.

"You shouldn't be working so late."

"It's okay, really. In fact, it's all quite interesting. You see, there's really a lot of controversy about the Vilnius Codex and the additions found in the Slavonic version of Josephus. There are English scholars who accept them, like Thackeray and Williamson; then there are those like Shurer, who think they are medieval forgeries; and then there's a third man, Eisler, who thinks that they're basically genuine but have Christian interpolations."

"What do you think?"

"Well, I think one's got to accept that the Slavonic version is derived from an early edition of Josephus written in Aramaic for the Jews in Babylon. There are passages that don't exist in the Greek version, but are unmistakably by Josephus. It's also clear how an Aramaic edition would end up in Vilnius. I don't know whether you want me to go into details . . ."

"Yes."

"Well, it boils down to the links between Babylon and the Byzantine Empire, and between the Byzantine Empire and Russia. It's more than likely that if such an edition of Josephus did exist, it would have ended up in Constantinople and been known there to scholars of the Orthodox Church. The most plausible theory is that it was translated into Old Russian in the fifteenth century by members of a heretical sect of the Russian Orthodox Church that, when finally suppressed by the tsar, took refuge in Catholic Lithuania."

"Might they have inserted the references to Jesus and John the Baptist?"

"It's conceivable, but it's hard to think of a motive."

"To prove that they existed."

"Of course, that's the obvious motive. But before the late eighteenth century no one doubted that they existed, so why should some medieval forger go to all that trouble?"

"So you think that the additions were definitely written by Josephus?"

"Yes."

"What about the Vilnius Codex?"

"That's more complicated. It existed up to World War One, but it was one among dozens of manuscripts scattered around in different places. They certainly knew that there was a Slavonic version as far back as 1893, but this man Alexander Berendts who was piecing it together died in 1912. Then came the war. The Germans invaded Lithuania and the Russians retreated, taking the Vilnius Codex with them. It was thought to have been given to the State Archives in St. Petersburg and destroyed in the fire there in 1917. That's why the publication of Berendts's work by Konrad Glass in 1920 did not include it. But given the chaos existing in Russia in 1917, it's quite plausible to surmise that the Codex was left in the monastery for safekeeping."

"So you think it's genuine, too?"

"It's impossible to be certain, but if it stands up to carbon-dating, then I'd say that on balance, yes, it's the real thing."

Henry rang off, elated by an extraordinary sense of relief. Only a forged Codex could justify doubting the integrity of Dagan. If the Codex was genuine, then the find was genuine, and Jesus of Nazareth had not risen from the dead. He was not, then, a superhuman being embodying the way, the truth or the light, but instead was a Middle Eastern sage with a number of interesting ideas that had been and always would be interpreted in a number of different ways.

Or rejected altogether . . . As Henry stepped back from the abyss of Christian belief he felt a sudden surge of physical well-being, like a man who wakes up to find himself cured of a debilitating disease. Life appeared once again as something of extraordinary beauty. Why had he faltered? Was there not art to entertain him, women to love him, men to esteem him and continents to be explored? What dreadful doubt had tempted him to accept the morbid philosophy of a crucified Jew? He was not a god but a man, a beast at the pinnacle of evolution, and he would live his life to the full until he returned, like Jesus of Nazareth, to the dust from which he came.

The telephone rang again. It was Sostakas. "Mr. Nash?"

"Yes."

"Are you alone?"

"Yes."

"Good. I have been talking to my friends in Vilnius. They have news of your friend, Natalija Vesoulis."

"Yes."

"She is, almost certainly, what we suspect. She was given the job at the State Library without proper qualifications."

"Is it known why?"

"She had powerful friends."

"In the Party?"

"Even more powerful."

"In the KGB?"

"That's what they think."

"And she was the one who discovered the Codex?"

"A month or so after she was appointed, the monks handed over their archives. There were many documents, and Miss Vesoulis was given the job of sorting them out. She quickly found the Codex, translated it and published her findings."

"It sounds as if she knew it was there."

"Not only that. My friends tell me that it is most unusual for someone so young to have a paper published in the *Soviet Archaeological Review*, and even more unusual for a paper to be published so soon after being submitted."

"So there are signs of a helping hand."

"Yes."

"Do they know whose?"

"It is suspected. A man named Gedda. A Jew."

"Ah."

"He is her lover."

"And what else is he?"

"He is a Soviet expert on Middle Eastern affairs."

"An academic?"

"At one time, but now a diplomat of some kind. You should ask our friend Meredith. He knows about Gedda, I am sure."

Henry telephoned Meredith. "I've been talking to your Lithuanian friend," he said.

"Did he help?"

"He's found a link between Miss Vesoulis and a man called Gedda."

"Gedda. Yes. I should have thought of him."

"Who is he?"

"A diplomat, so-called. He was here in the Russian embassy back in the seventies. We threw him out."

"For spying?"

"Yes."

"And now?"

"At one point he was in Damascus as part of the military mission."

"Would he have had contacts with the Israelis?"

"Not in Damascus, simply because there aren't any. But he would have had links with Syrian intelligence, and access to their agents in Israel."

"So he could have had the Codex forged?"

"Certainly."

"And planted the skeleton in the cistern?"

"Not without help from the Israelis."

"Dagan?"

"Yes. Unless Dagan himself has been duped."

"So we need to find a link between Gedda and either Dagan or some other Israeli."

"Yes. But since Gedda himself wouldn't have gone to Israel, it's a matter of finding an Israeli who was in Moscow some months before the Codex was found. Or if not Moscow, Damascus."

"I thought you said there were no Israelis in Damascus."

"None by choice. But the Syrians took prisoners during the war in Lebanon. Get one of your researchers to go back over copies of the *Jerusalem Post* to see if someone, say a student of Dagan's, was taken prisoner in the Lebanon and later exchanged."

Henry sighed. "It all seems far-fetched."

"More far-fetched than finding the body of Christ?"

"Perhaps not, except . . . it must be somewhere."

"What?"

"The skeleton of Jesus."

"Why?"

"Because he can't have risen from the dead."

"Nothing is impossible for God."

"Do you believe that?"

"If there is a God, it's only common sense."

"And is there a God?"

"That's a very deep question, Henry. We must talk about it some other time."

18

Anna was wakened at dawn by the cry of a mullah from a nearby mosque calling the faithful to prayer. She stretched, and in doing so sensed that she was naked. All at once she remembered everything that had happened the day before, remembered it vividly, yet she knew that dreams can leave a strong residue of feeling, and was therefore afraid to open her eyes for fear of finding herself in her parents' flat in Rehavya. But there were no mosques in Rehavya, and she could still hear the mullah. She could also sense the even breathing of a body beside her, and slowly moved one leg until it came up against Andrew's side.

She barely touched it; she did not want to wake him until she had put her thoughts and feelings in order. It was not easy. Usually when she first awoke, she went through a self-analysis that could be reduced to one question: am I happy or sad? Sometimes the answer was happy, more often it was sad, but today there were so many different factors to consider, so many undigested experiences, that at first she could not decide. She thought of Henry in London, then of her mother and her tacit admission that Anna had indeed been less loved than Jake, and finally, of course, of Andrew, his unspoken declaration and then the sudden metamorphosis from friend to lover.

The speed with which it all had happened had confused her, and it continued to confuse her now. In thinking about the night before, she could not quite decide who had seduced whom. Certainly it could hardly be said that she'd had designs on Andrew, since she had never thought of him as anything more than a friend; yet when it had become clear that he loved and wanted her, her body had reacted faster than her mind. Was this what was meant by falling in love?

If so, it was not at all how she had imagined it. She had always envisaged an older man, suave and masterful, who would bear down on her with glowing eyes and bend her to his will. Andrew, however, had made no demands; he had simply proceeded as if their making love was the natural and obvious thing to do. Clearly he had done it before, but he was neither awkward nor inept, hesitant nor apologetic. Nor did he act the part of the virile lover, as so many previous boyfriends had, tearing off her clothes and throwing himself at her body. Instead, he had been gentle, thoughtful and above all astonished, as if the sight and feel of her nakedness was even more beautiful than he had imagined.

When it was over, Anna's first thought was how little Andrew resembled his brother. But the memory of Henry had at once provoked both anxiety and shame, as if she had been unfaithful to Andrew retroactively. She was afraid of what he would think if he ever found out that Henry had been her lover, or how recently she had been in his brother's bed.

The same thoughts came back to torment her now. If she did not tell him, wouldn't he find out from Henry? If she did tell him, wouldn't he be disgusted that she had moved so easily from one brother to the other? In any case, wouldn't he come to despise her for the speed with which she had let herself be seduced? Yet she had not been seduced. They had known each other too long; they were too good friends; it had been as if the house were already built, and all that remained was to go through the door. But would he think of it in the same way?

She waited for Andrew to wake, listening to his quiet breathing. The sun shone through the curtains. She could not see a clock, but guessed it must already be eight or nine in the morning. Her thoughts returned again to her father, her mother and Jake, but now they seemed like beings in a different world. How could she have cared whether or not they loved her as a child when her childhood was over and a new life with a new love had begun? How could she have ever thought that she had liked Henry, with his cold manipulation of both her body and her soul? And all those beefy boys, the soldiers and the students? How could she ever have allowed them to defile what had been made so precious by his caresses?

Andrew stirred, turned, awoke. He sat up abruptly, looked out the window, rubbed his face, then turned to look at her and smiled. "*Benedicamus Domino*," he said.

"I beg your pardon?"

"It's what they say in the monastery to wake you up in the morning."

"*Benedicamus Domino?*"

"*Deo gratias.* That's what you answer." He kissed her, then took hold of the sheet beneath her chin and gently pulled it down to her stomach. "You know," he said quietly, "when at times as a monk I did let my thoughts stray a little down forbidden paths, they never went further than imagining how wonderful it would be to lay one's head on a girl's bosom."

She looked down at herself. "I'm afraid they don't make much of a cushion."

"They're fine," he said, smiling, resting his head gently between her small breasts. "Do you think that we could get breakfast brought up to the room?"

"Sure."

"I also used to dream of that—breakfast in bed on the first morning of one's honeymoon."

"Is this our honeymoon?"

"Isn't it?" He sat up and looked into her eyes. "Aren't we married, really, after last night?"

"If you say so."

"I do."

"And want to be."

"I do."

"So do I, I think."

He leaned forward and kissed her. "Then I pronounce us man and wife."

They both wanted to leave Jerusalem and return to London, but their tickets could not be changed without paying a great deal more money, so they moved to a cheaper hotel in West Jerusalem. Andrew insisted that Anna tell her parents where she had gone, but he did not himself tell Prior Manfred. "There's nothing much

I can do until I get back to England," he said. "Then I'll go see Father Godfrey and formally resign from the order."

The hotel was small and smelly, and their room intolerably stuffy, but the joy they each felt in the other's company made them oblivious to any discomfort. Privacy was all that they required. Already familiar as friends, their chief preoccupation was with the pleasure they could give with their bodies. They lived off falafel, coffee and Coca-Cola, and often ate and drank in bed.

On Sunday they took a bus to Jericho. Because of the *intifada*, there were fewer tourists than usual and Andrew became afraid that perhaps Anna was in some danger, but since he himself was so patently European and Anna leaned on his arm, the Arabs they met were friendly—too friendly, in fact, badgering them to buy postcards, carpets and Bedouin bracelets before the strike shut their shops at midday.

Before the Arab restaurants closed, they ate at a table shaded by an arbor. In the heat of the afternoon, they went to visit the ruins of the neolithic city uncovered by Kathleen Kenyon in the 1950s. There, for a moment, their conversation became that of two archaeologists, but as they walked back into the center of Jericho to take the bus back to Jerusalem, they returned to the tender inanities of lovers.

Anna was sick in the night. Sympathetic to her suffering, Andrew rose early to bring her mineral water and a glass of sweet tea.

"I already feel much better," she said, sitting up in bed and propping her slight body against the wall.

"Good."

"It must have been the salad in Jericho."

"Of course."

"Or a bug."

"Yes."

"Do you feel okay?"

"Me? Yes. Fine."

She frowned. "You look kind of funny."

"How?"

"Well, the expression on your face."

He gave up trying to hide his smile. "I'm sorry," he said, sitting down on the bed and taking her hand. "It's just that I know that sickness in the morning sometimes means that a woman is pregnant."

"Not in my case."

He blushed. "It's quite likely, isn't it, after what we've done?"

"Not unless . . ." She stopped and looked away.

"What?"

She turned to him again. "It isn't very likely."

He stood and walked toward the window. "It would be wonderful, wouldn't it, if our first child was conceived here in Jerusalem?"

"I suppose so."

"God knows where we'll live. Perhaps Henry will lend me some money for a deposit on a flat, and I think I could get a mortgage on my salary from Huntingdon."

She looked up at him from under her eyelashes. "You were serious, weren't you, about getting married?"

He turned to her, beaming. "We can't get married. We *are* married."

She looked away, avoiding his eyes.

Andrew smiled, mistaking the reason for her confusion. "I promise you, that's theologically sound. The Church only blesses a marriage. The state only registers it. A marriage itself is made between two people who commit themselves to each other forever."

"And you really feel committed to me forever?"

"For more than forever—for eternity." He came back to the bed. "I always thought it was a little unromantic of Our Lord to say that there was no marrying in Heaven, yet now . . . well, now I feel I am entitled to believe that there is."

"But what happens if I don't make it to Heaven?"

"Oh, you will. St. Paul said that Christian wives could save their pagan husbands, so it must work the other way around."

Anna looked down at the sheets. "Listen . . ." she began.

"To what?"

"To me."

He looked into her eyes with a mock-serious expression. "I'm listening."

"We've known each other for a long time."

"Yes."

"And in some ways we know each other very well."

"Yes."

"But there are things about me that you *don't* know."

"I'll have time enough to find out."

"But when you find out, you may not like it."

He smiled. "I can't imagine disliking anything about you."

"But you know, for example, that I've had other boyfriends."

He blushed. "Yes. In the past. Of course."

"In the recent past . . ."

"I don't really need to know."

"Are you *sure*?"

"Why do you ask?"

"Because I love you now," she said, "and I want to love you always, and I think that I can and will love you always, but I'm afraid that in a month or a year you might find out something about me that will give you a reason to leave me."

"I'll never leave you."

Tears had come into her eyes. "I've been left before."

"I wouldn't leave you ever, and I couldn't now that there's a baby."

"There isn't a baby."

"You can't be sure."

"Of course I can be sure. I'm on the pill."

"Oh." It was as if she had hit him.

"But that isn't all. I had a boyfriend in London."

"I didn't know."

"He didn't want you to know."

"Why not?"

"Because it was Henry."

He said nothing, but avoided her eyes.

She cried quietly. "I'm sorry, I'm really sorry. I wish to God I'd never known him or any of those other morons . . ."

He smiled at her. "It isn't your fault," he said.

"If I'd known, I'd have waited."

"For what?"

"For you."

"But you couldn't have known."

"I did dream of you," she said. "Not of you personally, Andrew, but of someone who would love me immediately and forever."

"And I *will* love you forever," he said. "All this really can't make a difference if you're sure."

"What?"

"Well, that you love me and not him."

"I *am* sure . . ."

"But a week ago . . ." He said this as if for the record, not as an accusation.

"Yes." She nodded. "A week ago I was with Henry. I didn't love him, but I didn't leave him, and he chucked me out after three months to the day. I won't pretend that there weren't times when I wasn't happy with him, up to a point, because I never knew if the kind of love I imagined actually existed. Now I know it does and . . . Well, just like you said, I feel that we're married, and I never felt that before."

He smiled. " 'If ever any beauty I did see, which I desired, and got, 'twas but a dream of thee.' "

She looked at him suspiciously. "Who said that?"

"John Donne."

"I guess that says what I was trying to say."

He kissed her lightly on the lips. "We both have a past, haven't we? So let's forget them now and think of the future."

"Sure." She smiled through her tears, leaned forward and hugged him. Then, because she wanted to sleep, she sent him off to visit the Rockefeller Museum.

19

Andrew could have taken a bus or a taxi, but he chose to walk, weaving his way between the other pedestrians on the crowded pavement of the Jaffa Road or stepping onto the street and dodging taxis and buses as he walked toward the Old City. He was in no hurry; he was only going to the museum to kill time while Anna rested. Yet he took long strides and had an anxious look on his face, as if he were late for some appointment or impatient to get to work.

Since it was a weekday morning, his businesslike manner blended with the bustle of those around him. Still, his thoughts were anything but businesslike. They were in complete confusion, for while he was not the first young romantic to discover that love sometimes follows an uneven course, there were ways in which his case was an exception, even unique. He had had no experience whatsoever of emotional exchanges with women. Even before he had decided to become a Catholic or a Simonite monk, he had been sufficiently shy, romantic and frightened of girls to have progressed no further than a quick kiss at the end of a teenage party. Whereas most of his contemporaries had, by the time they reached the age of twenty-eight, been through one or two affairs from which they had learned something about love, Andrew had experienced none. His only knowledge came, on the one hand, vicariously from his brother's cynical adventures, and on the other from the blend of romanticism and sentimentality that so often affects the attitude of the clergy toward the love they have sacrificed to pursue their vocation.

It was this innocence that had led Andrew to take Anna back to his room at the American Colony Hotel. There had seemed to him at the time an inexorable logic, which made it right and proper that he should do this. He had not considered that he had fallen in love with Anna since coming to Jerusalem, but that he had suddenly understood the true nature of the affection he had felt for her now for almost two years. His commitment to celibacy was, as he had explained to her, bound up with his belief in the divinity of Jesus. Purity, even virginity, was necessary for the sanctification of the body, which, like Christ's, would rise from the dead.

Even while he believed this, he had been aware of the argument against it that Henry, and also Anna, had tacitly presented: that celibacy was unnatural and therefore, by definition, the symptom of a neurosis. Hence, when he had seen the skeleton of a crucified man buried beneath the Temple Mount, and had believed that it was that of Jesus of Nazareth, he had found himself without the foundation upon which his commitment to celibacy was based. The first hypothesis being no longer tenable, the second took its place, and all at once he felt cured of that neurosis which had seen sexual longing as a serious sin.

The departure of the ascetic, however, did not mean the arrival of a cynic like his brother. There remained his idealism about love, unchanged since his adolescence. Therefore he had turned to the only girl with whom he could plausibly consider himself to be in love. Moreover, because he had not felt he was actually falling in love, but merely recognizing something for what it was, it never occurred to him that Anna would not recognize it too. Of course he knew that she had had boyfriends in the past, but she herself had told him how transitory and unsatisfactory these liaisons had been. But he had also thought she had no boyfriend in London, because she would certainly have told him if she had. He therefore assumed, because he had been not just her closest but almost her only male friend in London, that she too must have been deceived about the true nature of the bond between them, or possibly not deceived at all, but heroically reticent about the real nature of her feelings in deference to the vows he had taken.

Thus, with the sublime egoism of the young man in love, Andrew had taken it for granted that his love for Anna would not merely be requited, but consummated there and then. A blend of fashionable theology and heady romanticism had convinced him that after two years of sublimated courtship it would be wrong to wait a moment longer. As he had explained to Anna, a wedding only blessed a bond formed by a couple's commitment, and she had seemed to accept wholly his understanding of the way things were. If she had said very little that first evening as they had walked through the streets of the Old City, he had assumed it was because everything was clearly stated by the touch of their hands and the look in their eyes. Moreover, the certainty that she too had recognized that she loved him when they had only professed to be friends had given him great confidence as a lover. He knew that if he bungled things in bed, it would make no difference to such a deeply rooted affection. As a result, his body had not let him down, but had enhanced and strengthened the new-found emotions in ways he had not imagined. He had anticipated the delight of his own senses, but not the joy that it would give him to bring about such ecstasy in another, nor the beauty he would find, even after the demands of his instincts had been met, in the shape and texture of Anna's body. To be able to run his hand over her soft skin, or gently to implant kisses wherever he chose, made him happy in a way he had not envisaged and could not explain.

As they made love again and again, Andrew became almost afraid of the power he possessed to transform Anna from an alert, intelligent, sarcastic girl into a whispering, clinging creature craving his attentions. Even as he was absorbed in his own rapture, he was astonished, almost envious, of her complete oblivion as she murmured in an ecstatic trance, mouth half open and eyes half closed. No wonder, he thought, that sex so obsesses the human race. Why should anyone ever want to do anything else?

In those first days with Anna, they had indeed done little else, eating and sleeping only to recover their strength to make love yet again. However, from the beginning, thoughts had come unbidden into his mind that suggested all was not as straightforward as it seemed. For example, he had found that when he and Anna were discussing Father Lambert's seduction of Veronica Dunn, and he had told her how Father Lambert had apologized not for what he had done but for what he had done badly, a cruel grin had crossed his face, and a callous laugh had accompanied his conjecture about whether Father Lambert had been unable to finish what he had started, or whether it was all over before it had properly begun.

It was only the next morning, in that limbo between sleeping and waking, that Andrew had inwardly flinched as he recalled this ridicule of the man he had loved so much. Without mentioning it to Anna, he quickly repented of his uncharitable thoughts, even disowning the arrogant young male who had expressed them. Then, out in the street, he had been ambushed by another contradictory and shameful sequence of thoughts and emotions when he saw, walking toward him, wearing shorts and tight T-shirts, two tall European girls, either Dutch or German. One of them was not only pretty, but gave Andrew a fleeting glance of interest, that he involuntarily returned, wondering, before he was aware of what he was doing, what it would be like to sleep with her—wondering, and then wanting to give her the benefit of that skill and vigor which had left Anna with such a fresh complexion and happy smile.

Again he soon repented of these wayward thoughts, and even considered going to the nearest Catholic Church to say a decade of the rosary before the Blessed Sacrament, the kind of penance he would have imposed upon himself in his days as a Simonite monk. Now, however, such a practice seemed slightly absurd. Moreover, since he was constantly in Anna's company, he could hardly go into a church and fall on his knees without her knowing what he was doing, and for a reason he could not fathom, he felt inhibited, even ashamed, about being seen by her at prayer.

Clearly, on that first night in the American Colony Hotel, it would have been inappropriate to kneel at his bed as he usually did to say his evening prayers; and the next morning, since they had breakfast in bed and did not get up until lunchtime, he missed the moment to say his morning prayers. Nor, at midday, when he heard the Angelus ringing from one of the churches in the Christian Quarter, did he stop to say that ancient prayer as he had in the Simonite monastery. This omission came not from a deliberate decision to stop addressing the God in whom he still believed; rather, it seemed tactless to make these outward displays of an inward disposition in front of someone who did not share it.

The first excuse Andrew made to himself was that these practices were part of the discipline of a Simonite monk, and that since he had abandoned his vocation, he could abandon them as well. However, he knew that prayer was not simply for priests, and was obliged to admit that he had hardly thought of God at all since recognizing his love for Anna. Clearly he still believed in him; why else should he suffer from those stabs of remorse after scoffing at Father Lambert, or lusting after a girl who had flirtatious eyes and long brown legs?

One afternoon, on the pretext of buying a copy of the *Jerusalem Post*, he had gone into a church and said a quick prayer of repentance. He felt absurd as he did so, since it was Anna, not God, who had been cheated by his lecherous thoughts, and in recalling this sin he was perplexed to discover that he did not feel quite as ashamed of it as he should. It was as if the change he had made in leaving the Simonite order, and in sleeping with Anna, had not resulted in a straightforward metamorphosis from celibate monk to devoted lover, but instead had fragmented his personality so that two or even three different characters now existed within the same mind: the kind and humble Christian; the loyal and devoted husband of Anna; and this new, strutting embodiment of brute nature that gloried in what was healthy, strong and triumphant and despised what was feeble, needy and poor.

This confusion was made worse by the impossibility of discussing it with Anna. When he returned to the hotel after praying in the church, she had asked him why he had been so long, and he had lied incompetently about the difficulty of finding a newspaper. She had looked at him with an amused smile, as if realizing that he had been up to something, while knowing that it could not be anything particularly bad. He had longed to throw himself at her feet and confess his worthlessness, but could not bring himself to disillusion her by revealing that only days after declaring his lifelong love, he had fancied a girl he had passed in the street. Equally, it had seemed impossible to tell her about his remorse over scoffing at Father Lambert, for if to confess the first would make him seem lecherous and faithless, to admit the second would make him seem humorless and prim. Therefore he had kept silent about both matters, playing the role of a cheerful, debonair lover, sinking yet more deeply into a bog of deception.

Then came their trip to Jericho, Anna's brief sickness and the question of a child. If upon leaving the Simonite monastery Andrew had decided that everything Christ had taught was nonsense, it would have been easy to disown his Catholic conscience, but because he still thought of himself as a Christian, he still reacted involuntarily in a Christian way. Imbued with the Catholic teaching that sex was meant by God for procreation, he had justified the pleasure he took in it by the fact that it would end in the conception of a child.

Anna's blunt statement that she could not be pregnant because she was taking the pill had first shocked him for its reflection on the morality of what *he* had done; it was only later that he came to see what it implied about Anna. Not knowing that women sometimes take the pill simply to regulate their menstrual cycles, and Anna being too proud to pretend that this was the case, he assumed that she had been taking it because she had been sleeping with another man. He had not asked her who it was, but had turned the other cheek, and then had been struck a second, harder, blow when she had told him that the other man was Henry.

This had shocked him on so many different levels and in so many different ways that he had been quite unable to consider how to react or what to say. Anger, jealousy, embarrassment, disgust, disillusion, all swirled around in his mind to the extent that he might have said or done anything—strangled her, left her, kissed her—had not the lingering monk, whom he had tried so hard to shake off during the last few days, stepped forward with the reflexive gentleness and humility that came from the years of religious life.

This gentleness, however, was most tenuous; the violent emotions were not dissipated, but merely concealed. Certainly, in telling Anna it did not matter that she had slept with his brother and that the past was past, he had wanted it to be true. However, as he walked toward the Rockefeller Museum, he remained confused and tormented, both by the knowledge that Henry and Anna had been lovers, and by the exposure of his own credulity. He was embarrassed to recall his conceited assumption that she had been in love with him for the past year. Why had he not wondered about the men she might have been with before? He had known that she had boyfriends; he should have known that she had gone to bed with them. The answer was that he had not stopped to think about possible boyfriends and what they might have meant to her, because he had not really thought about her at all, and when he had said with such modesty that he could only claim to be a substitute, he had not meant a substitute for some other lover who had let her down, but for some more eligible candidate with better prospects who might present himself in the future.

That Anna had had lovers before, Andrew now acknowledged, should have come as no surprise; that she had had one so recently might be disagreeable, but if it was over it was something that might be quickly forgotten. That it was Henry was almost more than he could bear, because to exculpate his brother he had always explained his promiscuity by the depravity of his women. To make love out of wedlock was one thing; to make love out of lust was quite another, and since Henry clearly did not love his girlfriends, Andrew had always taken it for granted that they did not love him and slept with him simply to gratify their vanity or their sexual drive. Therefore it seemed that he had to look upon Anna as a girl of this kind, or else as an exception, but this alternative seemed almost worse, because it implied that she had loved Henry as sincerely as she now purported to love him—willing, perhaps, to marry him and bear his children. That Anna at some point might have been prepared to do this was even more painful to consider than that she was simply depraved. It was better not to think about it at all but to distract himself for the time being by concentrating on the exhibits in the Rockefeller Museum.

Andrew had been at the museum a number of times before, often with Father Lambert, and perhaps because of this he now found that the exhibits depressed him. He remembered how excited his professor had been when showing him the bowls, glasses, ossuaries and sarcophagi from the time of Christ, and he imagined the despair that must have entered Father Lambert's heart on realizing that the skeleton in the cistern might one day have pride of place between the prehistoric Galilee skull and the remains of the Bronze Age man from Mount Carmel. In the Northern Room he paused in front of two Romanesque friezes from the façade of the Church of the Holy Sepulcher. One of them depicted the life of Jesus; the other, figures of animals, plants and naked human beings. The dragons, he remembered from Father Lambert's explanations, represented heresy, the Antichrist and the Devil. The sirens were temptation and female lust, while male lust, as well as pride and arrogance, were represented by a centaur. The birds symbolized parsimony, and lechery was embodied in a naked man.

Andrew stood for some time staring at this marble frieze. Pride, heresy, lust—how simple things had been for these crusading craftsmen, and how simple they had been for him. How clear had been the distinction between truth and falsehood, good and evil, love and lust. Lust: there she was, the siren on the frieze. Was Anna such a siren? Had she herself not confessed that she could never distinguish love from lust? Had she gone to bed with him so easily just to satisfy a sudden urge of the flesh? And was he too no more than that figure of lechery, deceiving himself that he loved her because, like Father Lambert with Mrs Dunn, he was determined to indulge an instinct he had repressed for so long?

Further, was it simply his pride that was affronted by the knowledge that she had slept with Henry? He looked again at the centaur. Pride, arrogance and male lust: was that all that upset him—that another man had made love to her? That she had responded to Henry in the same way as she had responded to him? Yet how could he be jealous retrospectively unless conjugal love, like divine love, was outside the strictures of time? Was he so entrapped by Christian concepts that he must always think in terms of an eternity that was as much the past as the future?

Andrew went to the next room and looked at the stucco figures from the Hisham Palace near Jericho—snarling lions and big-breasted girls, whose jovial smiles seemed to ridicule the torments depicted in the frieze next door. Could he escape, he wondered, from the tentacles of a Christian conscience? Could he ever bring himself to enjoy pleasure for its own sake without seeking to give it some justification? Was love itself just an unreal idealization of a crude, atavistic instinct? Anna had said that even when she was sleeping with Henry, she had known she did not love him, and had dreamed of a love that was eternal, a love she now felt for *him*. It was only her body which had sought its own satisfaction, and the body, Andrew knew, was something distinct from the spirit. But was it? Why had she hidden her affair with Henry, and why had his brother also insisted that he not know about it? Had each felt embarrassed or ashamed? Had Anna sensed, as he had supposed, that already in her friendship with him there were the seeds of the love they now recognized and enjoyed? If so, then their friendship had already been corrupt, because she had deceived him daily about Henry, just as Henry had deceived him about her. The candor and trust that was both a sign of love and one of its principal delights was in reality only a sham. Always in the mind of the other there was some calculation, some pretense. Had he not hidden from her his lecherous feelings for the long-legged girl? Had he not lied about going to pray in the church? Did lovers often lie? Were there wives, perhaps, who faked ecstasy with their husbands, or husbands who, to allay suspicion, made love to their unloved wives?

Andrew looked at his watch. It was twelve. Never before had he felt quite so oppressed by the complexity of human relations, and while he did not doubt for a moment that he loved Anna, he left the museum and made his way back to the hotel with trepidation.

20

While Andrew was at the museum, Anna slept, tired out after a broken night and their anguished conversation. Soon after eleven, she was awakened by the ringing of the ancient telephone on the table next to the bed.

It took her a moment to realize where the sound came from, and then she hesitated to pick the phone up, knowing that only her parents knew where she was. But it continued to ring, and to silence it she answered.

"Anna?"

"Yes."

"This is Henry."

"Where are you?" His voice was so clear that it seemed as if he might be in the next room.

"In London."

"How did you know I was here?"

"Your mother gave me the number. Is it a hotel?"

"Yes."

"Why aren't you staying at home?"

"There wasn't room."

"Have you seen Andrew?"

"Yes."

"Is he all right?"

"Yes."

"It seems he's left the Simonite monastery and they don't know where he's gone."

"He's okay."

"Tell him to ring me."

"All right."

"Now listen. There have been some developments here in London."

"To do with what?"

"The Vilnius Codex. I can't tell you much over the telephone, but if you can I'd like you to make a few inquiries at your end while you're there."

"What kind of inquiries?"

"Have you heard of a man called Yehuda Lomish?"

"No."

"He was an officer in the army during the war in Lebanon who was captured by the Syrians and later released. Find out what he's doing now if you can."

"I'll try."

"Be discreet."

"Okay."

There was a pause, then Henry asked, "Are you all right?"

"Why shouldn't I be?"

"You sound funny."

"I've been ill, but I'm fine now."

"When are you coming back to London?"

"Next Friday."

"And Andrew?"

"He too."

"There's a lot I'd like to ask you, but it can wait."

"I'll have him call you."

"Good. As soon as he can."

Anna put down the telephone in a rage; yet she was not sure why she was angry. At first she thought she resented the nonchalant way in which the lover who had dumped her was so quick to make use of her in one of his investigations. Then she ascribed it to the retrospective remorse she felt when reminded of his existence and of their former liaison. Finally, after brooding about it some more, she realized that she was angry with Henry because his questions had implicitly suggested that the Vilnius Codex might be a fake. To be sure, he had not said as much, but what else could he have meant by "developments" concerning an officer in Israel? If the Codex was a fake, then the find might be a fraud, and if the find was a fraud, the reason for which Andrew had abandoned his vocation would be invalid.

It was this thought that filled her with dread, and that inspired her anger against Henry as the bearer of bad news. What to him was no more than a puzzle, an amusing distraction from industrial law and trade regulations, was to her a matter of life and death. It was not a question of whether Jesus of Nazareth had risen from the dead, but whether Andrew believed it or not. Certainly he had said that he would never leave her, and he had undoubtedly meant it. Certainly, too, despite all her disappointments in the past, she felt that she could trust him never to leave her for another woman, but that first wife, the Catholic Church, whom he had loved so well for so long—that was another matter. He had left the Church because he felt it had cheated him. What if he were now to discover that in fact it had been true, and that it was not Jesus who had deceived him by pretending to rise from the dead, but Anna's father and other unknown Jews?

As Anna considered the matter, the suggestion that her father would be a party to a hoax seemed absurd. She knew that his devotion to archaeology was more important to him than almost anything else, certainly more important than his feelings for his family. Then she remembered the conversation with her mother about her father's commitment to Israel. Was it possible that for the sake of his country he might take part in a deception, or at least turn a blind eye?

This idea redoubled her dread, not because it would put her father's livelihood and reputation in jeopardy, but because it threatened her bond with Andrew. To have found a love she had barely dared to imagine, a love that was fresh, equal and eternal, only to see it threatened almost at once, was more than she could stand. Weakened by her sickness and a sleepless night, she covered her head with the sheets and cried.

Even as she gave way to despair, certain practical considerations crept into Anna's mind. At any moment Andrew might return. He would ask her why she was crying. She would have to tell him of Henry's call. He might then phone Henry and learn what she suspected: that there was something suspicious about the Vilnius Codex. She sat up, suddenly convinced that if somehow she could get Henry the information he wanted, perhaps Andrew need never know. She jumped out of bed, her nausea gone, and splashed her face with the tepid water that trickled out of the tap of the basin in their room.

As she dressed, she wondered how she could find out about this man Yehuda Lomish. She could ask Jake, of course, but if there was a conspiracy of some kind, he was certainly in on it. Then she remembered Joel Abramovicz, a young journalist she knew on the *Jerusalem Post* who was a specialist on defence. She picked up the telephone, got through to Abramovicz, arranged to meet him for lunch, then left a note for Andrew, saying she had gone to see her father. It was the first lie she had told him since they had become lovers, and it pained her to deceive him, but she had no doubt that his happiness was irretrievably linked to hers, and no scruple should be allowed to inhibit her from doing what she could to protect it.

Joel Abramovicz was a sabra, a person born in Israel, but like Anna he had been to college in the United States and spoke fluent English with an American twang. He was small, with curly black hair, thick-lensed spectacles and an eager, earnest face. He was waiting for Anna at the bottom of Ben Yehuda Street, and they went to a sandwich bar nearby.

"What are you doing in Jerusalem?" he asked. "I thought you were studying in London."

"I am. I'm just here on a visit."

"To see the folks?"

"To see the folks."

"How are they? I haven't seen them in some time."

"They're fine."

Joel sat at one of the small tables and ordered a pita filled with salad and falafel, while Anna, her stomach still unsettled, had a glass of orange juice.

"So how can I help you?" Joel asked.

"Do you know anything about an officer called Yehuda Lomish?"

"You're asking *me* if *I* know anything about Lomish?"

"Yes."

"Yes, I know a little. But Jake's the one you should ask. He works for Lomish."

"Ah." His answer was like the stab of a knife in her stomach.

"At least he used to. The last thing I heard was that Jake had left the army to help your father."

"For various reasons," said Anna slowly, "I don't really want to ask Jake about Lomish."

"He probably wouldn't tell you anyway. It's all top-secret stuff."

"Mossad?"

Joel shrugged. "Or Shin Bet. I don't know. It's often difficult to know who answers to whom. During the war in Lebanon Lomish ran an outfit that reported directly to Sharon. He was one of his bright young men."

"And now?"

"I don't know. There are rumors that he runs some kind of dirty-tricks department."

"Against the PLO?"

"Yeah, but not just against the PLO. His speciality is covert propaganda."

"Give me an example."

Joel leaned forward and lowered his voice. "The planting of *agents provocateurs* in terrorist organizations, that kind of thing."

"What else?"

"War criminals. They know where they are and expose them as and when they're needed."

"Needed?"

"To remind the world what happened, and why we're here."

"And Jake works for him?"

"He certainly used to."

Anna looked down at her empty glass.

"Do you want some coffee?" Joel asked.

She shook her head and watched Joel as he turned to call the waitress and order some for himself. There was something lovable about him. He embodied everything that she liked about Israel; he was alert, cultured and humane. Suddenly she wanted Andrew to meet him, but the thought of her lover reminded her of the Codex. She leaned forward and asked Joel, "Is there any conceivable way in which Lomish could be linked to the Russians?"

Joel glanced at her with his eyebrows raised in surprise. "You seem to know everything about him already."

She felt the knife twist in her stomach. "You mean there is a link?"

"His parents came from Russia just before the war in Europe. Lomish speaks Russian as well as Hebrew, English and Arabic. He's a very clever guy."

"Is that the only link—that his parents came from Russia?"

"There's something else that has always seemed strange. In '82, when Lomish was in Lebanon, he was captured behind the lines."

"By the PLO?"

"No. By Amal, the Shi'ite militia. They held him for a while, and then he was handed over to the Syrians and taken to Damascus."

"How did he get back?"

"That's the mystery. Suddenly, four or five months later, he reappeared in Israel."

"Was there an exchange of prisoners?"

"That's what made it odd. Normally an officer of Lomish's rank would only be exchanged for several hundred Arabs. In his case, there were none."

"You mean they just *gave* him back?"

"So it seemed."

"Why?"

"No one knows. But the chances are that he made some kind of deal with either the Syrians or even the Russians, who would probably have interrogated him in Damascus."

"But how could anyone trust him after that?" asked Anna.

Joel shrugged. "Again a mystery. You'd think he would have been put on ice so far as counterintelligence was concerned, but in fact it was soon after he came back that he was given his own department."

Anna shook her head, as if in disbelief. In reality, she was beginning to see things all too clearly.

"Lomish also has some strange political affiliations," Joel went on.

"With the Likud?"

"Of course, and with the religious parties. But also with groups like the Temple Faithful."

"Who are they?"

"A bunch of zealots, mostly Americans, who want to rebuild the Temple."

"What about the mosques?"

"They'd be demolished."

"But that's crazy."

Joel shrugged. "In Israel there's a thin line between what's crazy and what's patriotic." He finished his coffee. "May I ask why you're suddenly so interested in Lomish?"

"When I can, I'll tell you, I promise."

"Is there a story in it?"

She frowned. "There could be. But I don't think it's one that can ever be told."

They parted outside the café, Joel to return to the paper, Anna to walk to a bus stop, where she stood wondering what to do next.

Her most urgent emotion was to hope against hope that what seemed possible would not turn out to be true. She knew Andrew better than he knew himself, and recognized that a resurrected Jesus was her most dangerous rival. Her first impulse was to telephone Henry and tell him that there was nothing to link Lomish to either the skeleton or the Codex. Her second was to question her father. However strong the grudge she still felt against Michal Dagan for his shortcomings as a parent, she still retained such faith in his integrity as an archaeologist that it seemed impossible that he would have perpetrated a gigantic fraud.

She walked the short distance to the Staedtler Institute and turned up at her father's office unannounced. His secretary ushered her in as if she was expected, and Dagan greeted her as if he knew that sooner or later she would come to see him. He looked perplexed, even guilty, and Anna realized that he must have been told about the bitter conversation with her mother. He came forward to kiss her, but then hesitated, as if afraid of a rebuff, and, to cover his confusion showed her to an armchair as if she was a student or a junior lecturer.

"I was worried about you," he said.

"I'm okay, I've been with Andrew."

"Yes. I was told. He is a good friend to you, that young man."

"Yes. A very good friend."

There was an awkward pause; then Dagan said, "Your mother told me about how you felt, and . . . I'm sorry."

Suddenly Anna was afraid that she might burst into tears, so she said sharply, "I didn't come here to talk about that."

"Very well," he said sadly.

"I'd like to talk about it some time," she said in a slightly kinder tone, "but something more urgent has come up."

"What is that?"

"The find . . . the skeleton."

He frowned. "What about it?"

"Dad, I need to know . . . I really need to know whether you found it by accident or not."

Her father's frown deepened. "It was not by accident that we went through the wall."

"But you had no idea there was a jar in the cistern or a skeleton in the jar?"

He avoided her eyes. "I had no idea there was a jar or a skeleton, no."

"Will you swear to that, Dad? To me—just to me—in the privacy of this room?"

"Why? I don't understand. Why to you?"

"I can't explain now, only that it's very, very important."

He hesitated and looked away from her. "I can swear, of course, that I knew nothing about the jar or the skeleton."

"And so when you knocked through that wall, it came as a complete surprise?"

"A complete surprise. We had not expected to find anything in the cistern."

She paused. She knew that her father was not lying, but sensed that he was holding something back.

"Were you the first to go through the opening?"

"Yes. First me, I think, then Ya'acov."

"Were you there when they removed the block?"

"Yes."

"Did you see them remove it?"

"Yes. It took some hours."

"Is it possible . . ." She hesitated, then frowned, trying to work out what might have happened. "Is it possible that someone removed the block the day before, put the jar in the cistern, and then put the block back again?"

"No."

"Were you there the day before?"

"No."

"So you can't be sure."

"Ya'acov would have known. He was there."

She paused, then asked, "When you found the skeleton in the jar, was it you who remembered the Codex from Josephus?"

"Yes."

"*You* remembered it?"

He looked confused. "Yes, it was me, or perhaps Ya'acov. I can't remember."

She leaned forward and looked straight into her father's eyes. "Dad, why did Jake get leave from the IDF?"

"It wasn't so much that he was given leave from the IDF, as

that for reasons of security the IDF wished to go beneath the Temple Mount, and Ya'acov quite rightly persuaded his superiors that it should not be done without an archaeologist in charge."

"Do you know why they wanted to dig beneath the Temple Mount?"

"Yes. It was to place listening devices to eavesdrop on the organizers of the *intifada*."

"Did Jake ever tell you who ordered the project?"

"He never told me precisely . . ."

"Was it Yehuda Lomish?"

"Lomish certainly is the officer in command of the department."

"Do you know Lomish?"

"I've met him. He lives in Rehavya."

"Did it occur to you, Dad, that Jake and Lomish might have faked your find?"

Never before had Anna seen her father look both so frightened and so ashamed. "You must understand, Anna," he said in a voice little louder than a whisper, "that there are sometimes lines of thought which we cannot follow."

"Because of where they might lead?"

"Yes. Because they might lead where you cannot go."

"So it *did* occur to you."

"Listen, Anna. You do not understand—you have never understood—what Israel means to me. It is everything, my dear, everything—not just a nation like any other nation, but the land of God's consecrated people. We have suffered for so long, for so very long—despised, humiliated, exterminated like vermin—until now, in this generation, we have won back what God gave us so long ago."

"Dad, that's . . ."

"Let me finish. You see, I know that you cannot see this, and for that I blame myself. I am not asking you to see it now, but only to understand how *I* feel when, for the sake of Israel, I am asked simply to suspend for a moment my disbelief, to restrain certain thoughts, to let certain suspicions escape without pursuing them, to leave a few questions unanswered."

"To perpetrate a fraud."

Dagan's eyes widened with anger. "A fraud? Is it a fraud? Or is the Christian religion a fraud? We know that the body of Jesus of Nazareth must have been buried somewhere, and I have found what I have found. It may or may not be the body of the Nazarene; that is not for me to say, and I have never claimed anything, one way or the other. I presented my evidence to the Christians. It is for them to decide."

"Christians like Father Lambert?"

He lowered his eyes. "Yes. Like Father Lambert."

"But you will be exposed, Dad, and ridiculed. We already know about Lomish . . ."

"Who knows about Lomish?" asked a voice behind her.

Anna turned and saw Jake standing by the open door. "I do."

He closed the door and came into the room. "What do you know?"

"Enough."

Jake smiled. "Would you like to meet him?"

"Ya'acov . . ." Michal Dagan began.

Jake ignored his father and said to Anna, "I'm sure he would be happy to answer your questions."

"I know enough."

"He could tell you more."

Anna hesitated, curiosity struggling with mistrust of her brother. "When could I meet him?"

"Right now."

She looked uncertainly toward her father, but his eyes, still afraid, were on his son. "Ya'acov . . ." he began again.

"We'll see you later, Dad," said Jake, and with an ironic bow toward his sister, he escorted her out of the room.

Jake drove her in his Subaru from the Staedtler Institute up through Mea She'arim, across the old Green Line and out of Jerusalem on the Ramallah Road. For a while neither of them spoke. Then Jake said, in the same sneering tone with which he had put down his sister as a child, "You should have kept out of all this, you know. You're way out of your depth."

"You got me involved."

"How?"

"In London. You asked me to ask Andrew to suggest a Catholic archaeologist to authenticate the find."

"That didn't mean you had to fuck him."

She turned to him, her face flushed with anger. "Do you have bugs in every bedroom in Israel?"

"Knowledge is power."

"Jesus Christ, Jake, what's happened to you? You were never nice, but now you're despicable."

"Who's talking?"

198

"I happen to love Andrew," she said with as much dignity as she could muster.

"Last week you loved his brother."

"Things sometimes happen that way."

"What's so special about Catholics? Do they fuck better than Jews?"

"Henry isn't a Catholic. He's an atheist."

"But Andrew's not just a Catholic; he's a Catholic priest."

She blushed. "He's not a priest. He's a monk. He hasn't taken his final vows, and he still thinks Dad's dug up Jesus."

"You haven't told him about Lomish?"

"No."

"Lucky for him."

"Why?"

"Because there are things it's better not to know."

Jake slowed down as the road ran parallel to the wire fence of a military compound, the top of it festooned with coils of barbed wire.

"Do you really think you can get away with this?" asked Anna.

"Why not?"

"Because it's crazy."

He stopped the car at the steel gates to the compound. "You don't live here," he said, showing his ID to a guard with a machine gun. "You don't know what we're up against."

"Nothing's worth destroying Dad's reputation."

"It won't destroy his reputation; it will make it."

The gates were opened. "Not when the world knows it's a fraud."

"The world won't know."

"It will if I tell it."

"And how will you tell the world?"

"I'll tell a journalist, I guess."

The gates closed behind them. Jake smiled.

21

The building the brother and sister entered, though superficially like a courthouse or a school, had the narrow windows of a fortress and the thick steel doors of a prison. They went up one flight of stairs, along a corridor, and came to a door Jake opened with the familiarity of someone who knew his way around. They entered a small anteroom, where a girl in uniform sat typing at a desk.

"Is the colonel busy?" Jake asked her in Hebrew.

She shook her head. "No. Go in."

They went through into a much larger room, with a table and some chairs at one end and a large desk at the other. Blinds covered the windows, dissipating the sunlight. There was no air-conditioning. One of the blinds flapped at an open window. On the desk was a fan, and behind it, on the wall, a large map of greater Israel.

As they came in, a man in uniform rose from his seat at the desk. He was aged around fifty, but looked vigorous and fit. His graying hair was shaved close at the back of his neck. His face and his hands were brown, but blurred margins of whiter skin showed at the open neck of his khaki shirt. As he crossed the room to meet them, he looked at Jake with a mildly puzzled expression.

"Colonel," said Jake. "This is my sister, Anna."

Lomish smiled and greeted her in Hebrew.

"My Hebrew isn't very good," said Anna.

Lomish nodded and pointed toward the sofa and chairs. "Then let us speak English." Jake and Anna sat down, while he looked into the anteroom and asked his secretary to bring some coffee. Then he too sat down and leaned forward, his elbows resting on his knees, ready to hear what they had come to say.

"I brought my sister to meet you," said Jake slowly, "because she had lunch with Abramovicz, that journalist on the *Post*, and then went to my father to ask about you."

The colonel nodded, his expression unchanged. "What did Abramovicz tell you?" he asked Anna.

"Nothing," said Anna. "It wasn't he who gave me your name."

"She had a call from London this morning," said Jake, "from the brother of the monk. He has been making inquiries about the Vilnius Codex."

Lomish nodded. "Has he made the connection?"

"Not yet, but he suspects it."

"Has he spoken to the monk?"

"No."

"So he is still convinced?"

Jake looked at his sister. "I think so, yes."

"And the cardinal?"

"Yes."

"So the leak is not yet large—simply the brother, Abramovicz and this young lady." He turned to Anna with cold eyes but a benevolent smile.

"Joel knows nothing," said Anna, "and Henry . . . well, I don't know what he knows or how he knows it, but if the cat's out of the bag in London, you can't put it back here in Jerusalem."

Lomish seemed to ponder this for a moment, then turned to Jake. "Have you any idea how the brother in London came up with my name?"

"He has a friend with contacts through the British Secret Service with Lithuanian émigrés in London."

"Would he have told them what he is after?"

"I doubt it."

"So we have only to deal with him, with Abramovicz and with you"—he turned to Anna—"to have a good chance of putting the cat back in the bag."

"Yes," said Jake, "but we must think of my father."

"Of course." Lomish continued to look at Anna like a headmaster pondering the problem of a troublesome child.

"The best solution," said Jake, "would be for Anna to persuade the monk's brother that you don't exist, or at least that you have nothing to do with the find."

"Why should I?" asked Anna.

"To save your ass," said Jake.

"To save Israel," said Lomish.

"How does it save Israel to involve my father in some half-baked hoax that sooner or later is bound to be exposed?"

Lomish frowned, but his tone remained calm. "I think you are wrong to say it would be exposed, because people believe what they want to believe, and at this moment there are many people who would like someone to dig up the body of Christ. These people are not atheists or Muslims or Jews, who know quite well that he did not rise from the dead, but liberal Christian theologians who want to adapt their faith to the modern world."

"So you're in the business of helping out Christian theologians?"

Lomish did not smile. "No, I am in the business of helping my people, the Jews."

"How does it help the Jews to dig up the body of Jesus?"

"I will tell you because I believe that when you understand what we are trying to achieve, you will help us to achieve it."

"Don't count on it."

"No, I won't count on it, but I would ask you for a moment to be patient and listen. You see, I know from what Jake has told me that you have never felt you belonged here, but you have the intelligence to understand that there are others, like your father, mother and brother, who love Israel and would willingly die to protect it."

"Sure."

"The problem is that dying is often not enough. If there is a lesson to be learned from our revolt against the Romans and the consequent obliteration of the ancient state of Israel—ending, as you know, when Masada was taken—it is that courage and determination are *not* enough. There are times when brute force wins.

"Now, however you may feel about Zionism, we do have a state that has survived for forty years, and survived despite the enmity of all the countries that surround us. We have fought three wars, and we were obliged to act in Lebanon, where, as you may or may not know, I was captured and taken to Damascus. For some months, I was held in solitary confinement. I had time to think, to consider the position of Israel, and compare the dangers that face us now with those facing us in ancient times. In both periods, we have shown courage and determination in pursuing our independence, but none of the countries now wishing to destroy Israel has anything like the power of Rome. The only nation in the modern era that can be compared to Rome is the United States, the champion, not the enemy, of Israel. If we have survived, it is because might as much as right has been on our side."

"I don't suppose even Arafat would disagree with that," said Anna.

"Of course," said Lomish, "all this may seem fairly obvious, but when you are in solitary confinement, inevitably some of your thoughts are obvious. However, they proceeded to less obvious territory—namely the future. When I looked into the future, I became afraid. The support of this great power on the other side of the world for a small band of Jews clinging to the edge of Asia arose from a set of quite fortuitous circumstances. The pogroms in Russia at the end of the nineteenth century drove hundreds of thousands of our people to emigrate to America. The descendants of these refugees in the most populous states of the Union ensure political support for Israel.

"What alarmed me was the realization that these fortuitous circumstances will change. In the United States there are only six million Jews. They cannot hold the balance of power indefinitely, whether in California or New York. The growth of other states in America—Texas, for example, or Florida, with their large populations of Catholic Hispanics, or the Southern states, with their Baptists—may alter the balance of power. Even if it does not, the chances of the United States continuing to dominate the world as it has since the end of the Second World War, seem small. Already the economies of the East are growing more vigorously than those of the West. With economic strength comes political power. Why should the Koreans or the Japanese care about the fate of the Jews? Why should they jeopardize supplies of oil from the Arab countries to satisfy the aspirations of a small sect in the West?

"Of course, if the situation in Palestine were to stabilize and our Muslim neighbors were to accept the state of Israel, the danger would recede with the passage of time. But as I looked into the future alone in my cell, I could only see further struggle and bloodshed. Sooner or later, I knew, there would be an *intifada* of the kind we see today, particularly if we were to exercise our rights over the land we had reclaimed.

"Israel, after all, has only been half completed. To be sure, we won back the territory we believed was ours, but are we masters in our own land? We have Jerusalem, and we have surrounded the city with Jewish settlements. In the city itself, however, there remain the towers, domes and minarets of other religions, and most blasphemous of all, there, where our Temple should be, on the site of the Holy of Holies, is the golden dome of a mosque. Clearly Israel can never be Israel, can never believe in her inalienable right to return, until we remove the mosque and rebuild our Temple on its rightful site on the Temple Mount."

"But that—" Anna began.

"Of course," Lomish interrupted. "It will double the number of our enemies and enrage the world. Yet how can we ever say that we have really returned, how can we prove that we have a God-given right to this land, if we dare not demolish a mosque and rebuild the very symbol of God's Covenant with our people?"

Anna glanced sideways at Jake, to see if he too realized that this man was mad, but the eyes of her brother were fixed on the face of his superior officer with an expression of exhilaration and awe. She turned back to Lomish. "Are you really serious?" she asked. "You really want to pull down the Dome of the Rock and rebuild the Temple?"

"Don't you see," said Lomish, "that it has to be done, not as an exercise in archaeological reconstruction but as the tangible proof that our people are reborn?"

"But that's crazy," said Anna. "You can't just pretend that nineteen hundred years haven't happened."

"Certainly you can," said Lomish. "Look at our language. Who spoke Hebrew a hundred years ago? A few old rabbis, and, even for them, it was not their mother tongue. Now we all speak it."

"I know—"

"It was the vision of a few men that achieved this, and it is precisely their work that is only half completed. Israel still has some way to go before she is truly in possession of the promised land, and as we proceed, we are certain to make still more enemies. That is why it is so important to consider how to make useful friends—or, at least, to keep the friends we have, particularly the United States, during a period when the influence of the Jews in America is likely to diminish."

"And is digging up Jesus going to make you friends?" asked Anna.

"Yes." He hissed out the word. "Because in America, besides the six million Jews, there are two hundred million Christians, and in South America there are millions more. In India, the Philippines, South Korea, China and Japan, the Christians are an influential minority. The whole of Western Europe is Christian, and so, beneath the surface, are the countries of Eastern Europe and even the Soviet Union itself. The one thing they all have in common is their belief that Jesus of Nazareth rose from the dead, a belief that is incompatible with any fundamental sympathy with Israel, because at the root of Christian teaching is the certainty that God's Covenant with us, his chosen people, ended with the death of Christ. He was the Son of God. He abrogated the old Covenant and substituted a new one, replacing us Jews as his chosen people with all those who accepted that he was the promised Messiah.

"What struck me in Damascus, was that if these hundreds of millions of Christians could somehow be convinced that Jesus of Nazareth was *not* the Son of God, but merely one among other Jewish prophets, like his cousin John the Baptist, then they would have to accept that he was in no position either to make a new Covenant or to abrogate the old one. I also realized that the only article of Christian belief that confirms him as a superhuman being is his resurrection from the dead. If it could be shown that he had *not* risen, then it would have to be accepted that the old Covenant still stands."

"You mean," said Anna, "that a billion Christians are suddenly going to become Jews simply because you dig up the body of Jesus?"

Lomish laughed. "I hardly think so, no. They would still be Christians, but the followers not of a God but of an unusual man. They would no longer have grounds for the supposition that lies behind all Christian thinking: that somehow the obliteration of Israel by the Romans, culminating in the destruction of Jerusalem and the demolition of the Temple by the soldiers of Titus, was not only no more than what the Jews deserved for killing the Son of God, but was also predicted by Christ as the necessary demonstration that the old Covenant was at an end."

Anna again looked at Jake, and although her instinct told her that it might be wise to appear convinced by what Lomish was saying, her irritation at the smug look on her brother's face got the better of her. "If you'll excuse me saying so, Colonel," she said scornfully, "I think solitary confinement sent you slightly crazy. I know many Christians, and most of them don't think like that at all."

Lomish did not seem discouraged by her reaction. "Consciously they may not, but unconsciously they do. In any case, for us time is running out. The sympathy we can still count on for what we suffered under Hitler will not outlive those who remember the last war. Certainly we can remind the young of what happened with the trials of war criminals like Demjanjuk, but soon there will be no war criminals to uncover, and the images of suffering Jews will be replaced in the newspapers by images of Palestinians suffering as we put down their *intifada*. All that the world will care about is the danger of war and the threat to their supplies of oil, and then the age-old hatred of the Jews by the Christians will rise to the surface once more, and it will be *''raus mit den Juden'* all over again—*'raus* not from the ghettos of European cities but from this ghetto here, between the River Jordan and the Mediterranean Sea.''

Anna scrutinized Lomish with a puzzled look on her face. She still thought that he must be mad, but he did not appear so, and she had to acknowledge that everything he said had a kind of inner coherence. It was not that she felt persuaded to approve of the hoax—she did not feel sufficiently involved with the plight of her people for that—but she could appreciate the logic of what Lomish was saying. People's attitudes and convictions *are* malleable, and if marshaling support for Israel was his job in counterintelligence, she could accept that the plan to find the skeleton of Jesus became a plausible project for covert propaganda.

Her attention turned to the mechanics of the conspiracy. "Okay," she said to Lomish. "I see now why you did it. But how was it done? How did you come up with the Vilnius Codex?"

"Here," said Lomish, "providence came to my assistance. As you know, I was originally captured by the Shi'ites in Lebanon. After a certain amount of rough treatment by them, I was handed over to the Syrians, who sent me to Damascus for interrogation. They were rather more sophisticated—certainly less violent—and seemed to accept quite quickly the limits I placed upon what I would tell them. They were principally interested in what they could extract in exchange, in terms of prisoners we had taken and hard currency.

"Our people, I like to think, wanted me back, but at first the demands were so exorbitant that they had to pretend for a time that I was not of much value. That is why I was kept waiting in Damascus. After a while, however, the Soviets in Damascus learned of my capture and expressed an interest in what I might know. One of their men used to visit me almost every day, an urbane and intelligent man called Leon Gedda, who spoke excellent

Hebrew as well as Arabic, English, Russian, Polish and even Lithuanian because he had lived there as a child.

"His method of interrogation was far subtler than that of the Syrians. Where they had put quite straightforward questions, which told me immediately what they wanted to know, Gedda never asked any questions at all. He always referred to my interrogation as 'a chat,' and arranged for it to take place in a relatively pleasant room, with comfortable chairs and decent coffee, and he left an open pack of cigarettes on the table from which we each helped ourselves. He also gave the impression of being genuinely more interested in me than in what I had been doing behind the lines in the Bekaa Valley. To get me to talk about myself, he told me about his own life, and it turned out that we had several things in common. Not only were we both Jews, but his grandparents, like mine, came from Brest; mine had gone to Israel as Zionists, but his had joined the Bolsheviks. His father, having fought against the Whites, had joined the Cheka, ending up in Vilnius as the coordinator of the Soviet campaign against the partisans. In 1949, his father was taken prisoner in an ambush. Five days later his mutilated body was dumped in the main square of Kaunus. Gedda was then ten years old. From that instant he vowed he would follow in his father's footsteps and one day take his revenge.

"I cannot pretend," Lomish went on, "that after two months of solitary confinement I was not vulnerable to Gedda's technique. He not only had great charm, but he also had a most infectious nonchalance, which seemed to suggest that he did not care what he said, so why, I thought, should I? I realized, of course, that this put me off my guard, and that I might easily forget what was secret and let slip some piece of classified information. Therefore, to protect myself, I decided to talk to him about what I had been considering alone in my cell—my plan to undermine the central tenet of the Christian religion by digging up the body of Christ.

"This idea seemed to interest Gedda at once. At first I thought it was only out of historical or political curiosity. We went back over the precedents for this kind of thing—the Protocols of the Elders of Zion, for example, or the Piltdown man. Then we moved on to the technology, and for a while I thought he was trying to find out what techniques we had evolved for forging documents or frustrating the efforts of carbon-dating. He boasted of Soviet skills in this field. But even as we talked, he seemed to adopt my project as his own, returning to it day after day, often with answers to the questions of the day before.

"We soon decided that the problems were not technical, because it would not be hard to find the skeleton in Israel of a man crucified in the first century of the modern era. The difficulty would be to identify it as the body of Jesus of Nazareth. Our first idea was to fake the pieces of wood or papyrus Pilate had nailed to the cross that said that this was Jesus of Nazareth, King of the Jews. The objections to this were not technical, but were the same as any that could be made in respect to corroborative evidence found at the actual site—the whole thing could be a hoax.

"We arrived at two necessary conditions for the scheme to have a chance of success. The first was that the discovery should be made by an archaeologist with an international reputation whose integrity was beyond reproach. The second was that the critical corroborating evidence should be quite independent of the find.

"As to the archaeologist, there were several possibilities, but my mind settled upon your father first because of his reputation, and second because I knew that I could call upon Ya'acov to help me. More intractable was the question of corroboration. We thought about it for days on end and came up with various ideas, all more or less improbable. Then Gedda remembered Josephus and the Slavonic additions to his *Jewish War*. What poetic justice if the man who so shamelessly betrayed his people in the first century could be used to help them in the twentieth! If I could think of a place where the body could be discovered that had some unique features not hitherto made public, then Gedda would arrange for the discovery to be made in Russia of a hitherto unknown Codex that referred to the burial of the Nazarene in the same place.

"For days I racked my brains to consider where the body might have been hidden. Our hypothesis was the same as that of the chief priests at the time—that Christ's own disciples had stolen the body and smuggled it out of the city. I thought of sites in Galilee or Samaria where the skeleton might be found, but not being an archaeologist, I was not familiar enough with any of them to know which would best serve our purpose. The choice of a site in which to place the skeleton would have to await my return to Israel.

"By this time it had become clear that Gedda would arrange my release. What he told the Syrians or his superiors in Moscow, I do not know. He had no assurances from me that I would go through with the plan, but he was so eager to see it put into effect that he seemed prepared to take the risk that I might let him down. Only at the very end did I ask him why he or his government were willing to embark on a venture of this kind, and he then explained to me quite candidly the difficulties being faced by the Soviet Union. The economy was inefficient, and its failure to produce not just consumer goods but the minimal requirements of its people had led to widespread disillusion with the theories of Marx and Lenin, upon which the whole legitimacy of the Communist state depended. There was a grave danger that the Soviet Union would disintegrate, each republic falling back upon the racial, national or religious ideologies of its bourgeois past to justify seceding from a now unwanted union. Russia itself, and even Byelorussia and the Ukraine, might survive the demise of Marxist thought because they shared the same heritage of Orthodox Christianity, but the Muslim republics—Azerbaijan, or those whose populations were Lutheran like Latvia, and above all Lithuania, with its links to the Roman Catholic Church—would be overwhelmed by a popular desire to secede.

"Of course, behind all this reasoning were Gedda's personal motives for wanting to frustrate the rebirth of a nationalist, Catholic Lithuania. He was quite candid in his determination to prevent the ideological heirs of those who had murdered his father from once again taking power in Vilnius. There were others, he said, who thought like him, but how much my scheme had the backing of the Kremlin I was never able to tell.

"Gedda accompanied me as far as the border with Jordan. There we parted with a handshake, two Jews whom ideology had taken in quite different directions but who remained brothers all the same. Back in Jerusalem, I worked out with Ya'acov just where the skeleton should be found. Three months later, in Geneva, I handed Gedda the text of the new Slavonic addition. Five months after that came the news that a lost Codex of the Slavonic version of Josephus's *Jewish War* had been discovered in Lithuania."

Lomish sat back in his chair, his explanation over. There was no expression of conceit on his face, simply the somber look of an officer who had described the background to a necessary mission.

His eyes, however, remained fixed on Anna, studying her reaction. If they had been alone, he might have seen in her expression a certain admiration for the audacity of his scheme. She had no interest, after all, in sustaining the dogmas of the Christian religion; indeed, it was essential to her happiness that Andrew, at least, should continue to believe that there had been no Resurrection. However, Jake sat next to her, and the feelings of rivalry he provoked in her proved stronger than her caution. She turned away from Lomish, and with a look of sneering disdain said to him, "I suppose you provided the skeleton?"

"It wasn't hard to find."

"And put those scratches on the skull?"

Jake shrugged.

"Did Dad never suspect what was going on?"

Jake shook his head. "People don't ask questions when they might get answers they don't want to hear."

"And you thought that if you could fool him, you could fool the world?"

"We don't need to fool the world," said Lomish. "Just some of the people some of the time will do."

"Like Father Lambert?"

"Yes. If he had announced the find, it would have been front-page news, and any doubts expressed later would take up only a couple of inches on an inside page."

"And now you expect Cardinal Memel to announce it instead of Father Lambert?"

"Yes," said Jake. "He was completely taken in."

"It didn't bother you to use him in that way?"

"No."

"Or that it drove Father Lambert to suicide?"

"There are always unforeseen eventualities," said Lomish.

"Like me."

"Like you."

"Well, I won't kill myself, I can promise you that."

Lomish smiled. "Certainly not while you're under my protection."

"Thanks," said Anna, "but I can look after myself."

"Given what you now know, I'm afraid that won't be possible."

She looked from Lomish to Jake, who glanced away. "You mean I'm a *prisoner*?" she asked.

"You avoided the draft," said Lomish. "You are liable to three years in prison for that alone."

"I was deferred . . ."

"Your deferment just expired."

"But you can't keep me quiet for ever," said Anna. "And then there's Henry. What are you going to do about him?"

Neither Lomish nor Jake replied.

22

Michal Dagan returned home late that night in a state of some agitation. Rachel seemed to realize this and served his supper in silence. Only when they were sitting at table did she say that Andrew had telephoned an hour earlier, asking after Anna.

"What did you tell him?"

"That I didn't know where she was." She said this in a tone that suggested that her husband *did* know, but Michal Dagan said nothing. "He thought that she might have had lunch with you," she went on.

"She came *after* lunch," said Dagan, as if the exact moment mattered, "and then she went off with Ya'acov."

Again Rachel waited for him to say more, but when he remained silent she laid her fork aside and said, "Did she come to talk?"

"Yes."

"About you and her?"

"No."

"About what, then?"

"The dig."

"She wanted to talk *archaeology*?"

"Yes . . . Except that it was more than archaeology."

Rachel picked up her fork and put a piece of boiled potato in her mouth, eating methodically as she always did, waiting for her husband to go on.

"She asked me about Lomish," said Michal.

For a moment, Rachel stopped eating. Then she once again laid aside her fork. "Why should she ask you about Lomish?"

"Because she suspects what we suspect . . ."

"Suspect?"

He flinched. "Very well. What we know."

Rachel shook her head. "You must get out of this, Michal, before it gets worse."

"Get out? How? I have found what I have found."

"You have found nothing," she said with an unusual vehemence.

"How can you know that?" asked Dagan miserably.

"Because I know my son, and I know the influence that Lomish has over him."

"Of course, of course, but if it is for Israel . . ."

"Israel can survive without lies."

"You don't understand . . ." He got up from the table and crossed the room, as if unwilling to hear any rejoinder, but Rachel said nothing, remaining at table and finishing her food.

Michal sat down on the sofa and opened the evening newspaper, but his eyes would not focus on the words. It was as if, quite independent of the mind that directed them, they were terrified of reading the story of his extraordinary find. For some time the couple sat like this, the husband pretending to read the newspaper on the sofa, the wife methodically eating the supper she had prepared. The silence was like a low cloud hiding peaks of antagonism and troughs of recrimination. It was finally broken by the sound of a key turning in the front door, and both of them looked toward the hallway as Jake came in.

"Ah, Ya'acov, good," said Michal, his expression changing to one of mute admiration for his heroic son.

Jake greeted his parents, then went into the kitchen.

"What happened to Anna?" shouted Michal after him, almost jovially.

"She's okay," said Jake. He came back holding a glass of milk and sat down at the table next to his mother.

"Where is she?" asked Rachel.

"With Lomish."

"Still?" asked Dagan.

"She's been detained."

Dagan went pale. "Lomish detained her?"

"Yes."

"Why?"

Jake shrugged. "Because she asked too many questions."

Dagan put down the unread newspaper. "That is going too far."

"She should have minded her own business."

"It *was* her business. We made it her business."

"Just as we made it the business of Father Lambert and drove him to suicide," said Rachel, handing Jake a plate of fish and boiled potatoes, but looking over at her husband as she did so.

Dagan, his elbows resting on his knees, hid his face in his hands.

"He didn't kill himself," said Jake, with an anxious glance toward his father.

"He's found hanging out of the window of his cell," said Rachel, "and he didn't kill himself?"

Dagan looked up at his son.

"We now know that he was murdered," said Jake.

"How can you know that?" asked Dagan.

"Lomish told me. We have his notebook."

"But how? Where did you find it?"

"They killed him to shut him up."

"Who?"

Jake shrugged. "Some Catholic fanatic. A Yugoslav. They caught him at Heathrow checking in for a flight to Zagreb. One of our people was working on security and found the notebook in his suitcase."

"He knew what it was?"

"He had been briefed."

"So what did he do?"

"He switched the notebook for a gun and then called the British police."

"But who was this man?"

"A Croatian, a defrocked Franciscan from Mostar."

"How did he know about the find?"

Jake shrugged. "The Franciscans run the holy places here, don't they? Someone must have got wind of it, perhaps from Father Lambert."

"But then why . . ."

"Whoever knew about it here must have alerted the order."

"And they *killed* him?"

"Those Croatian Franciscans worked with the Fascists during the war. If they could massacre hundreds of thousands of Serbs and Jews, why should they hesitate over a crazy priest?"

Dagan looked at his wife to see if she believed their son's story, but at that moment she rose to take the dirty plates into the kitchen. He stood, meaning to follow her, but instead paced up and down the room. "Of course it makes much more sense if he was murdered, because I knew from his tone of voice when he called me that afternoon that he couldn't have thrown himself out the window immediately afterward. He was very polite, of course—he didn't want to disappoint me—but he made it quite clear that after thinking it over, he felt sure it could not be the body of Christ. So why, after that, would he kill himself?"

"It had to be murder," said Jake.

"Yes. But if only the Croatian had known."

"What?"

"That Father Lambert no longer believed in the find."

Jake nodded. "Then there would have been no need to kill him."

Dagan returned to the sofa, sat down and once again covered his face with his hands. Finally he asked, "But what made Lomish suspect he had been murdered?"

"He knew about Father Lambert's call to you."

"How?"

"He knew."

"He tapped his telephone?"

"Perhaps."

"Or mine?"

Jake did not answer.

"Of course," said Dagan. "It would have to be mine."

"He has to know what's going on."

Dagan did not argue, but once again covered his face, as if blocking out the light would help him think. "So, Lomish thought Father Lambert had been murdered," he said to Jake, "but how did he know that the notebook had been stolen?"

"If someone had taken the trouble to kill him, they would hardly have left the notebook with evidence that he believed in the find."

Michal nodded. "Yes, that's true."

Rachel came back from the kitchen with a pot of coffee. "It seems to me," she said quietly, "that Lomish had a better reason to kill Father Lambert than any Croatian."

Jake frowned. "Why?"

"Because Father Lambert must have realized that the find was a fraud."

"He never said that," said Michal Dagan.

"But he said he was sure, didn't he, that it could not be the body of Christ?"

"Certainly, but as a matter of faith, not of fact."

"How much better for Lomish, then, to have people think that Father Lambert killed himself in despair, or that his fellow Catholics killed him to keep him quiet," said Rachel.

"Then why wasn't the notebook left there," asked Jake, "for the monks to find with the body?"

"Because he had written nothing . . ."

"Then why take it?"

"To add something later, or . . ." She hesitated.

"Or what?" asked Dagan.

She turned to her husband. "To persuade you that Father Lambert was murdered by someone else."

Dagan looked at his son.

"You make things too complicated," said Jake.

"Perhaps Lomish is a too-complicated man," said Dagan.

"He is a simple man who would die for Israel," said Jake.

"And kill for Israel," said Rachel.

"Of course," said Jake, looking defiantly at his mother.

"And expect others to do the same."

"Of course," said Jake again.

She stared into the eyes of her son. "You were in London, Ya'acov . . ."

"Rachel, please," said Dagan. "How can you suggest such a thing?"

"And Anna?" she asked, without taking her eyes off Jake, "is the same thing going to happen to her?"

Jake looked away. "He won't harm her," he said with exaggerated bluster.

"Then what will he do with her?"

"Keep her out of the way until the story has broken."

"And afterward? Can he ever let her go, someone who knows exactly what has happened?"

Jake scowled. "If he thinks she'll be sensible, he'll let her go."

"When has Anna ever been sensible?"

Jake said nothing. His father got up from the sofa. "You must speak to Lomish, Ya'acov, and tell him that things have gone far enough."

"I can't," said Jake. "I'm going back to London."

"To London? Why?"

"To fetch the notebook."

"When?"

"Tomorrow at six A.M. on the British Airways flight."

"Then *I* shall speak to Lomish."

Jake shrugged his shoulders. "Please yourself."

The building where Lomish lived was not far from the Dagans' apartment, and, being one which housed several important officials, was guarded by a man wearing jeans and sneakers, a machine gun slung over his shoulder.

Recognizing the professor, the guard let him pass. As Dagan climbed the stairs, the cool air, scented by pine and eucalyptus trees, came in through the open windows at each landing. He rested for a moment at the first floor, and again at the second, but at the third walked straight to the door of Lomish's apartment. He knocked and waited, his face squarely in front of the peephole in the door.

Lomish himself opened it. He was still wearing his uniform, but had changed his boots for sandals. He stood aside and asked Dagan to come in, as if he had half-expected such a visit so late at night, then led the way toward the living-room. Before either had sat down, Dagan said, "Where is my daughter?"

Lomish raised his hand and made a soothing gesture. "She's perfectly comfortable and perfectly safe."

"If she has been arrested," said Dagan, "I would like to know on what charge."

"There is no need of a charge," said Lomish, sitting down. "There are the emergency regulations."

"To deal with Arab agitators," said Dagan, "not patriotic Jews." He was thinking more of himself than of Anna when he said this, because he felt that her detention was an affront to him, but it enabled Lomish to recover from the defensive posture he had adopted since the professor had appeared at his door.

"But is she a patriotic Jew?" he asked. "If I could be sure of that, I would let her go."

Dagan was confused. "She may not see things as you or I do," he said lamely, "but that is no reason to detain her."

Lomish sighed and gestured to Dagan to sit down. "You know quite well, Professor, that what you have discovered in that cistern is of considerable political significance. Already one man has died as a result—your friend Father Lambert was murdered, we now know, to prevent his authenticating the find. If this news gets out in the wrong way, it could lead to riots and bloodshed, and destroy much of the good will that is felt toward Israel in other parts of the world."

"There is no need to pretend any more," said Dagan, his voice rising with his growing agitation.

"Pretend what?" asked Lomish coldly.

"That this whole thing is not a preposterous deception."

Lomish neither frowned nor smiled. "You only say that because your daughter put the idea into your head," he replied. "That is why she must be detained. We cannot have her influencing others in the same way."

"It won't work," said Dagan. "No one will be taken in."

"No one?" Now Lomish smiled. "Didn't *you* believe in what you found? Didn't Father Lambert? Father van der Velde? And Cardinal Memel?"

"Yes. But they didn't know about the Vilnius Codex."

"But you are a scientist, professor, and I am a soldier. We deal in facts, not silly unsubstantiated rumors. There is the Codex, and it will undoubtedly be subjected to rigorous tests. There is the cistern. There is the jar. They too will be open to examination. And there is the skeleton, which, as you know, is certainly that of a man crucified in the first century of the modern era. What else is asked of you but that you should attest to these facts as facts, and leave rumors and conjectures out of the equation?"

"I was confused, deceived . . ."

"Deceived? By whom?"

"By myself. By my own wish to discover something that would help establish our right to Palestine."

"And your wish has come true," said Lomish. "If the find is announced by the right people in the right place—that is, by Cardinal Memel or by the pope in Rome—it will establish beyond doubt in the Christian mind that God's Covenant with Israel still stands."

"It still stands," muttered Michal Dagan. "Of course it still stands, and we know that Jesus of Nazareth did not rise from the dead—that his bones lie somewhere, or the dust from the bones that were his. And I wanted the bones in the cistern to be his. I was so determined that his was the body I had uncovered that I ignored all my instincts as an archaeologist, instincts that told me the whole thing was too improbable, too coincidental, too good to be true."

Lomish shook his head sadly. "Those were the right feelings, professor, not the selfish ambitions you now suppose them to be, but the culmination of all those aspirations you have had for our people since you were a child. We have suffered, professor—your parents and my grandparents, herded into gas chambers, then shoveled into ovens. They had no nation to protect them, nowhere to go, because for nineteen hundred years it had been accepted that God's gift of a nation for the Jews had been withdrawn, that the promised land was no longer Palestine but some mirage of paradise in another world. Yet you know—you *know*—that this *is* our land, and that the rock where our father Abraham was ready to sacrifice Isaac for the sake of the God of our people, and where Solomon built his Temple to house the Holy of Holies—you know, as I do, that this rock is the heart of Israel and the foundation for a new Temple, which must be built before our people can feel that they are truly home."

Dagan shook his head. "I don't know, I don't know," he moaned.

"We both know," Lomish went on, "that somewhere there must lie the bones of Jesus of Nazareth. You also know that the longer those bones remain undiscovered, the longer a billion Christians are encouraged to believe that he was the Son of God whom *we* killed by crucifixion, thereby bringing upon ourselves the well-deserved punishment of expulsion from our homeland. Only when those bones are found again can it be demonstrated that he was not superhuman, but a minor political agitator and would-be prophet. The bones have to be found, and people have to believe that they are the bones; whether the bones you found in the cistern are the actual bones or not does not matter. What matters is that they *could* be the bones, because the bones do exist, and that because of the Vilnius Codex many will believe that they *are* the bones. Only then, after nineteen hundred years, will the vile blood-libel that we Jews killed the Son of God be disproved once and for all, and all the wretched humiliation and persecutions which followed from that libel, right up to the gas chambers and ovens in which your parents died, will be brought to an end as Israel is reestablished as the land promised by God to his chosen people."

Dagan sat in silence, his head bowed, as if crushed by the weight of Lomish's argument. There seemed to be nothing he could dispute. What was asked of him except that he should connive at a lie? What sacrifice was that if it saved his people? Then he remembered that his reason for coming to see Lomish that evening had been the detention of Anna, and wondered if he might not be expected to sacrifice something more.

"Ya'acov told me," he said, "that Lambert was murdered after all."

"Yes," said Lomish. "By a Croatian."

"My wife does not believe you."

"We have the notebook to prove it."

"She thinks that Ya'acov killed him."

Lomish was silent for a moment, then asked, "And what difference would it make if he did?"

"It would make a difference to me."

"Struggle demands sacrifice, professor. You sent your son to fight in Lebanon. You knew he would kill there."

"I know."

"And you were prepared to see him die."

"Of course."

"Do you love him less than you loved Father Lambert?"

"No."

"Then why complain if it was his life and not Ya'acov's that was lost to further our cause?"

"Did he have to die?"

"He was the foremost Catholic archaeologist, and the first to see your find. His judgment was critical. If he had believed the skeleton was indeed that of Jesus, his Church would have found it hard to deny it—and at first, as you know, it seemed that he did. But then he called you from London and said he had changed his mind, and we had to resort to our second option and make it seem that he had committed suicide."

"Why did you take the notebook?"

"Since he had written nothing in it about the find, no purpose would be served in leaving it there. Later it could emerge that he had left the notebook here in Jerusalem, with a final entry giving the reason for his despair."

"And this story about the Croatian?"

Lomish smiled. "That was Ya'acov's idea, to spare your feelings."

"To spare my feelings?" asked Dagan incredulously.

"And to allay your suspicions. He knew you would wonder why Father Lambert had killed himself so soon after calling you to say that he no longer believed in the find."

"How considerate of my son."

"He is a fine young man—not just brave, but also clever."

"And Anna?"

"The same qualities, but slightly distorted. Foolhardy, and too clever by half."

"For which she must die like my friend?"

"Die? No, it won't come to that," said Lomish. "But she must serve her sentence for avoiding the draft, and then . . . we shall see."

"And what am I to do?" asked Dagan. "What am I to tell her mother?"

"Tell her that no war is won by those who let pity rule their hearts. Tell her that she must be prepared to sacrifice her daughter just as you, like Abraham, have been prepared to sacrifice your son."

"I don't think she can bear it," said Dagan.

"Then let us hope that Yahweh provides a ram caught in a thicket," said Lomish, "so that you can sacrifice it instead."

23

Michal Dagan left Lomish at around two in the morning and started to walk home. When he had gone less than a third of the way, however, he was stopped by the thought that Rachel would be waiting for news of Anna. Knowing that she would see through any pretense or procrastination, he felt unable to face her.

He turned, not toward Lomish's flat but in the general direction of the Staedtler Institute of Archaeology. He was very tired, but so painful and confused were the thoughts tormenting him that even if he had been in bed he would not have been able to sleep. He walked in the cool, quiet streets, hoping that a steady stride would bring order and calm.

If only he could be governed either by emotion like Rachel or by reason like Lomish, and yet what contradictions there were in both reasoning and feeling. He had been prepared to sacrifice Ya'acov for Israel, so why not Anna? Was it because he loved her less that he felt so reluctant to lose her? Or was it because he was afraid of Rachel's reproach? He knew that she felt he loved his daughter less than his son and that if Anna disappeared she would never believe that he had done all he could to save her. What had Abraham said to Sarah, he wondered, as he had set out with Isaac, their only son, with the fire and the knife in his hand? Had he told her what Yahweh had commanded him to do? Had she seen anything odd about the look in his eye? And if, like Isaac himself, she had known nothing of what he intended, what would Abraham have said when he returned?

Dagan shivered, not because of the cool night air, but with dread as he anticipated Rachel's reproach. She would know that he had connived at whatever Lomish had done, and she would think that he had abandoned Anna not from an excessive zeal for Israel, but from the lukewarm affection she inspired in him. And of course there would be truth in her suspicions. Dagan had to acknowledge that while he had always been ready to sacrifice Ya'acov in Lebanon, he could never have raised his hand to cut his son's throat.

Was he less reluctant to sacrifice Anna? As Rachel had admitted to Anna, Dagan had never felt as fond of his daughter as he had of his son. To defend himself for this lack of affection, he sometimes blamed her for growing into someone so unlike what he thought a daughter should be. In a more honest frame of mind, he would recognize that the reasons he had put forward for leaving her to be educated in the United States had really been pretexts for banishing this cuckoo from the nest.

What would Abraham have done, he wondered, if he had had ambivalent feelings about Isaac? Would he have felt, as Dagan now did, the sour bile of bad conscience as he prepared to sacrifice what was in fact no sacrifice at all? No, it was inconceivable, because Yahweh spoke so clearly to Abraham, and Abraham to Yahweh. If only Yahweh would make himself as clear to Michal Dagan.

Yet to Dagan Yahweh was not someone who spoke in the ear or even the mind of a man. To him God's intentions were made manifest in the history of his chosen people. It was by studying the past that one could discern his will for the future, and since the greatest evil of the age was undoubtedly Hitler's attempt to exterminate the Jews, so the greatest good must be its antithesis: the reestablishment of a Jewish nation. It was inconceivable that Yahweh could want anything different. Why, then, did he feel so unhappy when he thought not only about the fate awaiting Anna, but about the murder of Father Lambert? Why had Lomish admitted that Ya'acov had killed him? Was it to test the inexorable logic of his reasoning? Did he boast of his ruthlessness in order to prove his patriotism, or to draw others into complicity with what he had done?

As with Anna, Father Lambert had aroused ambivalent feelings in Michal Dagan. Certainly he had been his friend, but he also was his rival. Was it not true that Dagan had asked Father Lambert to come to Israel to authenticate his find not just because he was the one archaeologist who could persuade the Christian churches that the skeleton was that of Jesus Christ, but because Dagan had exulted in showing the Catholic monk that his beliefs about Christ's resurrection were absurd?

Had Dagan had no doubts about his own hypothesis? By now he could not remember. If there had been any scepticism in the back of his mind, it had been quickly silenced by his Zionist zeal and professional ambition. What were Yadin's discoveries at Masada or Kenyon's at Jericho compared with his uncovering of the body of Christ? And what were the accomplishments of Christian archaeologists like Father de Vaux, Father Vincent and Father Lambert compared with those of the Israeli, Michal Dagan?

Of course, when he had seen the effect of the find on Father Lambert, Dagan realized that any professional rivalry he might have felt paled beside the theological significance of what had apparently been uncovered. He had also noticed that despite the destructive effect of the discovery upon his own beliefs, Father Lambert had been sincerely pleased that such a triumph should crown his friend's career. Indeed, it was perhaps this humility, this fear that his own professional pride might impede his acceptance of what Dagan had found, which had prompted Father Lambert to authenticate the find so promptly and return to London in despair.

This would explain why only a day later he had telephoned Dagan to say not just that he had changed his mind, but that he now felt that the skeleton could not be that of Jesus of Nazareth. The call, made only an hour before Father Lambert died, had been relayed by Dagan to Ya'acov, and then presumably by Ya'acov to Lomish—or, more likely, had been recorded through a tap placed on his own telephone at the Staedtler Institute, and replayed at once to Lomish. It would then have been a simple matter for Lomish to call Ya'acov in London and order the priest's execution.

Now Dagan, who until that moment only knew that he was walking away from Lomish and from home, suddenly came in sight of the floodlit walls of the Old City. He was on Mishkenot Sha'ananim, near to the Montefiore windmill. He sat down on a low stone wall facing the city, and forgot for a moment that he was cold—forgot even that he was tormented by so many contradictory emotions, and simply looked with rapture at his beloved Jerusalem. How could anyone who was not Jewish understand what this city meant to him? It was not merely the site of his people's historical glory, nor the tangible proof after two millennia that they had regained what was rightfully theirs. Rather, it was—like the empty tomb of Christian myth—the proof that even after their own crucifixion, the Holocaust, the Jews had risen from the dead.

As he always did when he looked at the Old City, Dagan thought of his mother and father, and prayed that somehow from the mysterious depths of She'ol, the next world, they might see through his eyes that their suffering had not been in vain. This time, however, conjuring up the image of his dead parents did not bring comfort and reassurance, but instead induced a spasm of the bad conscience that had disturbed him since parting from Lomish. However hard he might try to invest his memories with his own aspirations and ideas, he could not so mold them that the honest and amiable lawyer from Hamburg would condone what he had done. Moreover, his memory of his mother merged with the image of Rachel, and both women rebuked him with the same silent look of reproach.

"But I did it for you," he said aloud, as if his father were standing there. "Did what?" the old lawyer seemed to reply. "Lie? Deceive? Murder? Your friend? Your daughter? For stones and rocks and sand? No, not for me. That is what was done to *us* for generation after generation—by Titus and Torquemada, by Ignatiev and Hitler—but however many of us died, they never triumphed. We triumphed because we did not put our trust in stones, rocks and sand, in castles, palaces, synagogues or even a Temple, but because we put our trust in faith, rectitude, patience, humility and resignation to the will of Yahweh. Remember, Michal, the man I was as you sat on my knee and I puffed at my pipe—a victim, certainly, who was to be kicked out of the park by the Brownshirts, but warm, humorous, affectionate, kind, just, decent and honest. Those qualities are better monuments than all the stones, rocks and sand you will ever cheat and kill to conquer. What are you, Michal my son, but cold, loveless and afraid? And what is Ya'acov, raised in your image and likeness, but ruthless, fanatical and cruel? What monument are you to my suffering, whether or not you hold Jerusalem or live in Israel, whether or not you demolish the Dome of the Rock to build a new, air-conditioned Temple of marble-faced, prestressed concrete? No, Michal, my son, your mother and I suffered, and it brought us close to Yahweh. If you must build a monument, build one to us within yourself so that when we meet in She'ol we may know and love you as our son."

With no onlookers to inhibit him, Michal Dagan wept, sobbing not just at the rebuke implicit in the memory of his dead parents, but also because he was tired, distraught and confused. Until that moment he had been propelled through life by the clear and urgent mission to exact revenge and retribution for everything that his parents had suffered as Jews. Now, in just one day, he had been forced to count the cost. In doing so, he had come to wonder not merely whether the game was worth the candle, but whether it was worth playing at all. In seeking to punish the elusive male-factor who had persecuted his people throughout history, he now recognized that he had become malign himself, conniving by the most devious logic at the sacrifice of his daughter and the murder of his friend. The shock of understanding that unwittingly he had become party to something so patently wrong returned strength to his conscience, which, like Samson in the court of the Philis-tines, pulled away the two pillars upon which the edifice of his convictions had rested.

The tears that now trickled down Dagan's weatherbeaten cheeks came not just from fatigue and remorse, but also, to his own astonishment, from an extraordinary sense of relief and joy, as if a spring that had been blocked for many years had suddenly opened. What he saw for the first time was that the finest accom-plishments of men and women lay not in nations and empires, wealth and culture, in palaces, temples, churches or mosques, but in those invisible and intangible thoughts and emotions that are imbued with gentleness, unselfishness and love. He now under-stood that for fifty years he had suffered from a misconception. His father was not a Joshua who had failed, but a Job who had succeeded, a man defeated and humiliated in the terms of this world, but heroic and victorious by the values of the next. Though persecuted by vile men, he had not been infected by their hatred. The pity he had felt was also for them. For this reason he had triumphed even in Auschwitz.

Slowly it began to grow light. The street lamps lost their pointed brilliance and the moonlight evaporated like a morning mist as the first rays of the sun rose from behind the sparse hills of the Judaean desert.

Michal Dagan got to his feet. There were still traces of tears on his haggard face but the tears themselves had stopped. He shuffled out of the park away from Mishkenot Sha'ananim, not in the direction of his home in Rehavya, but past the almshouses into the valley of Hinnom. Already one or two cars and buses were passing as he stumbled across the road encircling the Old City and climbed up the path toward the Zion Gate. He reached it just as the sun rose to shine obliquely onto the city wall, and stood there for a moment to recover his breath. A policeman looked askance at the unshaven old man coming so early to the Old City, but made no attempt to stop him as he walked through the gate.

Bent with exhaustion, Dagan walked toward the Temple Mount. There, in a shaded spot, two or three Jews were already praying at the Western Wall. He too went to the Wall, putting on his yarmulke as he entered the enclosure. He did not stop to pray, but passed straight through to the cavernous space below Wilson's Arch.

At the gate to the passage there was a sleepy guard, one of Lomish's men, who looked surprised to see the professor. "None of your people are here," he said.

"It doesn't matter," said Dagan. "I can manage on my own."

The man looked perplexed but unlocked the gate and switched on the lights.

The air, which usually felt cool compared to the heat outside, now seemed hot and stuffy. Already exhausted, Dagan set off down the long tunnel. "Vanity of vanities, all is vanity," he muttered as he stumbled along beside the massive blocks of Herod's Western Wall. "What profit has a man of all his labor which he takes under the sun? One generation passes away and another generation comes, but the earth abides for ever . . . All things are wearisome . . . what was will be again, what has been done will be done again; there is nothing new under the sun."

He reached the entrance to the cistern. Here there was a switch for the lights inside, and since they had always been turned on for him by one of his assistants, it took Dagan some time to find it. When he did, he heard through the rectangular hole in the wall an echoing pop as the bulbs were lit. He crouched, climbed through and then paused for a moment, standing upright on the ledge of rock, remembering the emotions which had overwhelmed him when he had stood there with Jake after finding the skeleton— the feelings of excitement, exaltation and triumph.

Now it was as if that had occurred not a month before but in some other life. As he climbed down the ladder onto the shale floor, he felt excitement, exaltation and triumph of quite a different kind—and a sense of vindication, too, which went far beyond his own memories and experiences, or the memories and experiences of his family or his race—reaching down into the innermost kernel of his being and outward to the extremities of space and time.

Yet while this emotion was overwhelming, it was hardly coherent, and the thoughts that accompanied it were jumbled. It was here, just above him, under the Dome of the Rock, that Abraham had been prepared to sacrifice Isaac, and had instead found a ram caught in a thicket. To Dagan it seemed as if the ram had fallen into the cistern and was darting in and out of the shadows made by the lamps. At the same time, the spade he found at the foot of the ladder leading down from the ledge became the knife held in Abraham's hand as he raised it to sacrifice not his son but the ram. But it was also a spade with which to dig a grave for his parents, and to bury with them the rage and anguish that had possessed Michal since he had seen his father humiliated in the park as a child. And the skeleton he now saw, as he approached the contents of the broken jar laid out on the plastic sheet, became in his mind's eye the relics of those millions who had died, relics so terrible until this moment that he had never recognized them as an enduring and indestructible monument to his parents' quality of soul.

With a great groan of final anguish, Michal Dagan raised the spade and brought it down, again and again, to slaughter the sacrificial ram, to exorcize the black spirit of vengeance, and to reduce the skeleton of a crucified man into a thousand fragments of dust and bone.

PART
III

24

It was already midday in Israel, but ten A.M. in Britain when Jake arrived in London on the British Airways flight. He was not armed, but had in his hand-luggage all the equipment carried by a diabetic: a packet of disposable syringes, indistinguishable from the kind found in a doctor's office, that were used for daily doses of insulin, and another, smaller syringe looking something like a fountain pen, with which a diabetic could give himself an extra shot while sitting at a table in a restaurant. There were also four small bottles labeled INSULIN, three actually containing the drug, the odd one being filled instead with a poison that stopped the heart. It was easily administered, left no trace in the blood, and had been used successfully to dispose of terrorists and their mentors in different countries of the world.

Jake passed through customs and immigration control without difficulty. The stamps on his passport showed that he had been in and out of Britain many times before. Since his only luggage was the bag he had carried on the plane, he went straight from Terminal One to catch the underground into central London. If he had been in a hurry, he would have taken a taxi, but Lomish always scrutinized his expenses on missions of this kind, and reacted to any unnecessary extravagance as if it were a blow aimed deliberately at the faltering economy of Israel. Since he knew that his target,

Henry Nash, would already have left his flat for his office, and that he would have no opportunity to deal with him until he went out for lunch, there was no reason for speed.

Jake sat reading *Newsweek* as the train made its way through the suburbs of Hounslow and Hammersmith. At South Kensington, he changed to the Circle Line, catching a train to Victoria. There he went to the public lavatory, shut himself into a cubicle, took the portable syringe out of his bag and filled it with a dose of the poison. He screwed on the cap, clipped the syringe to the inside pocket of his blouson, and then left to deposit his bag in a storage locker. He was booked on the El Al charter flight from Gatwick to Tel Aviv that evening. He studied the railway timetable to check the times of the express to the airport, then returned to the underground and caught a train to Piccadilly Circus. From there he walked to Leicester Square, went into a café and sat down.

It was here that Aron, the operative who had helped him with Father Lambert, was to bring a photograph of the target. Jake already knew a certain amount about Henry Nash, and had formed a picture of him in his mind, but that was not enough to make a positive identification. Lomish would be angry if he killed the wrong man, and if there was one emotion that dominated the many thoughts and feelings flitting through Jake's restless mind, it was the desire to earn Lomish's approval. His regard for his father amounted to nothing beside his admiration for his commander. Certainly the professor was a zealous Zionist who had raised his son to be brave and heroic, but this vicarious ambition had exposed him to Jake as a man who himself was neither.

Lomish, on the other hand, was as decisive in action as he was in analysis; the logic of the thought led inexorably to the enactment of the deed. No misgivings were allowed to impede the attainment of an objective; pity, his commander said, was merely cowardice in a pleasing disguise.

Jake did not like to kill. The first time was supposed to be the most difficult, but in his case it had been the easiest, in the heat of battle in Lebanon, where his victim, given the chance, would have happily killed him. Later, in cold blood, on missions in Athens and Geneva, it had become harder, but even there the targets had been strangers in a crowd. The worst had been the last—Father Lambert, because he had been kind to Jake since he was a child, and because he had looked at him and Aron as they had dragged him to the window, not with hate or even fear, but with a pity that did not seem at all like cowardice in a pleasing disguise.

Jake had understood quite clearly why Father Lambert had to die. There was never a flaw in the logic used by Lomish. He could also see why it was necessary to kill Henry Nash, and he told himself over and over again that he should no more flinch from sticking a needle into the arm of this Englishman than Judith had hesitated to hack off the head of Holofernes. Time might separate the one deed from the other, but the cause remained the same.

Only one thought worried Jake: that Lomish might judge it necessary to eliminate Anna too. It was unlikely that if he did he would involve her brother in her execution, but this did not resolve his anxiety. However much his sister had exasperated him over the years, she remained a member of his family, his people, his nation. Wasn't she one of the people they were fighting to defend? Could it really be right to kill her? Or was it possible that Lomish's logic was somehow flawed?

He looked at his watch. It was a quarter to twelve. Aron should have arrived by now. What if he did not turn up? Jake could find the office, but how would he identify the man? He looked for a public telephone, but there were none in sight. If he left the café, Aron might arrive and miss him. In any case, he knew the habits of a man like Henry Nash: he would not leave for lunch before half-past twelve. He could afford to wait. He could even wait until the evening—these matters were more easily done in the rush hour—and take a later plane, but he wanted to get back as soon as possible because he was afraid of what his father might do in his agitated state of mind.

Aron still had not come, and it was now five to twelve. He stood up, left money for his coffee on the table, and went outside to look for a telephone. There was one in Leicester Square, but it was being used by a swarthy Lebanese. Jake could tell this from the man's accent as he chatted in Arabic, apparently to a girl, trickling a loathsome flow of pornographic innuendo down the line, unaware that anyone around him could understand what he said.

Jake turned away. He loathed London and longed to be out of these gutters filled with human rubbish, and back in Israel, in the desert, with his comrades in arms. How pitiable were those who had never known what it was to fight in the heat, side by side with friends, for a cause that had been ordained by Yahweh himself. How majestic it was when they camped under the stars to know that their lives were not to be lived out as insects in the ant heap of a city like London, but as the heroes of Providence, reconquering and rebuilding the land of God's chosen people.

He found a telephone and dialed Aron's number. A girl answered: Aron had left over an hour before. There had been a call from Tel Aviv that had held him up. Or it could be the traffic or the tube; she did not know how he had traveled. Jake told her to tell Aron if he rang her to meet him outside the offices of the *Soho Newsletter*.

It was now a quarter past twelve. He had to start his surveillance soon or risk losing the chance of executing the job during the lunch hour. He walked up Dean Street, past a nightclub advertising nonstop stripteases by big-busted girls, and shuddered. How vile this wantonness of the Philistines was. Never would Jerusalem become like London. Never would a new Isaiah be able to say, "What a harlot she has become, the faithful city . . ."

He came to the building housing the office of the *Soho Newsletter*, walked straight past it to the corner, crossed the street and came back down the other side to a small sandwich bar, with three or four stools in front of a counter. He could sit there and watch, but how would he know who to look for? He would have to go to the office and try to find out. He crossed the street again and went straight into the old brick building, then up the stairway to the first floor. He did this with all the confidence of someone who worked there. Only at the door to the office of the *Soho Newsletter* did he hesitate for a moment, not because he was afraid, but because he had not planned what to do. He knew that Henry was the managing director, and that he was Andrew's brother; he also knew that he was unlike Andrew in almost every way—an atheist, not a Catholic; a roué, not a prig.

Jake pushed open the door and found himself in a small foyer. He looked at the walls. Perhaps there would be a photograph of the board of directors. Instead there were framed prints, modern, tubular chairs, a table with magazines on it, and a desk behind which a sharp-nosed girl sat answering the telephone and putting through calls.

She looked up as if to ask what he wanted, but as she did so the telephone burbled and she picked it up—her eyebrows still arched in the interrogatory look she had directed at Jake.

"*Soho Newsletter*," she said in the singsong voice of the trained receptionist. "Mr. Nash? One moment, please." She pushed a button on the board in front of her, and turned back to Jake. "I'm sorry . . ."

"I was wondering . . ." Jake began.

She was not listening. The light was still flashing on her console. She smiled up at Jake. "I won't be a minute." She picked up the telephone again. "Sandy? Is Mr. Nash in his office? Oh, I see. He can take it here, then. It's that young chap—Alistair something or other. Will you take it? Good."

She pushed another button and another light flashed for a moment, then stopped.

She turned back to Jake.

"I was wondering . . ." he began again.

Again she was distracted. Two men, both in suits, one blue, the other gray, entered the foyer from the hall behind the desk. "There was a call for you," the girl said. "I put it through to Sandy."

"Was it Alistair?" asked the man in the grey suit.

"I think so, yes."

"About time," said the man in the blue suit.

"Sandy can deal with him," said the man in gray, and they left.

"I *am* sorry," said the girl to Jake.

"I wanted to see Henry Nash."

"Oh, that was him who just went out."

"Which one?"

"The tall one."

"I'll run and catch him."

Out in the street, the two men were sauntering away from the office. Jake walked behind them, cursing the girl because neither seemed taller than the other. They were both about the same age and type. The gray suit was better cut; the blue suit seemed crumpled. As he came closer, he noticed that the man in the gray suit was an inch or two taller.

They came to the corner, stopped for a moment, finishing what they had to say and then parted, the man in the blue suit turning to the west, the man in the gray suit to the east. Jake went east, a short way behind, convinced that the man in the gray suit was his target. He felt for the syringe in his inside pocket and found it, but left it there. The street was neither empty nor crowded enough for him to prick his target without running the risk of being seen. In a moment he would turn into Frith Street, or even better into Oxford Street, and there it could be done quite safely.

Jake removed his gaze from the back of the man's head, knowing that people can sometimes sense when they are being followed. When the man hesitated before crossing a street, he too stopped, and then followed him and entered Soho Square.

The man walked through the garden in the center, where bunches of office workers sat eating sandwiches and drinking juice out of cartons. This would do. If he sat down on a bench, Jake would sit next to him, but from what he knew of Henry it seemed unlikely that he would take a sandwich from the pocket of his well-cut suit. But the man did not stop, walking straight through the gardens and crossing the street on the other side. There he hesitated and looked at his watch, then slipped furtively through the door of a red-brick church.

Jake frowned, wondering why an atheist should go into a church. He had looked at his watch, so perhaps he had an assignation. Churches, after all, were often used as a meeting place for lovers or spies. Henry's newsletters involved covert connections, so he could be using the church to meet a cautious informant. He crossed the street and followed the man into the church. He had been in churches before and always had loathed them. However beautiful the building or rich the decoration, they were the temples of the enemy, stewpots of that malign ideology which had persecuted the Jews since the death of Christ.

This one was ugly, and smelled of incense and candlewax. There was a lobby, empty except for a large marble bowl of holy water, and stands selling tracts of Catholic propaganda. Beyond, through double doors of glass, was the nave itself, painted stucco, aping the baroque, with portraits above the altar of the Holy Family who looked Irish or Italian—anything but Jewish.

At first the church seemed empty, but then he saw two Filipino women kneeling before a statue of the Virgin Mary; and, in the front pew at the foot of the altar, the man in the gray suit, staring up at the figure of Christ on the cross.

Once again Jake felt for the syringe in his inside pocket. This seemed as good a place as any. He took out the syringe, unscrewed the top, and holding it behind his back with two fingers and the thumb of his right hand, walked quietly down the left-hand aisle. When he was within fifteen feet of his target, he stopped and looked around. The church was still empty but for the Filipino women, and their eyes were fixed on the statue behind the bank of flickering candles. He looked back at the man, brought the syringe out from behind him and stepped forward, but at this moment the figure in the gray suit went down on his knees before the cross, lowered his head and clasped his hands together in prayer.

Jake cursed inaudibly, turned, and retreated down the aisle. Henry Nash was an atheist. He would not pray. He had followed the wrong man. In the foyer, he put the top back onto the syringe and the syringe back into his pocket, and then went out into the sunlight of Soho Square. As he did so, he caught sight of Aron looking for him among the people sitting on the benches. He crossed the street, came up behind him and tapped him on the shoulder.

Aron turned. He looked afraid. "I was held up," he said. "There was a power cut on the Bakerloo Line."

"Never mind. Did you bring the photograph?"

"Yes." Aron reached into his pocket. "But Lomish called. The mission is off."

He took the photograph. "Why?"

"I don't know. There are developments in Jerusalem. The whole thing is definitely off."

Jake looked at the photograph. He had followed the right man.

"I'm not too late, am I?" asked Aron. "You haven't done it?"

"No, I haven't done it." He gave the photograph back to Aron. "Did Lomish say what I was to do?"

"Go back as planned."

25

Three weeks later, Henry met Anna when she returned to London, arriving on the same flight from Tel Aviv that Andrew had taken two weeks before. Henry greeted her as he might have greeted a sister or a very old friend. Neither said much as they walked to the parking lot, and even as they drove through the tunnel beneath the runway they were silent, Henry apparently concentrating on driving his silver-gray BMW, Anna staring ahead with a wistful look in her eyes. It was only when they were on the highway that he asked, "Are you all right?"

"Fine," she said shortly, but with a shrug, as if to add, "As well as can be expected." She turned toward him, and for a moment the wistful look left her eyes to make way for an expression of pained apprehension. "But what about him? Is *he* all right?"

Henry could not return her glance since he was driving in fast-moving traffic, but he nodded and said, "Yes, I think so. For the time being."

They drove on for some time in silence until finally, with some reluctance, Anna said, "Did he tell you?"

"What?"

"About him and me?"

"Yes."

She paused, then said, "I suppose you think I behaved badly."

"No, I don't."

"I really loved him."

"I know."

"But once he knew about the hoax . . ."

"Why did you tell him?"

She gave a sad smile. "At first I didn't. When Lomish let me go, he was waiting at the hotel, and he was so happy to see me and I was so happy to see him that I just couldn't bring myself to tell him that everything Dad had found had been faked. I told him that Dad had had a nervous breakdown and had destroyed the skeleton because Father Lambert's suicide had made him think that the find would lead to more suicides, riots and civil wars."

"Did he accept that?"

"Yes, but by then he would have accepted almost anything."

"Why?"

"Because he needed to believe that Jesus had not risen from the dead. It was all a package—the priesthood, celibacy and the Resurrection on the one hand; sex, me and the skeleton of Jesus on the other."

"You realized he saw it that way?"

"Yes."

"Yet you told him?"

Anna sighed. "It's hard to lie to someone you love, especially someone like Andrew. Then the whole thing got out of hand. Andrew felt he had to tell the Simonites what I had told him. He went to see the prior and then telephoned the cardinal, who gave a press conference in Rome . . ."

"What did he say?"

"Didn't you read about it?"

"No."

"He came out in favor of the theory that the Risen Christ was just a kind of ghost, not a reanimated corpse; and when he was rebuked by the pope the next day, Andrew felt that it was all his fault."

"Did Cardinal Memel mention the find?"

"No. How could he? The evidence was destroyed. It was all theological theory, but Andrew felt sure that he would never have said what he did about the Resurrection if he hadn't seen the skeleton in the cistern. So he was all set to go to Rome and tell the pope the whole story, and I could see him getting deeper and deeper into a lie, so I told him the truth."

"You knew the risk?"

"I suppose I did, but I thought . . ." She sniffed. "You see, one of Andrew's favorite sayings of St. Paul is that the truth will set us free."

"He still loves you," said Henry.

"I know. Like a sister."

"What happened after you told him?"

"It was terrible. Much worse than I had imagined."

"How?"

"He withdrew into himself, but at the same time pretended nothing had changed. But I knew that he was suffering, that he was even forcing himself to make love to me when he didn't really want to."

"He felt guilty?"

"Guilty, ashamed, disgusted. He came to look on me as Eve, the woman who had inveigled him into eating the forbidden fruit, and as a result he'd never make it back into the Garden of Eden."

"The idea of Hell has always been very real to Andrew," said Henry.

"You can say that again. But you see, he'd promised never to leave me. He'd said we were married in the eyes of God, so he was completely caught."

"Poor Andrew."

"Yes, poor Andrew, going to bed each night as if he was getting into his coffin, making love to me with a look of doom on his face, and afterwards . . . well, it wasn't a matter of postcoital sadness but of postcoital despair."

The trace of a smile came onto Henry's lips. "Poor Anna," he said.

"In the end I couldn't bear it. I told him to go."

"And he agreed?"

"He didn't want to, and he didn't want to stay, either. But he felt he had to go to Rome anyway, in order to tell Cardinal Memel that the whole business was a fraud, so I suggested that he go back from there to the monastery in London—for a while, at any rate, to think things over."

"And he agreed?"

"He didn't want to leave me, but I persuaded him that Dad was still in a bad way, and that I needed to be alone with him for a while."

"Which was perhaps partly true?"

She shrugged. "Sure. Dad did have a kind of breakdown. I think he still can't forgive himself for Father Lambert's suicide.

I'm sure that's why he smashed the skeleton, though Ma says he did it to save me from Lomish. He's certainly fed up with Jake for landing him in the whole shemozzle, and only wanted me and Ma to be with him. So we went off to Galilee and Andrew came back here, miserable but relieved."

"Yes," said Henry. "That's how I found him. Miserable but relieved." They had reached Kensington. "Are you staying with your aunt?" he asked as he waited at a red light.

"Yes, but you don't have to take me all the way there."

"Of course I will, but perhaps you'd like some supper first."

"I'm not hungry, but I'd like to talk."

The car moved forward again.

"What I really hate about the Christian religion," said Anna, "is that it talks about loving one's neighbor, but when it comes down to the business of Heaven and Hell, it's every man for himself."

Again a slight smile came onto Henry's lips. "*Sauve qui peut*," he said.

"Precisely."

"To give him his due," said Henry, "I think that Andrew's dilemma is a little more complicated than a straight choice between being saved as a priest and being damned as a lover."

"Have you talked to him about it?"

"Yes."

"What did he say?"?

"His thoughts were very confused," said Henry. "I was worried that he was heading for a breakdown."

"So was I. That's why I thought he should go home."

"I'm sure it was the right thing for him to do at that moment."

"And have you seen him recently?"

"Yes. He's much calmer."

She scowled. "I bet the monks are glad to have him back."

"I'm not sure they know how nearly they lost him."

"His confessor must know."

"Of course."

They turned into Eaton Square and stopped outside Henry's flat.

"I feel as if I've been away for years," said Anna.

"A lot has happened in a short space of time," said Henry.

He brought her suitcase up to his flat because she said she wanted to take a shower. It was a sign of how much had changed that neither was embarrassed by the intimacy of the situation. The condition of Henry's flat suggested that he too had altered in some way that was not at once apparent. Where before the living room had been kept scrupulously tidy, with every rug and cushion in place, there was now a certain chaos in the room, with odd books in haphazard piles and letters left unopened on the table. But Anna was so preoccupied that she did not notice the untidiness, nor that Henry's manner had subtly altered from the sardonic charm that had once so enraptured her to a kindlier, more tentative approach. When she returned from taking her shower, wearing fresh clothes, he handed her a glass of wine with a look of solicitude, as if he cared for her now far more than he ever had before.

As she took it, she said, "You said you thought that things were more complicated with Andrew than they seemed."

Henry sat down opposite her, but rather than sink back into the cushions of his sofa, he perched on the edge, holding his drink between his knees.

"Do you find Andrew naïve?" he asked.

She seemed hurt. "No, I don't think he's naïve."

"Perhaps that's the wrong word," said Henry.

"He's kind of unspoilt and uncompromising . . ."

"Yes. Uncompromising and unspoilt. That's what I mean. He has never had to live his life at odds with his ideas. He has never had to settle for anything other than a clear conscience."

"No."

"Whereas others—most of us, I would say—muddle along, if only because we are not quite clear what our conscience is telling us to do."

"Yes," she agreed.

"Some of us are not even sure that there *is* a right path or a wrong path . . ."

"Yes."

"Most trust to a kind of gravity, which will pull us, like a meandering river, down to the sea," he said.

"I guess that applies to you and me . . ."

"But not to Andrew. Ever since he was a child he has been determined to be on the right side of the law, and he was always anxious that there should *be* a law to give an inflexible structure to his life."

"Why?"

"I don't know for sure; I'm not a psychoanalyst, after all. But I think one could say that it was partly because our mother was such a bully, and yet so erratic, that we never knew where we stood with her—what would make her pleased with us, or what would put her in a rage."

"He told me . . ."

"While our father, who might have provided some consistency in our lives, was a weak man who couldn't stand up to her and eventually, as you know, ran off with his secretary, leaving us at the mercy of our mother until, in Andrew's case, he came upon Father Lambert."

Anna drank from her glass and nodded to Henry to go on.

"Father Lambert not only exemplified all those qualities which had been so poorly represented in our father; he was also the priest of a religion which offered a definite and detailed code. Inevitably this appealed to someone like Andrew, who had always wanted to know whether he was doing right or doing wrong."

"Of course."

"So he found, both in the man and in the religion, a clear answer to what the Freudians might call the yearning of his superego, and a way to cope with the frightening urges of his libido. However, the libido can never be successfully repressed or denied. If it cannot flow on the surface, then it runs underground, and in his case, I suspect, it expressed itself in his affection for you . . ."

Anna nodded.

"It only surfaced again as undisguised sexual desire when, for a moment, your father's claim about his discovery enabled Andrew to throw off the inhibitions implicit in his commitment to a priestly vocation . . ."

"Go on."

"At first he thought he was in paradise, but he quickly discovered that life outside a monastery is neither as innocent nor as simple as it seems."

She blushed. "Because I told him about you?"

He looked at her, but did not blush. "Yes. He said nothing at all to suggest that he blamed either of us for what had happened, but clearly he'd had as idealistic a conception of sexual love as he had of everything else, and to discover so soon that we make mistakes—or rather that we settle for the relative while awaiting the absolute—threw him into confusion."

"For me he was the absolute," said Anna.

"I know, and I'm sure that in time he would have realized that. But before he could recover from that first confusion, he suffered the second setback, discovering that the find was a hoax, and he felt impelled to return to the structure that had served him so well before, but which committed him to the celibate life of a monk."

Anna stood up. "Shall we go eat?" she said abruptly to hide her impending tears from Henry.

"Yes." He finished his drink, and together they walked to a restaurant in Chelsea.

After they had ordered, Anna described in detail what she had learned from Lomish.

"Will the story get into the press?" Henry asked.

"I don't think so. Cardinal Memel didn't mention it, and Lomish certainly won't leak it. Nor will Dad."

"What about you?"

She shook her head. "No. It would ruin Dad."

"What will he do now?"

"Ma wanted him to go back to the States, but he won't hear of it. He says he now loves Israel more than ever before."

"But not in the same way?"

"Not at all in the same way."

"And Jake?"

"He's gone to Gaza."

"And you?"

She looked sad. "After the Congress of Biblical Archaeologists at Oxford, I suppose I'll go back to the States."

"You're giving up on Britain?"

"I think Britain's given up on me."

"I'm sorry."

"It's funny," Anna said. "I've been dropped before, and felt bad about it at the time, but I've never before felt that it needn't have turned out like this, and I've never hated a rival the way I hate the Catholic Church."

Henry looked perplexed. "Can you blame the Church for our emasculating mother?"

"No. But as you always said, the Simonites are short of vocations, so don't tell me that now that they've got Andrew back in their clutches, they aren't painting me as a Jezebel who will lure him out to lead him into damnation."

"And will you?"

"What?"

"Try to lure him out?"

"I don't even know if he'll see me."

"I'm going to see him tomorrow. I'll find out."

26

At ten the next morning Henry went to the Simonite monastery, where Gerry, the porter, called Andrew down from his cell. He was wearing the gray habit of the order, with a rope tied around his waist. Though calm, he seemed thin, and had a tired look, as if he had been fasting or keeping an all-night vigil. He greeted his brother with a kind of measured friendliness and led him back to his cell. Henry, who loathed all institutions, but felt particularly repelled by the mixed smell of floor polish, incense and the monks' breakfast, which always permeated the air, followed him obediently up the stairs.

"They moved me to another cell while I was away," said Andrew as they walked along the corridor on the second floor.

"Promotion?"

"In a way, I suppose."

They reached the cell, and Andrew opened the door to let his brother enter before him.

Henry looked around at the book-lined walls. "Who was here before?"

"Father Lambert. It was much simpler to move me up here than to move all his books and papers down to my old cell."

"But doesn't it give you the creeps?"

Andrew frowned. "It reminds me, naturally . . . but that's as it should be." He directed Henry toward the wooden armchair and himself sat down at the desk.

"You seem to be busy," said Henry, glancing at the pile of papers.

"I've not only been asked to clear up his papers, but also to take over some of the tasks he was to perform for the Congress of Biblical Archaeologists."

"They must be relieved that you came back."

Andrew blushed. "I'm also relieved to have something to do."

"Of course, and I won't waste your time. I just wanted to see that you were all right, and to tell you that Anna returned last night."

"Ah, good. I must call her," Andrew said in a tone of contrived detachment.

"She'll be at the Congress. Her father's coming too. But after that she means to go back to the States."

Andrew frowned. "Won't she finish at Huntingdon?"

"I don't think so."

"No, well, I can see why she might not want to. After all, she only came to study under Father Lambert. Without him, it's only to be expected that she might go elsewhere."

"I don't think that it's because of his death that she's leaving," Henry said.

Andrew looked out of the window. "No. There must be other reasons. I realize that."

"Do you realize that she still loves you?" asked Henry.

Andrew's expression did not change, and he still looked out the window at nothing in particular. "And I still love her," he said in a flat tone of voice. "There was never any question of an absence of love."

"I know, but . . ."

"It was only a matter of what kind of love it should be."

"Are you sure . . . are you absolutely sure that you now know what kind of love it should be?"

Andrew sighed and looked back into the room. "She agreed," he said in an irritated, almost exasperated tone, "we both agreed that we weren't meant by God to be man and wife."

"How can you be so certain?"

"I can be certain because—well, because at the root of what took place between us was the lie, the biggest lie of the Prince of Lies, that Jesus did not rise from the dead. I believed that lie because I wanted to, just like Father Lambert, and like him I ignored all the usual procedures and spurned all reasonable doubt, and I seduced Anna just as Father Lambert seduced Mrs. Dunn. But while he died in despair and in mortal sin, God in his mercy has given me the chance to redeem myself and repent."

"I can see that," said Henry gently, "or rather I see clearly how it can seem like that to you. But I wonder if God would want you to save your soul at Anna's expense."

"But don't you see," said Andrew urgently, "that it isn't just a question of *my* soul? If it was just that, it would be easy."

"You mean that hers is at risk?"

"Not hers. *His*." He looked back toward the window.

"Father Lambert's?"

Andrew nodded.

"You feel that by becoming a Simonite monk, you can save his soul as well as your own?"

"Yes. By seeing it through right to the end—my life for his life—a return for what he did for me."

"But that's . . ." Henry was about to say "mad," but stopped himself for fear of tipping his brother over the edge. Instead he said, "It does make God seem vengeful to try to placate him in that way."

"It's not to placate God; it's to cheat the Devil."

"You mean the Devil can claim the soul of Father Lambert . . ."

"Unless I offer up my life to expiate his sin, just as Jesus did for the sin of Adam."

"So it's not to save *your* soul that you have returned?"

"No. His."

"And if you were to somehow discover that he had died in a state of grace?"

"Then, of course, there would be no debt to pay. But I found him hanging there, and I heard from her lips of his sin with a woman, and I saw the skeleton. Like him, I doubted, and denied Christ's divinity so easily, so quickly, so shamelessly . . ." He shuddered.

Henry shifted in his chair. "You might like to know," he said, "that I went to see Veronica Dunn."

Andrew looked up suspiciously. "When?"

"Yesterday. Before I picked Anna up the airport."

"Did she ask to see you?"

"No. I had promised to tell her how things turned out . . ."

"Of course. She must have been relieved to know it was a hoax."

"She knew that already."

"How?"

"From faith. She said she'd always known. In fact, I'd made a

247

bet with her about it, and saw her to tell her that she'd won."

"And was she all right?"

"Yes. She seemed fine."

"I'm glad."

"She was worried about you."

Andrew frowned. "She shouldn't be."

"We agreed . . ."

"What?" asked Andrew, almost irritably.

"It's awkward for me to say this," said Henry in a quiet but deliberate voice, "given what passed between Anna and me, and what passed between Mrs. Dunn and Father Lambert, but we both agreed—we both felt quite certain—that you are not meant to be a priest or a Simonite monk, but to be Anna's husband and the father of her children."

"Meant by whom?"

"By . . . God."

"But you don't believe in him."

"I'm no longer so sure . . ."

"Take care," said Andrew gravely. "Don't believe unless you must. Faith is a terrible burden."

"Didn't Christ say that his yoke was easy and his burden light?" asked Henry.

"Yes," said Andrew sadly, "and at times it is. But at other times he withdraws and the Devil renews his temptations . . . to give up, to abandon one's vows and solemn resolutions."

Henry smiled. "Am I an agent of the Devil?"

Andrew did not smile. "Are you? I don't know. Not knowingly, certainly, but perhaps . . . You mean well, I realize, but love is so complicated—so selfish, sometimes, and at other times so pure."

"Has it occurred to you," asked Henry, "that perhaps before making any final decision you should seek advice of some kind?"

"I have my confessor."

"A Simonite?"

"Yes."

"Perhaps, you should consult a priest who is not a Simonite, or a lay counselor of some kind."

"Do you mean a psychiatrist?"

"I suppose I do."

Andrew laughed. "I'm not mad," he said, "or only in so far as anyone who aspires to be holy will always seem mad."

"I didn't mean to suggest that you are mad," said Henry, "but only that you are unhappy."

"Of course I suffer," said Andrew. "If I didn't suffer, what would I have to offer to save Father Lambert's soul?"

"And *her* suffering?" asked Henry. "What should she do with that?"

"Endure until it passes," said Andrew, "and then find a better man than me."

Sensing that the conversation had become too painful for his brother, Henry talked a little longer about other things and then said that he must leave. He insisted he could see himself out and left Andrew at the door of Father Lambert's cell. Impatient to escape the claustrophobia that always came over him in an institution of this kind, he made his way back along the polished corridor and down the heavy wooden stairs. At the entrance, however, he was waylaid by the porter, who asked if he could spare a moment to speak with the prior. He was led back along the corridor on the ground floor and shown into Father Godfrey's study, with its comfortable armchairs and the portrait of St. Simon Doria on the wall.

Father Godfrey rose from his desk as Henry entered, and with a friendly gesture guided him to one of the chairs. "I'm so glad you could stop in," he said. "I knew you must be worried about Andrew . . . So were we, so were we . . . I wondered how you found him, whether, indeed, you are reassured?"

Not knowing what the prior knew—or whether he was Andrew's confessor—Henry looked at him uncertainly. As if realizing that Henry might feel constrained, Father Godfrey lowered his voice and added, "He has told me everything, I think, of what happened in Jerusalem—certainly about the skeleton, the deception and Miss Dagan."

"It seems clear to me," said Henry, "that the two are very much in love and should get married."

Father Godfrey frowned, as if pained that anyone should speak so bluntly. "You may be right, you may be right," he muttered, "but it seems to us that it was an aberration . . ."

"What?"

"The love affair. A result of the shock, surely, at seeing what appeared to be the skeleton of Our Lord."

"A shock some might say brought him to his senses."

Again the prior frowned. "I know, of course, that you are not sympathetic to the idea of the religious life, but I would have hoped for your brother's sake that you would try to judge his case with some objectivity."

"I am no longer so opposed to the religious life as you assume."

"You can see its value?"

"Clearly, if one accepts that Jesus was God, then one might feel that he wishes some of us to devote their lives to him in an uncompromising way."

The prior looked relieved. "Then you accept that his vocation might be genuine?"

"It could be, but I am convinced that it isn't."

"Even though he has felt it now, apart from this short falling away, for over six years?"

"Yes."

"What makes you so sure?"

"I know him very well. He is very open, affectionate and kind."

"Of course, but those are qualities that may suit a priest as well as a married man."

"I know, and if I felt that God *did* want him as a priest, I would do nothing to dissuade him. But I can see so clearly the psychological forces that have driven him to this step—above all, his obsession with Father Lambert . . ."

"I know, I know. He was always very influenced by Father Lambert, and naturally feels an obligation to him."

"But is that a proper basis for a religious life?"

"Not in itself, no, but as a manifestation of love . . ."

"To give up his life for the sake of another?"

" 'Greater love hath no man . . .' "

"But does God bargain in that way?"

"He does, yes, or so it would seem from Scripture. Look at Lot, who haggled to save Sodom, or even the barter implicit in the new Covenant, our salvation in return for the sacrifice of Christ."

"And are you happy to have Andrew back on that basis?"

The prior, avoiding his eyes, said, "It is not for me to turn away someone whom God has called to join our order."

For a moment Henry felt impelled to argue further, but he knew that it would be futile, not just because Father Godfrey seemed so determined to hold on to Andrew, but because he himself no longer felt certain that what the prior said was untrue.

Henry left, and escaped from the gloomy monastery into the street. He walked toward his car, which he had parked at a meter.

When he reached it, he stopped, turned and looked back, not at the grim monastery in which Andrew was imprisoned, but at the shabby church that stood next to it, with grass growing in its gutters and weeds from the crevices between the wide, worn steps. Then, just as three weeks before he had felt curious enough to enter St. Patrick's in Soho, he turned and went back into the church of St. Simon.

It was cool and musty, filled with the somber green light of dawn. It had a particular smell, a mixture of condensation on the tiles of the floor and smoke from the guttering candles in front of the statue of the Virgin and St. Anne. He walked down the right aisle, looking up at the stained-glass windows representing the Father, Son and Holy Spirit, then at the painted bas-reliefs at each Station of the Cross depicting the suffering of Jesus in Jerusalem. What trouble and expense had gone into the decoration of this church with works of art that were now ignored. How incongruous that at a time when man finally seemed to have mastered the world with steam, gunpowder and reason, these painters and sculptors of the Victorian era should have returned in their imaginations to the Middle Ages.

Yet even as he thought this, Henry found himself kneeling at the foot of the altar, just as he had at St. Patrick's in Soho. Then he had not prayed; he had merely been curious to see how it felt to adopt such a posture before an invisible deity who might or might not exist. Even now he did not pray, but looked at the stone table at the top of the flight of steps. Behind it was the tabernacle, a little cupboard covered with an embroidered cloth, and beside it, on a bracket set into the wall, was a brass lamp in which burned a candle in a red glass bowl—the sign, Henry knew, that there was consecrated bread in the tabernacle. So this, he thought, is the Holy of Holies of the new Covenant, just as the innermost courtyard of the Temple in Jerusalem was the Holy of Holies of the old one. That had been at the heart of one of the greatest monuments of the ancient world; this was at the center of a decrepit old church in Paddington. Yet the first, for all its magnificence, could hardly be compared with the second if it did indeed house the living God.

Henry looked above the tabernacle to the figure of Christ on the cross. He imagined Andrew kneeling before this same cross, begging to be forgiven for the sin of loving Anna. As he imagined this, and thought with despair of his own inability to help her or to save his brother, he found himself speaking not to the figure on the cross nor to the man it depicted, but to the presence hidden in the tabernacle. "Let him go," he said in the silence of his mind. "Let him go, and I will believe in you and in what you taught— yes, even in your Resurrection. Let her be happy with Andrew, and let Andrew be happy with her; if you need a life to atone for Father Lambert, then take mine. Show him the way out, as you are showing me the way in. Cut through his guilt and neurosis as you cut through my egoism and doubt. Is it too much to ask? Didn't you walk on the water? Didn't you feed five thousand on a few loaves and fishes? Didn't you bring Lazarus back to life? Didn't you raise yourself from the dead? Then please perform a small miracle: raise Andrew from this gloomy mausoleum and let me give my life in his stead."

27

Among the delegates to the Congress of Biblical Archaeologists at Oxford was Father Stephen Driffield, a Jesuit
from a Canadian university, whom even Father Lambert in his
most charitable frame of mind had found difficult to endure, not
because he was malicious or cantankerous, but because he was
such a tenacious and indefatigable bore. He had once been told
that he looked like Teilhard de Chardin, and the comparison had
gone to his head. He walked with a furrowed brow, as if he were
considering the deepest mysteries of existence, and he spoke with
the slowness and the solemnity of a sage. During the first days of
the Congress, Andrew always had to have his wits about him to
avoid being cornered by Father Driffield in one of the halls or
quadrangles for one of his "little chats." Luckily, having taken on
Father Lambert's duties as one of the coordinators of the Congress,
he had an excellent excuse to move away whenever the old priest
approached him.

Andrew's duties also distracted him from the more painful presence of Anna, who was there with her father as a member of the
Israeli delegation. He did what he could to avoid her, since every
glimpse provoked anguish of a most confused kind. He could also
see that she was doing what she could to shun him. This com-
pounded his remorse, for it seemed to prove that he still caused
her to suffer. There were moments when he thought that they
should meet alone, but he was afraid that if they did so all his

pious resolutions would crumble, that he would feel powerless not to embrace her and kiss her and drag her to his room.

Every night during the Congress he lay awake on the narrow bed that belonged to a student during termtime, tormented no longer by gentle fantasies of laying his head upon Anna's bosom, but by savage, unsubtle sexual desire. Even when he was able to banish these coarse fantasies, he could not rid himself of the memories of her perfect face and sour smile. He knew, of course, that they were sent by the Devil to tempt him. He recognized, too, that the longing he felt to care for her, protect her and make her laugh, that came over him when he caught sight of her across a quadrangle or at one of the lectures, was merely a subtler wile of the same Satan who, having won the soul of Father Lambert, was determined not to be cheated.

Andrew's resolution to save the soul of his patron and mentor was bolstered by his role as his understudy at the Congress. The delegates had been told that Father Lambert had died of a stroke the month before. Many of them, who had known and admired him, came to Andrew to express their sorrow, among them the dreary Father Driffield. Luckily there were so many others around that Andrew could escape from him without seeming impolite. He avoided him again when the old Jesuit tried to collar him after Andrew had delivered the paper that Father Lambert was to have given. On this occasion too there were many others who also crowded around him to discuss the paper or to talk of Father Lambert—among them Michal Dagan, who clasped Andrew's hand and held it, saying in a low, hoarse whisper, "What I would give to have had him read that paper."

Andrew nodded. "I know."

"But at least there is no Cardinal Memel."

"No." He glanced at Anna, but she had moved behind her father so that her face was hidden.

Dagan turned to his daughter. "Have you arranged to see Andrew while we are here?" he asked.

"He's very busy," said Anna drily.

"But not *so* busy, are you," asked Dagan, turning back to Andrew, "that you can't have supper with old friends?"

"No, of course not," said Andrew.

"Come this evening and we will have supper."

"That would be kind, but . . ."

"No buts. Come to my room in Balliol at seven. We will drink a glass of sherry—isn't that the thing to do?—and then go out to a restaurant."

Andrew looked again toward Anna, who still remained hidden behind her father. "Thank you, yes," he said lamely. "At seven. I'll be there."

They moved away and Andrew turned to the other delegates, and then went to the organizer's office to deal with a furious quarrel that had broken out between a Frenchman and an Iraqi as to which of them had first uncovered the entrance to a Hasmonean tomb. He had intended to listen to a paper by an American archaeologist, an old friend of Father Lambert's, on cuneiform tablets from Carchemish, but realizing that he had already missed the first half hour, decided to go back to his room.

As Andrew passed through the gate, he saw the figure of Father Driffield walking slowly along the other side of the quadrangle, holding his conference papers in one hand and his empty pipe in the other. Since the route to his room led through the passage between the two quadrangles, he stopped and stepped back into the shadows of the porter's lodge for fear that the Canadian Jesuit would see him. When he saw him disappear beneath the arch, he cautiously continued.

The senior common room of the college, in which the delegates to the conference could take tea, gave on to the passage between the two quadrangles. As he passed it, Andrew saw through the door the solitary figure of Father Driffield sitting alone at a table. The sight of the garrulous old Jesuit, whom the other delegates undoubtedly found as boring as he did, and went to the same pains to avoid, gave him a pang of bad conscience, so though neither hungry nor thirsty, and with a number of other things he wanted to do, he went into the common room himself, filled a cup with tea from the urn on the trolley, and sat down next to the priest.

"Ah," said Father Driffield, his face lighting up as he saw Andrew. "Playing truant too, eh? Couldn't face old Dormer riding his hobby horse about the Hittites?"

"No."

"Well, I've always thought he made much too much of that find of his, which was, what, fifteen years ago? And he's been giving the same paper ever since."

"Yes."

Father Driffield glanced from his half-empty teacup to his empty pipe, the prop he used to string out his endless stories, sucking it, lighting it, puffing at it in the middle of a sentence to prevent anyone else breaking in. Now, however, because he was in the common room, he hesitated to light it, but instead took up his tea. "You know, Lambert didn't think much of him—Dormer, that is. He never said it in so many words—he was too charitable a man for that—but I could tell, I could tell . . . No, he didn't think much of Dormer."

"He had to be invited."

"Of course, of course. You couldn't avoid it but"—here he sipped his tea—"there are a great many men in our field who hold chairs at important universities, but who, when you come down to it, have accomplished very little, while others, like Lambert—well, of course, Huntingdon is important, very important, but he should have been here at Oxford."

"Yes," said Andrew, scorching his tongue in his impatience to finish his tea.

"Do you know," said Father Driffield, "that I must have been one of the last people to have seen poor Father Lambert alive?"

Andrew put down his cup. "When was that?"

"I'd been in Rome, at the Institute, but I stopped off here on my way from Montreal—when was it? About a month ago—to see a colleague at Farm Street, and as I was leaving I ran into Father Lambert. He was leaving too, so we walked up to Grosvenor Square and sat on a bench and had a chat."

"But when was that?" asked Andrew again.

"I can't remember the date exactly, but he'd just got back from Israel, and someone told me he died later that very day. If he did, he certainly went straight to Heaven, because he'd just received the sacrament of reconciliation from that old priest of ours—I forget his name, a severe old man. Father Lambert said he always went to him because he was one of the few who didn't make your excuses for you."

"But what time of day was it?" asked Andrew. "Can you remember?"

Father Driffield picked up his cup and slowly sipped his tea, delighted to have aroused Andrew's interest and determined to spin out the story. "It must have been, well, around four or five in the afternoon, and overcast, a little cool for that time of year, so after we parted, I went for some tea at the Connaught. You know, it's part of my English heritage as a Canadian that I always like a cup of tea around four or five in the afternoon . . ."

256

"And you say he'd been to confession?"

"Yes, although we call it reconciliation now . . ."

"Are you sure?"

"Well, of course I'm sure, because he told me about that old priest—I wish I could remember his name—and then went on for some time about the sacrament—how important it was, and how neglected these days. He said hardly anyone goes because they're happy to settle matters in their own conscience. Yet it's one of the promises which Our Lord made to his disciples—'those whose sins you forgive, they are forgiven'—that proves to us that he really was the Son of God."

"Did Father Lambert say that?"

"Actually he did. He was in a funny mood. As you probably remember, he wasn't usually talkative, but that afternoon I could hardly get a word in edgeways. He went on about faith and doubt and Almighty God retiring momentarily from our lives to teach us that we are lost without him. Then he returns, and you feel the warmth of grace all over again, and all doubt and confusion vanish, and you realize how extraordinary and wonderful it is that there is a God who loves each of us enough to bring us into existence, not just as an animal or an insect or a plant but as an eternal being who can choose to love him or reject him, but who, even if he does reject him by sin, just as St. Peter, St. Paul and St. Augustine did—in fact, almost every saint has sinned in his time—but how even then one can repent and know with absolute certainty, after the words of absolution, that every sin is forgiven."

Andrew was silent, his head bowed. Father Driffield glanced at him, as if expecting an interruption, but seeing that there was none, he drank from his cup and continued. "He was also very interesting about Grierson's discoveries in Ugarit. I'd wanted to tackle him on that for a long time, and as soon as he'd said his piece about reconciliation, which was, I have to admit, a little pre-Vatican II for my taste, I managed to get him onto the question of Grierson's method, which I criticized in a paper you may have seen in the *Saskatchewan Archaeological Review* . . ."

Andrew left Father Driffield still talking and staggered back to his room, his mind grappling with all that he had just been told. How could he make sense of what had happened? Father Lambert had returned from Israel convinced that Christ had not risen from the dead. In his despair, he had turned to Mrs. Dunn. Had he then repented? Had he then believed in the Resurrection? If he had believed, repented and then confessed his sins, how could he in the space of an hour have fallen back into a state of such despair as to buy a clothesline and hang himself?

But if he had not hanged himself, then someone must have killed him, and all that hope returned that Andrew had felt at the beginning. If Father Lambert had been murdered, it must have been to prevent him from denouncing the find. It followed that he must have died for his Christian witness, and far from being ensnared by the Devil, his soul was already in Heaven wearing a martyr's crown.

Andrew knelt and prayed as he had never prayed before, a mixture of thanks and pleading for what he now suspected to be true. For if it were true, he was released, and could run to Anna as he had so longed to do, and beg her to have him after all. How could he find out? How could he know for certain? Who could have killed him and why? These thoughts and prayers ran around and around in his head until he suddenly realized that it was seven o'clock, and that he was expected by the Dagans at Balliol College.

He washed, changed his shirt and combed his hair, and walked from his college to Balliol, his mind still in a turmoil. Some of the delegates returning from Dormer's lecture greeted him as he passed but he did not see them. Indeed, so pressing was the riddle which obsessed him that no sooner had Michal Dagan admitted him to the large paneled room to which he had been assigned for the Congress, than he blurted out what he had heard from Father Driffield.

Michal Dagan was alone—Anna was expected momentarily— and listened to what Andrew said with a bowed head.

"Of course it must all seem nonsense to you," said Andrew, "but to me it is completely confusing because, if Father Lambert really repented, confessed his sins and believed them forgiven, then why on earth would he hang himself from the window of his cell?"

For a while Michal Dagan sat in silence, his head still bowed, his face hidden. Andrew, who until then had been so preoccupied with his own agitation that he had not noticed the older man's reaction, realized that his words had had a considerable effect. He waited in silence for Dagan to reply.

Eventually Dagan looked up. There were tears on his cheeks. "I shall tell you," he said slowly, "no matter what happens as a result. Lambert did not hang himself. We killed him—not me, but Ya'acov, on the orders of Lomish—because he had telephoned me in Jerusalem that afternoon to say that he now believed that the skeleton I had found could not be that of Jesus of Nazareth. But my telephone was tapped. Lomish heard this and thought that his purpose would be served just as well if he made it seem that Father Lambert had taken his own life in despair. There was his notebook, you see—Lomish thought that Lambert would have written in it that he accepted the find—but Ya'acov found that he had written nothing in it, so he took it away to forge some entries and plant it, if necessary, on someone they could make responsible for his murder."

Andrew was weeping.

"Poor Father Lambert," said Dagan.

"No, no," said Andrew. "You cannot imagine how happy he must be."

"Happy?"

"Yes, now, in Heaven."

Dagan shrugged. "In Heaven, yes, perhaps. Who knows?"

Half an hour later, Anna entered her father's rooms to find Andrew and the Professor laughing together, having drunk two-thirds of the bottle of sherry.

"You know, I think it is because he is drunk," Michal Dagan said to his daughter, "but this crazy young man says that he is no longer going to be a monk and wants instead to marry you. I warned him that life would be more peaceful as a priest, and that you aren't an easy person to live with, but he says he knows you very well. He thinks you will get along, and he asks me if I will let you get married."

"Actually I asked him if he minded if I were to ask you," Andrew said.

"Of course, of course," said Michal Dagan. "But what notice would she take of my opinion now, when she has never paid any attention before?"

"I'm sorry," said Andrew, blushing and hardly daring to look at Anna, "but might you—I mean, after everything—might you consider—well, marrying me after all?"

This time Anna did not hide behind her father, but caught Andrew's eye and smiled.

ABOUT THE AUTHOR

PIERS PAUL READ was born in 1941, brought up in Yorkshire and educated at Cambridge. In addition to two years spent in Germany and one in the United States, he has traveled extensively in Eastern Europe and Israel. He is married, has four children and lives in London. *On the Third Day* is his eleventh novel.